CARTER A. VAUGHAN
BRINGS AN ERA OF INTRIGUE AND
ADVENTURE TO VIVID LIFE

This rousing tale of adventure and romance is based on the actual events leading up to the Louisiana Purchase.

Carter A. Vaughan has captured all the exuberance and excitement of these years in the character of Andrew MacCullough— physical giant, daring adventurer, irresistible lover.

And he has woven into his story fascinating sketches of the most influential men of the time . . . men like Napoleon, Talleyrand, James Madison, John Adams and Thomas Jefferson.

The River Devils

BY CARTER A. VAUGHAN

POPULAR LIBRARY • NEW YORK

DEDICATION:
For Cleo and Dick

With the exception of actual historical personages, the characters are entirely the product of the author's imagination and have no relation to any person in real life.

Americans are in the great debt of the river devils, who prevented the bankruptcy of the West, and perhaps its loss to a foreign power.

THOMAS JEFFERSON

ONE

October 1799

Except when he was angry, Andrew MacCullough hated violence, so it was unfortunate for his peace of mind that he had a hot temper and was equally expert with a long rifle, a pistol, a knife, and his fists.

The attempt of the Spanish officials to prevent American guards from returning to their own barges, which were tied up at New Orleans' wharves, was intolerable, a deliberate provocation intended to discourage the settlers of the American West from shipping their corn, wheat, tobacco, and vegetables to the states of the Eastern seaboard by way of the Mississippi, which was far easier and cheaper than sending wagon trains across the mountains. Had the incident been an isolated one, Andrew might have been able to accept it philosophically in a manner befitting a young man who had attended Harvard College for a year, the University of Paris for another eighteen months, and had been forced by necessity to become a barge guard.

But the Spanish customs officers, military, and constabulary had been making life unpleasant for the Americans ever since they had arrived at the great port town on Mississippi delta three days earlier. Self-respecting river devils allowed no one to browbeat them, and the senseless order to keep their distance from their own barges was too much.

Andrew's temper exploded, and it was easy for a giant of six feet, four inches to reach down, pick up the pompous little assistant port director for New Spain and set him down on his heels with such force that he looked stunned.

Twenty customs men in yellow tunics, plumed brass helmets, and black breeches, all of them carrying muskets, poured out of their headquarters shed and raced toward the Americans at the foot of the wharf. Apparently they had been waiting for some show of resistance that would give them the excuse to show their authority.

A wild light of battle appeared in Andrew's blue eyes,

and as he braced himself for the assault he ran a huge hand through his blond hair. "River devils, to me!" he called, but retained enough common sense to add, "No firearms, boys! Use your fists!" Governor Almonaster y Rojas of Louisiana was fair, farsighted, and efficient, but, like his subordinates, he was a loyal Spaniard, and would not hesitate to send Americans to the gallows if some of his customs men were killed in a waterfront brawl.

Shaggy, buckskin-clad frontiersmen from Kentucky and Tennessee, America's newest states, hurried to join Andrew, and formed in a circle, their backs to the center.

The momentum of the Spaniards sent six or seven of them into the American position, and Andrew, with a joyous roar, smashed a fist into the face of one and sent him staggering off the foot of the dock into the water. Within a few moments the rest of the vanguard had been knocked down, too, and the bulk of the Spanish customs force lost its appetite for combat.

Andrew flexed his hand and reached down to pick up his long rifle, which he had dropped to the ground. "I reckon nobody is going to bother us again, boys," he said, and swaggered down the wharf.

His cousin, Billy MacCullough, two years his junior and only an inch shorter, followed him, as did the nine other Americans. They climbed aboard their three barges, and several disappeared into the crude cabins of logs built amidships, reappearing shortly with earthenware jugs of whiskey. No river devil would pay two Spanish *dolars* for a half-gallon of the liquor in New Orleans when he could buy the identical product in Nashville for only thirty-five cents in United States currency.

Andrew remained at the foot of the dock, and there Billy joined him, wiping his mouth on the back of his sleeve. "Sure you don't want a drink, Andy?"

Andrew did not bother to reply. Billy well knew that a fondness for liquor, gaming, and women had caused him to squander his inheritance, leave New Haven, where his future seemingly had been assured, to live a precarious existence on the frontier. *"Le meilleur vin a sa lie,"* he said.

"You know I don't understand French, and if that's another of your damned proverbs, I don't want to hear it."

Andrew was unruffled. "It means there are dregs in the best bottle of wine."

8

"If you weren't my own kin—"

"But I am," Andrew said, and grinned. "What's more, we haven't seen the last of this little ruckus, and I've never yet known you to object when I stand with you in a fight."

"I've got to admit there's nobody I'd rather have on my side."

Billy drew in his breath. "Look up the road. I knew they wouldn't like it when you gave that yellow-coat a bath."

A full company of Spanish infantry in black uniforms trimmed in yellow was marching toward them, and, as always, looked impressive. The troops helmets, buckles, and buttons gleamed, and they marched in perfect step, their muskets held on their shoulders at precisely the same angle.

But the river devils, climbing back onto the dock, were unconcerned. "There's about fifty of them," one said, "so the odds are equal." Laughing, he raised his jug to his lips.

Andrew jabbed a finger at him. "Tom Hammond, go back onto your barge, and keep your mouth shut. The rest of you do the same. I'll handle this."

Two or three of his comrades jeered good-naturedly.

"I'm just as anxious as the rest of you for a dish of lamb broiled on a spit and some yellow rice," Andrew replied. "And I have me an appointment with a lady this afternoon that I aim to keep."

"Since when have you known any ladies, Andy?" Tom Hammond called to him.

Andrew joined in the general laugh as he jumped onto the barge that he, Billy and Tom had been hired to guard.

The troops, still in formation, wheeled onto the wharf.

"If they don't break step," Billy muttered, "they'll smash the boards."

"It won't be the first time," Andrew said, and moved to the stern of the barge, which was tied to the end of the wharf.

An officer called an order, the troops halted and another officer with lace ruffles showing beneath his cuffs came to the edge and peered down, his manner haughty. "It has been called to my attention," he said in the pure Castilian of a Madrid accent, "that these foreigners resisted the authority of His Spanish Majesty's customs officials. Do you admit the crime?"

9

"No one committed a crime, Captain." Andrew, gravely polite, answered in equally faultless Spanish. "There was a slight misunderstanding, I believe. The customs men tried to prevent us from boarding our own barges, which are our property, American property."

"We do not recognize the authority of the United States in New Orleans."

Andrew remained patient. "We don't claim any authority. We just wanted to come aboard our barges, that's all."

"For what purpose?"

"I don't know of any law, Spanish or otherwise, that requires us to explain our purpose!" Andrew returned the Spaniard's steady glare.

"His Majesty's customs officials are not required to explain their orders, either. They give the orders, and you foreigners must obey them."

Andrew resented being called a foreigner; like everyone else who lived in the American West, he considered the Mississippi an American river that happened to be under the jurisdiction of a European nation, an unfortunate circumstance that should be rectified at the earliest convenient opportunity. But he kept his temper in check. "Surely you can't blame men for wanting to use their own property."

The officer ignored the statement. "I am also informed that an attempt was made to drown one of His Majesty's customs officials," he said. "Do you deny it?"

"Of course. There was an unfortunate little scuffle," Andrew said, "and the customs man happened to fall into the river." He shrugged and smiled.

The Spaniard was not amused. "Who threw him into the river?" he demanded more stridently.

"He wasn't thrown, as I've just told you. He fell. But if you insist on knowing which of us was responsible, I did it!"

The Captain jumped down onto the barge. "In the name of His Majesty," he thundered, "and under the authority granted to me by His Excellency, Don Juan Almonaster y Rojas, I place you under arrest. Come with me!"

Planting his feet apart, Andrew rested his hands on his hips but made no other move. "This barge is American

10

territory, so you have no authority here. I deny your right to arrest me."

"I am not jesting!" The officer was becoming red-faced.

"Neither am I. Spanish law is very explicit in this matter, Captain, and if you will take the trouble to speak to the Governor's advocate-in-chief, you will discover that I am entirely correct in this matter."

"You are in my custody!" the officer shouted, drawing his sword with one hand and clamping the other on the American's shoulder.

"I don't like to be pawed," Andrew said, and his friends realized from his soft tone that he was rapidly losing his own temper. They had known him to speak in a voice scarcely above a whisper when he was really enraged. "Take your hand off me."

The officer tightened his grip.

"I reckon," Andrew said, "you need a cooling off." He moved so swiftly he caught the Spaniard by surprise, disarming him and, as the sword clattered onto the deck of the barge, bending forward and heaving the officer over his shoulder.

The Captain landed in the river, went under water and rose again to the surface. He clutched at the line that held the barge fast, managed to grasp it and sputtered.

A sergeant hurried to the edge of the wharf and hauled him up. Meanwhile several soldiers snickered, turning away to escape the wrath of their other officers.

"You forgot something," Andrew called, and threw the sword onto the wharf. He hurled it as he would a knife, and it landed at the Captain's feet, the point burying itself in the soft wood, the quivering blade standing upright.

The officer shouted an order, and the soldiers raised their muskets to their shoulders.

The river devils needed no order to aim their long rifles at the troops.

"All of you are under arrest!" the humiliated Captain shouted. "Surrender yourselves at once, or stand the consequences."

Andrew quickly weighed the situation. He felt certain that he and his friends could give far better than they received, but in a shooting match men on both sides inevitably would be hurt and some might die. Even if the

Americans could escape up the Mississippi, which was probable, they would risk arrest and hanging if they returned to New Orleans. So it would be the lesser evil to submit without a struggle.

"Boys," he called, "stash away your firearms. Hide them where they'll be safe in the cabins. I'll use up as much time as I can for you." He tossed his rifle and the brace of pistols in his belt to Billy, but did not remove the knife he carried in his boot-top, hoping the Spaniards would not see and confiscate it. Then, moving very slowly, he climbed up onto the wharf and bowed.

Again some of the soldiers laughed quietly. The sight of the American giant in buckskins, his hair tied at the nape of his neck with an eelskin, making a courtly bow that would not have been out of place at the Governor's palace, was too much for them.

"I place myself in your custody, Captain," Andrew said. "I am your prisoner, sir."

The drenched officer called out another command, and two soldiers came forward, seized Andrew and pinned his arms behind his back. It would have been easy for him to break their joint hold, but he submitted quietly.

His comrades, who were straggling ashore, were ready to put up a fight when they saw him taken captive, even though they were unarmed.

But Andrew knew that a free-for-all fight similar to those held at Tennessee county fairs would cause more problems than it solved. "Don't start a ruckus, lads!" he warned. "We might want to come back to New Orleans one of these days."

Although he had no official authority over them, they heeded his advice and allowed themselves to be made prisoners. A half-squad surrounded each American, the bedraggled Spanish Captain went to the head of the line, and the strange group paraded down the wharf as it started toward the center of town.

New Orleans, founded in 1718 by the French, had become one of the largest cities and busiest ports in North America, and its population of more than twenty thousand was exceeded only by Philadelphia, Boston, New York, and Charleston, all of them in the United States. In 1764 the Louisiana Territory and its capital had been ceded to

Spain, and the city showed the influences of both French and Spanish cultures. The houses, many with interior courtyards, boasted grilled balconies and gates of wrought iron which had been imported from Madrid at considerable expense, the names of streets, daubed on corner buildings, were bilingual, and the younger generation, half-French and half-Spanish, called itself Creole and was proud of establishing a new breed.

Most of the houses, shops, markets, and storage buildings were new, the better part of the community having been destroyed by major fires in 1788 and 1794. Almost miraculously, the orange and fig trees, many of them planted by Jesuit missionaries a half-century earlier, had survived the two catastrophes and were flourishing; they lined most of the main roads, and were nurtured on the extensive grounds of government buildings, monasteries, and hospitals. A walk leading to the main entrance of the Ursuline convent was decorated with tall, graceful palms that rustled gently in the autumn breeze.

Andrew, long a city dweller who had enjoyed the comforts of Boston and Paris, London and Philadelphia, had developed a fondness for New Orleans, where taverns served a wide variety of dishes prepared by experienced chefs, where theaters and concert halls provided entertainment unequalled elsewhere on the Continent, and where the girls were as sophisticated as the barmaids of the University of Paris district on the Left Bank of the Seine.

He had known his pleasures, however, when he had been free to wander where he pleased on the narrow, winding streets. It was far different to be marched as a prisoner by young, self-important soldiers who prodded him in the back occasionally with the muzzles of their muskets. The whole town seemed to be watching the procession from balconies, the entrances to houses, and produce markets. Men shouted insults, women and girls with elaborate hair styles, low-cut gowns that would have been considered immodest in the United States and huge, hoop earrings burst into gales of laughter, and small boys, accompanied by their dogs, fell in at the rear of the column and marched solemnly, too.

Andrew was the only American prisoner who under-

13

stood French, Spanish, and the local language, a jumble of the two, so he alone knew what the residents of New Orleans were saying. Easygoing men who had lost money in trades with alert Americans urged the troops to castrate their captives; women who were ignored by all but the roughest of visitors from the United States, who treated even the most respectable of them as harlots, obtained a small measure of revenge by calling offers to the officers, requesting the right to buy the prisoners as slaves.

Andrew's face burned, and he told himself that, once again, he had been too civilized for his own good. Even though he was twenty-eight years old and had spent several years on the frontier since fleeing from the bankruptcy courts of his native Connecticut, he was still being forced to learn that the meek had not yet inherited the earth. Had he met threats with even stronger threats, he and his friends would not be suffering the indignities of degradation now. There were times when it was better for a man to risk the consequences of losing his temper than to remember he once had been a gentleman.

A light rain fell as the group turned off the Rue St. Charles, which ran parallel to a canal, and onto the Avenue de Bienville, named after the city's founder. Ahead was the Place d'Armes, the center of New Orleans, where the military headquarters, cathedral, and other important buildings were located. Andrew quietly breathed a sigh of relief: the company was taking him and his companions to the Hall of the Cabildo, the headquarters of the colonial and town governments.

He and his comrades would be taken before a magistrate, he decided, and he would persuade the justice to set them free. Most residents of New Orleans might be as savage as the raw wilderness of the interior, but the judges, elderly Spanish nobles who had come to live in the New World in semiretirement, prided themselves on their urbanity. So Andrew felt certain he could persuade even the most dubious magistrate that the incident on the waterfront had been a misunderstanding. No one had been seriously injured, after all, and if eleven Americans were sentenced to prison terms, there would be a storm of protest when news of the affair reached the United States. Magistrates who treasured the tranquillity of their lives preferred

14

not to ask too many questions and avoided controversies.

The Captain led his column past the Charity Hospital and the new, two-story brick buildings recently completed by the Governor, which housed some of the city's more expensive shops and wealthier merchants' offices. But, instead of continuing across the Place d'Armes to the Hall of the Cabildo, he made a detour behind the Army headquarters, marched past the barracks of the 133rd Andalusian Foot, and approached a low, wooden building with barred windows.

Andrew realized he and his companions were being hauled off to prison, and he protested loudly. "I demand the right to be taken before a magistrate!"

The Captain and his subordinate officers appeared to be deaf.

"You have no right to take us to jail until we've been given a fair hearing and a magistrate sentences us!"

No one, it seemed, could hear him.

The door of the jail was unlocked by a uniformed soldier whose tunic collar was unbuttoned, and who showed so little respect for his superiors that he continued to smoke a long *segaro* of the type made in Spain's Caribbean colonies. Then the prisoners were herded into one cell, and the Captain, who was supervising the operation, stood aside to permit the jailer to shut the door.

"I demand justice!" Andrew said. "You can't imprison us without a trial!"

"If you know as much about the law as you claim," the officer replied with an unpleasant smile, "then you must realize Spain does not observe the legal code of the English and Americans. You will stay here until I decide to set you free. And in your case, that means you will remain until you rot!" In a vain attempt to recapture his dignity he wiped a smear of mud from a boot, then nodded to the jailer.

The door of the cell slammed shut, and a heavy bolt slid into place on the outside. Andrew MacCullough and ten of his fellow river devils, a group reputedly the roughest brawlers in the West, had been taken captive and imprisoned without putting up even a token struggle.

15

TWO

October 1799

"In less than three months," Billy MacCullough said morosely, stretching out on a straw pallet, "there's going to be an important change in the calendar of the whole Christian world. The only change of its kind we'll know in all our lifetimes. All of a sudden, at midnight on the last day of December, it'll be a new century. The nineteenth century. In Nashville there'll be real doings, I can tell you. They'll have a jamboree that'll last three days. They'll roast venison. And oxen. And sides of beef. They'll cook corn and potatoes in the coals—"

"—and there'll be free whiskey and ale for all," Tom Hammond added gloomily. "Maybe sack for them as likes it."

"It'll be the same everywhere," Billy continued. "At Louisville, over in Kentucky, river devils will be welcomed at every house in the town. They've never forgotten how a party of devils saved the old fort when it was still the Falls of the Ohio, and a band of Cherokee attacked the place one night. Even that miserable town we helped to capture last year and made the capital of the Mississippi Territory, Natchez, will have a grand celebration. Folks there will forget they're the neighbors of New Spain, and they'll feast, and sing—"

"—and drink," Tom muttered.

"Yes, and drink to their hearts' content," Billy said. "But we won't be in Nashville or Louisville or Natchez. Not us. We'll be right here in this damned cell, getting so weak and cramped we won't be able to walk."

A young man with a long scar on the left side of his face raised himself to one elbow on a pallet at the far side of the cell. "We'll be hungry, too. Hell, I'm hungry right now. I wonder if that meal they gave us at noon is all we'll get until tomorrow. Or maybe they'll feed us again tonight. Not that it matters, if all they give us is like the dinner we just had."

"I swear it was dish water, not soup," Tom said. "I thought I saw some vegetables floating around in it, but they was dead worms."

"I didn't mind the soup as much as I did the bread. How can anybody get bread that stale?"

"They set it up on a shelf for a month or two after they bake it," Billy said, "and if the rats don't get it in that time, and I don't think any self-respecting rat would touch the damned stuff, then they feed it to the prisoners."

Andrew, leaning against the outer wall of the cell and staring out across the Army's parade ground, paid no attention to the prattle. Finally, when there was a pause in the conversation, he said quietly, "I wouldn't advise you lads to lie down on the pallets. There are sure to be lice in them."

"Listen to him!" one of the others said bitterly. "Do you expect to stand up the whole time you're here?"

"I don't intend to be here long enough to find out," Andrew replied.

As the significance of his words dawned on his companions they turned, one by one, to stare at him.

"When I left Connecticut," he said, "I learned to enjoy being in places where there's enough room to breathe. But I'm afraid if I inhale here, it would crowd some of you boys against the wall over yonder."

No one laughed.

"Are you aiming to leave, Andy?" his cousin asked.

"Could be."

"If you're getting out," the man with the scar said, "you've got to get us out, too. We wouldn't be here at all if you hadn't gotten so blamed polite to the Spaniards."

"*Al agradecido más de lo pedido*. To the grateful man give more than he asked. I wouldn't think of leaving without you, Ed."

The man with the scar grinned, but said no more.

Others, however, were curious. "What do you have in mind, Andy?" his cousin wanted to know.

"An engagement I had for this afternoon, that I aim to keep. I don't believe in making a lady wait."

Tom started toward the window.

"If you don't mind," Andrew said firmly, "I'll hold this post alone."

Tom held his ground for a moment, then retreated when Andrew looked at him coldly. Any man who had fought beside Andrew MacCullough knew better than to cross him.

The others remained silent, knowing he would tell them what he had in mind when the appropriate moment came.

At last Andrew stirred and moved still closer to the window. Crossing the parade ground, letting her see him yet not venturing too close, was a young woman with a willowy figure, a lace mantilla covering her red hair, the dark shade of red so often found in Toledo and Madrid. She was wearing a daringly low-cut gown of green satin that clung to her body, outlining its every curve, and although the high heels of her matching slippers dug into the soft ground, she did not break her sauntering, hip-swaying stride.

Tom caught a glimpse of her, and whistled softly.

Andrew silenced him with a curt gesture, and then she disappeared from sight.

"Is that your friend, Andy?"

"Yes, I—"

"Does she know you're here?"

"She saw us from a window in her house when we were being brought here. Now, lads, I want you to listen carefully. Make no move until I give you the signal. There are two pairs of sentries who patrol around the jail. Ed, you and George will take care of the two who march clockwise, facing as I'm facing right now. Billy, you and Tom will see to it that the other pair cause us no trouble. I don't want anyone killed or maimed, so be careful. Bind and gag them, and drag them in here, where they'll be safe. Any questions so far?"

"What about the head jailer and his assistant?" one of the men asked.

"I'll be responsible for them," Andrew said.

The others were satisfied.

"When you leave here," he continued, "go straight to the river. In pairs. Not in a body, as you don't want to call too much attention to yourselves. When you get to the barges, cast off and get yourselves out of New Spain as fast as you can."

"Suppose the customs men try to stop us," Ed said.

18

Andrew smiled. "I'd be surprised, after their experience of this morning, if they'd come within fifty feet of you. If they should, though, I reckon you'll know what to do."

Billy thought he detected something out of the ordinary in his cousin's instructions. "Are you coming with us, Andy?"

"As I've already told you, I have an engagement with a lady, and I don't want to disappoint her."

The river devils gaped at him.

"Are you mad?" Billy asked.

Andrew shrugged. "I believe it was Publius Syrius who said, *Amare et sapere vix deo conceditur.* To love, and to be wise at the same time, is scarcely possible even for a god. Besides, I'll be in her debt after she's helped us."

"She's—"

Andrew again demanded quiet with a gesture, and the men froze when they heard the bolt being moved, very slowly, as though the person manipulating it found the task difficult. Then a key grated in the heavy lock and turned.

Two or three of the men started toward the door.

Andrew, still at the window, halted them. "Wait," he said softly, and did not move until he saw the red-haired girl strolling back across the parade ground in the direction from which she had come. "Now," he said, and was the first to reach the door.

He opened it, the others behind him, and headed alone to the small office at the end of the corridor. The door was ajar, and he peered in, ready to spring, but to his astonishment saw the *segaro*-smoking soldier crumpled unconscious on the floor.

Andrew took a loaded pistol from the man's belt and another hanging from a wooden wall peg. Then, using strips of the jailer's own tunic, he bound the man's hands behind him, tied his feet and pushed a gag into his mouth. Slinging the man over his shoulder, Andrew carried him to the cell and dumped him inside. The assistant jailer, whom some of the others had noticed on their arrival, was nowhere to be seen.

Before he could leave the cell, the men to whom he had assigned the task of disposing of the sentries arrived with their trussed victims. "It was easier than we thought,"

Billy said. "Ed will have a bruise on his face, but he's so blamed ugly it won't matter."

Andrew shook hands with them and urged them to leave at once. He waited until they departed in pairs, as per his instructions, before he himself started toward the front door. The escape was more effective than he had dared anticipate; not only had the river devils carried out their assignments well, but the girl had done more than her share. How she obtained the key to the cell was a mystery, and how she had managed to knock a rugged, armed man unconscious was completely baffling.

As Andrew approached the entrance to the prison a large figure in a Spanish Army uniform suddenly loomed up directly in front of him. The assistant jailer, armed with a musket, had found his superior missing and the sentries absent, so had decided to investigate, and was making an inspection of each occupied cell.

Both men were surprised, and both acted at the same moment. The soldier, bringing his musket to his shoulder, opened his mouth to shout for help. Andrew, knowing his own future would be jeopardized and that his friends would in all probability be recaptured if an alarm was raised, lunged at him. They grappled, and the assistant jailer tried desperately to fire his musket as a means of calling attention to his predicament.

Andrew concentrated his full attention on seizing the weapon, and they fell to the floor together as they grappled. The American was strong, but the Spaniard was powerful, too, and while hugging the weapon to him with one hand, battered at his assailant with the other. Andrew was willing to absorb the beating because he could use both hands to gain control of the weapon, and eventually he wrested it from the Spaniard.

The soldier pummeled him with such ferocity, however, that Andrew was forced to drop the musket, but, in desperation, managed to kick it away a short distance down the corridor. Now, evenly matched at last, both men were free to fight as they saw fit. The burly Spaniard, although shorter than Andrew, was heavier, and it quickly became evident that he was no novice in the art of personal combat at close quarters.

A short, vicious punch to the body made Andrew wonder if his ribs had been broken, and an even harder blow to the head momentarily left him dazed. Not only was his opponent gaining an advantage, but he was afraid their scuffle would attract attention in the nearby barracks, so he knew he had to win an immediate, clear-cut victory.

Brute strength without guile would not help him achieve his goal, he reasoned, and although his mind was slightly hazy, he forced himself to remember the techniques of the free-for-all fights that were a prominent feature of every American frontier jamboree and picnic. He allowed his body to go limp, and the Spaniard, thinking he was winning, pounced on his prostrate victim.

At that instant Andrew brought up a knee, driving it hard into the pit of the soldier's stomach, and doubling him over. Almost simultaneously he drove a series of hard punches at his foe, raining blows on his face and head that closed one eye and rendered him helpless. Again Andrew used a knee, which landed in the Spaniard's groin, and the man groaned as he toppled backward onto the floor, writhing in agony.

Andrew finished him with several more blows, putting all of his waning strength into each. This was no time to remember he had been a gentleman before his own folly had led him to the wilderness of the West; if he failed now, he felt certain he would be executed by the Spanish authorities, and the will to survive made him ruthless. Not until the soldier lost consciousness did Andrew relent and shakily pull himself to his feet.

The sounding of a trumpet somewhere in the barracks made him realize a new danger threatened. He recalled vaguely that a ceremony of some sort took place before Spanish troops, like everyone else in New Orleans, retired to their beds for a rest of several hours. If new sentries came to replace the guards who had been hidden in the cell, he would be trapped, and not even his skilled improvisation would save him from recapture.

In order to complete his escape he would have to disguise himself in the defeated soldier's uniform, and he hastily ripped off the man's outer clothing, donning the various items over his buckskins. The boots were a trifle too large and the breeches and tunic were a little too

21

short, but the man's helmet, which was on the floor near the musket, fitted reasonably well.

Andrew hurried out of the jail, the musket on his shoulder, cautioning himself not to run. As he had feared, a full company was moving into formation only twenty yards away, so he hastily turned a corner, reached the rear of the building and then made his way across the parade ground, aware that he was conspicuous, and that, if accosted, he could offer no valid excuse for leaving the military bivouac, no matter how fluent his Spanish.

Off to the left he saw two officers walking in the direction of the barracks, so he veered away from them, even though he was being taken farther from his destination. He felt rather than saw the officers looking at him, and could only hope they assumed he was being sent somewhere on official business. Where would a Spanish soldier go for this purpose? His mind working swiftly, he turned in the direction of the Hall of the Cabildo, even though a heavy sentry detail was maintained there at all times.

Out of the corner of his eye he saw the officers continue toward the barracks, so the immediate crisis had been averted, but another, far more serious, remained to be surmounted. An officer of the rank of major was always in charge of the guards at the Hall of the Cabildo, and although Andrew had spent at least one-third of the past year in New Orleans, he had never paid much attention to Army ceremonies and was not certain he could imitate a Spanish salute.

Necessity forced him to make a wide detour around the government building, and he kept a healthy distance from the sentries. At last he reached the relative safety of the city's streets, and increased his pace until he remembered that he had never seen a Spanish soldier hurrying anywhere. A young woman with heavily rouged lips called out to him, two small, admiring boys fell in beside him for some yards, and a middle-aged man and woman, who appeared to be strangers in town, addressed him in French, asking directions.

He replied in rapid Spanish and, not waiting to see whether they understood him, proceeded around the rear of the cathedral to the Avenue de Bienville. There a number of officers were promenading with ladies, and Andrew, instantly aware of his mistake, was forced to leave the thoroughfare and use smaller, winding streets. Ordinarily he could have reached his destination in ten minutes, but the long, circuitous route he took caused interminable delays, and a half-hour passed before he finally reached St. Charles Street.

Making his way to a small but substantial two-story house of red brick, he rapped at the door. The helmet felt heavy on his head, perspiration streamed down his face and his buckskins, beneath the uniform, were soaked. He rested the butt of the musket beside him, realizing that if no one answered his summons he would be compelled to maintain his disguise for a long time, perhaps the rest of the day.

The red-haired girl opened the door a few inches, saw the uniform and started to close it again.

"Beatriz!" Andrew took care to address her in Spanish for the sake of casual passers-by who might overhear him. "Don't you know me?"

Beatriz de Santos peered at him through a crack in the door, then opened it. "Come in quickly," she said. "My reputation is bad enough, but it will be ruined, completely ruined, if the neighbors think I entertain members of the garrison."

Andrew needed no second invitation to enter the house, and the door closed behind him. He removed the helmet, wiping a film of sweat from his forehead with the sleeve of the uniform tunic, and turned to face the girl.

Her enormous green eyes, which he ordinarily found exceptionally attractive, were troubled. "Go in there," she directed, pointing to a room he had never visited, "and don't come out again until I call you. I must send my servingmaid on an errand before she sees a soldier in the house."

Andrew obeyed, and found himself in what appeared to be her dressing chamber. Rows of lotions, pots of rouge and other cosmetics, and several small jars of perfume filled a table, and at one side of the room, on a rack, were Beatriz's gowns and cloaks. He had never seen such a large feminine wardrobe and wondered, not for the first time, what her source of support might be. Perhaps she

23

was one of New Orleans' more expensive courtesans; he had heard that a small handful of young women in the city were becoming wealthy associating with high-ranking government and Army officials, fur traders and ship owners. There were more rich men in New Orleans than in any other town on the North American Continent, and he resented the ownership of Louisiana by a foreign power. Most of the Mississippi River country, the principal source of New Orleans' income, was American, so it seemed only right to him that the city and its hinterland should belong to the United States, too.

Beatriz seemed to be taking a long time, and Andrew paced up and down in his buckskins after stripping off the uniform. Finally, when she did not reappear, he tried the door and found it locked. It occurred to him that, even though she had made possible his escape and that of his friends, she might, for reasons of her own, be notifying the authorities of his presence under her roof. Unable to trust any woman after his experiences in Paris and London, he would not put it past Beatriz to turn him in so she could pose as a patriotic heroine.

The room's one window was too small for him to crawl out in case of need, and the only entrance was the locked door. It was premature to batter it down, he decided, but checked the pistols and musket to make certain they were primed and loaded, and he cocked them. Now, if the Spaniards tried to recapture him, he could give a good account of himself before they shot or overwhelmed him.

A key turned in the lock, and Andrew picked up the pistols just before the door opened.

Beatriz looked into the muzzles of the weapons and laughed. "You have no faith in anyone. Put away your weapons and come out. I sent my servingmaid shopping, and had to make out a list of things for her to buy at the market. She'll be gone for at least an hour or two. Come with me and tell me exactly what happened."

Andrew accompanied her into a small but handsomely furnished parlor, where a wood fire was burning in the hearth, and related everything that had occurred from the moment the door of the prison cell had been unbolted and unlocked.

Beatriz listened intently, shifting in her chair occasionally and so absorbed in his account that she paid no attention when her gown slipped from one shoulder, revealing a large expanse of creamy skin. The moment he concluded his tale, however, she jumped to her feet and hurried from the room, returning a few moments later with the uniform of the sentry he had overpowered.

"We'll have to burn these things at once," she said, and threw the breeches into the fire before turning to open a window in order to remove the odors.

"The brass buttons won't burn, and neither will the helmet."

"I know." There was a hint of contempt in Beatriz's voice as she stooped to take the knife from Andrew's boot-top and began cutting buttons from the tunic.

"I had to keep his boots and left mine," Andrew told her.

"We'll get rid of them later. The first task will be to bury the helmet and buttons behind the house."

"I'm not sure that's wise," he said. "Wouldn't it be better to weight them and throw them in the canal across the road?"

Beatriz considered the suggestion, faint frown lines appearing on her smooth forehead. "All right," she said, "provided we don't drop them anywhere near this house. Governor Almonaster y Rojas is an intelligent man, and so is his chief constable."

Andrew watched her in silence as she threw the tunic into the flames. Only once, in Paris, had he encountered a girl with her allure. Her attraction was so great and she was so confident of her powers that she could draw any man to her by displaying a mildly flirtatious attitude, even a cursory interest in his activities. "What I want to know," he said at last, "is how you immobilized the chief jailer, who is at least twice your size."

Beatriz giggled, and a mischievous expression appeared on her sensuous face. "I had no problem persuading him to let me come into his office," she said, "and it was easy enough to take one of his pistols from him."

Although she offered no details, Andrew could imagine them. She had strolled into the prison office, her hips swaying, a promise in her eyes, and the jailer had been delighted to admit her. Then she had suffered his embrace,

25

and while he had fondled her she had encountered no difficulty in taking a pistol from his belt.

"When I told him to stand against the wall and raise his hands over his head," she continued, still laughing, "he was so startled that he leaped backward too quickly, and his head struck the wall. You'd have thought someone had hit him with a club. It was far simpler than I'd hoped. All I had to do was take his keys and open the cell door."

Andrew stared at her, grinning slowly. "What would you have done if he hadn't knocked himself unconscious?"

Beatriz shrugged prettily. "I find I'm more successful when I make one move at a time rather than plan a whole campaign in advance." The amusement faded from her eyes. "Now I must leave you for a short time. Stay here, and admit no one to the house."

His suspicions came to life again.

"I've already compromised myself," she said with asperity, "and there is no one else in New Orleans who can help you. I assume you want to know whether your American friends have left the city or have been recaptured. Unless you go to the wharves yourself—and you can't without taking the risk of being arrested again—I'll have to go in your stead."

Andrew was forced to admit, grudgingly, that her argument made sense.

"And while I'm out, I shall buy some new clothes for you. An alarm will be given for an escaped American who was last seen in a greasy hunting shirt and trousers of skins, and since rewards are usually given when the constabulary believes a man may be dangerous, you must disguise yourself. I believe," she added, scrutinizing him, "that I shall dress you as a Creole."

Her calm assumption of the right to take charge made Andrew uneasy. He had to concede that her logic was unassailable, however, and he had no arguments to offer in rebuttal. In essence he had two choices: he could steal out of New Orleans or stay for a time so he could see more of Beatriz. Bored with his endless journeys up and down the Mississippi, the occasional skirmishes with parties of Indian warriors and the somewhat more frequent encounters with river pirates intent on taking the grain, tobacco, furs, and other cargo of barges, he was fascinated by the daring of this young woman whom he had met on only one previous occasion.

"Here," he said, digging into the worn money pouch hanging from his belt, "I have eight dollars, American. Take all of it, but don't buy anything fancy." It had been so long since he had worn the attire of the gentry that he had no idea how much might be purchased for eight dollars, but New Orleans was an expensive town, so he didn't think the sum would go far.

Beatriz took the money without comment, went to the front hall for her mantilla and a fringed shawl, and departed.

Andrew returned to the parlor, where he watched the remains of the jailer's uniform burn in the hearth. The house was unfamiliar, and he reflected that his safety demanded an investigation. Undecided whether to take the musket with him or leave it in the parlor until he returned, he carried it under his arm on a tour that proved surprisingly brief. In addition to the parlor and dressing chamber he had already seen, only a dining room was located on the ground floor. Above were two large bedchambers and, between them, still another dressing room in which so many gowns were hanging that he realized the chamber on the ground floor was used for the overflow.

Only someone of considerable means, he thought, could afford such a large wardrobe.

From a second-story window he saw the kitchen, a separate out-building, and behind it a snug, one-story edifice that, in all probability, was the servingmaid's dwelling. At the rear of the property, near a fence, stood a little barn; a breeze had blown open its door, and it appeared to be unoccupied.

Feeling a trifle more comfortable now that he had learned something of the physical plans of the house and its auxiliaries, Andrew returned to the parlor. Sitting down, he made a review of all that happened in the past few hours, the sudden turn of events that had transformed him from a free American, proud of his status as a river devil, into a fugitive from Spanish justice.

Certainly Beatriz de Santos was responsible for his continuing presence in New Orleans, and he knew he wanted her, but there was much in their relationship he found baffling. They had met on only one previous occasion, when he had prevented her from being trampled by a runaway horse on the Avenue de Bienville, and she, in gratitude, had allowed him to buy her a bottle of wine and a light supper at a nearby, expensive tavern. They had agreed to meet again today.

When Beatriz had seen Andrew and his companions being marched to jail she had indicated in pantomime that she would help him. But those scanty gestures, he knew in retrospect, could not account for the confidence, the almost absolute assurance he had felt that she would keep her word. Nor could he understand how the escape itself had evolved with literally no communication between them. His puzzlement increased when he realized he had relied on her to find some way to unlock the cell door and remove the bolt; similarly, Beatriz appeared to have understood how he would react, too.

How was it possible for two people who scarcely knew each other to have established such a close rapport? And why was she taking risks—great risks, that might involve her own disgrace and imprisonment—for a man who was a virtual stranger? He did not know the answers, but promised himself he would find out.

Time dragged, and Andrew repeatedly returned to the windows to gaze out into St. Charles Street, where the fashionable Spanish, French, and Creole residents of New Orleans were strolling. A sudden panic came over him when a middle-aged woman in a servingmaid's uniform, laden with vegetables and parcels, approached the little house. He was not afraid of fighting a whole platoon of soldiers singlehanded, if necessary, but the prospect of dealing alone with a woman in her forties and silencing her was too much for him.

He heard her entering the rear of the house, and when she began to store her purchases in the small pantry adjoining the dining room, he knew it would be only a matter of time before she came into the parlor. Again he had two alternatives, that of leaving at once or hiding. Not bothering to analyze his motives, he crept up the stairs and searched for a place of concealment. Only the dressing room proved relatively satisfactory, between two rows of silk and satin gowns.

28

He was still there when Beatriz returned a half-hour later, and when she came into the chamber, obviously looking for him, he stepped into the open.

"This is the first time I've ever hidden behind a woman's skirts," he said.

"I was afraid you'd gone," Beatriz said, "and I didn't dare ask Lucille if she'd seen anyone."

Lucille, he gathered, was the servingmaid.

"I have your things in here," she said, beckoning, and he followed her into the smaller of the bedchambers, where a pile of clothing lay on a chair. "Join me downstairs when you're ready, and I'll think of something to tell Lucille. Just be sure you don't speak English when she's within earshot."

Andrew was faintly amused as he dressed in breeches of pale blue silk and white silk stockings, a tailcoat of darker blue silk with pewter buttons, a shirt and stock that were lace-edged, a yellow waistcoat, and buckled shoes. He was surprised by the fit of each item, and concluded that Beatriz had a sharp eye. She had missed no detail except a sword, and had even provided him with a ribbon to match the waistcoat so he could get rid of the eelskin at the nape of his neck.

Placing one of the pistols inside the waistcoat and stuffing the other into the tail-pocket of the coat, he went downstairs, carrying the musket but laying it aside when he saw Beatriz waiting for him in the parlor.

"Your servant, ma'am," he said, and bowed.

She was delighted. "I knew you were a gentleman!"

"Long ago, maybe," he replied, and had no idea there was a faintly wistful note in his voice.

But Beatriz heard it.

The unexpected compassion in her eyes flustered him. "You're a lady," he said, "and you're also a spendthrift. These clothes cost more than eight American dollars. I'm in your debt."

Beatriz smiled. "You'll repay me in good time, I'm sure."

"What do I owe you?"

"I'll need to add it up. Another time."

"Now, if you please," Andrew said firmly. The very idea of being in debt was anathema to him, and he was reminded of the nightmare years in Paris and London when, no matter how many hours he spent at the gaming tables each day, he had fallen deeper into insolvency.

Beatriz heard the urgency of his tone and, although she failed to understand, did some quick mental arithmetic. "Your debt is very small. You owe me only four dollars and a half, American."

Andrew was able to relax slightly. He knew a loan shop often patronized by river devils that would pay him at least that much for one of the pistols. "You shall have the sum before tomorrow."

She inclined her head, and the long, red curl that came forward across one shoulder brushed against her breasts. "That leaves only one small matter to be settled. Your French is faultless, so I advise you to speak it rather than Spanish in front of Lucille. I've told her you're a French plantation owner from the hinterlands."

"I see," he said, but actually saw nothing. All he knew was that the servingmaid seemed accustomed to visits paid to the house by strange men.

"Now that we're finished with business, will you join me in a glass of brandywine?"

"Help yourself, but I won't have any, thank you. I don't drink."

"So you said the other evening, but I didn't believe you."

"Why not?"

"Well, it's rather strange—" Beatriz stopped short, then laughed. "To tell the truth, I thought you had designs on me, and wanted me to become giddy while you stayed sober."

Andrew looked at her, his gaze steady. "I have designs, but I need no help from liquor."

"I don't believe I care for any brandywine just now," she said quickly.

"Maybe you'll tell me something else. Why did you help me today?"

"I was curious about you."

"Do you always take such chances when you're curious?"

"Jeanne Valdéz, my closest friend, tells me I'm the most cautious girl in New Orleans."

30

"I haven't had the pleasure of meeting the lady," Andrew said, "but I deplore her judgment."

Beatriz giggled.

"I wonder if you realize you could have been imprisoned yourself," Andrew said sternly.

Her shrug caused her gown to drop and momentarily exposed a shoulder. "I wouldn't have been there long. Don Juan would have released me as soon as he heard."

Andrew looked at her inquiringly.

"The Governor," she said.

He wondered whether she was the mistress of Almonaster y Rojas or a wealthy thrill seeker. Perhaps she was both.

Beatriz seemed to read his mind. "Life has been very dull in New Orleans since the 3rd Castilian Cavalry went home and the squadron of Admiral de Toledano transferred its headquarters to Cuba."

Andrew told himself he was insane to have stayed on in New Spain. Bitter experience had taught him that girls like Beatriz de Santos invariably caused trouble for a man, no matter how great their allure, and sometimes because of it. He should have fled from New Orleans with the other river devils, grateful for the bold assistance she had rendered, but carefully keeping his distance from her.

Instead he was a guest in her house, virtually her prisoner, dressed in the latest gaudy Creole fashion while Spanish troops prowled the streets and kept a watch on the river for a tall American who had escaped from the city's main prison. He was literally penniless in one of the Western Hemisphere's most outrageously expensive communities, and there was no need to remind himself that this was not the wilderness, that he could not shoot game or take fish from the river for his supper. Even if he found some way to acquire funds, every meal he ate here would cost him as much as a Tennessee or Mississippi Territory frontier family paid for an entire month's staples of flour, cornmeal, and bacon.

But he could not attempt to earn money in a place where he was wanted by the authorities as a fugitive from justice, and he was further handicapped by his new clothes. A man posing as a member of the gentry could not seek work on the waterfront. For that matter, he could not rent himself a room at an inn without incurring debts he was incapable of repaying, and to top it off, he owed the girl four and a half dollars in American money.

Nevertheless he was here. He rose from his seat, crossed the room in three strides and towered above her.

Beatriz read his intentions in his eyes, but made no move. "You're curious, too," she said calmly.

"You could call it that, I suppose."

Her smile was enigmatic. "I had imagined you'd be romantic, but you aren't."

"I've learned that a man creates problems for himself when he indulges in romantic fancies. They aren't real."

"Never?" she inquired softly.

"Never!"

"We seem to agree in many things," Beatriz said. "I feel as you do."

Andrew raised a bushy eyebrow.

Suddenly she stood and, before he could reach out to stop her, crossed the room, placing herself behind a table for protection. "Women are taught to be gentle and soft and yielding, but those who follow custom are always hurt. Men take advantage of them."

"I believe we differ," he said, inching toward her. "In my opinion the women seek every advantage, and secretly rejoice when one of us makes a fool of himself."

"Then you've been hurt, too. I'm sorry." She circled the table, edging away from him as he came toward her.

"Are you? I wonder." Suddenly Andrew reached out, his long arm stretching across the table, and grasped her arm.

Beatriz made no attempt to break away from him; instead she stood very still, her head high and her smile proud.

He swept her into his arms and kissed her.

She neither fought him nor responded, but remained limp, virtually lifeless.

Andrew felt challenged and, still kissing her, began to caress her.

All at once Beatriz reacted, curling her arms around his neck, pressing close to him and actively receiving his kisses.

Their joint fervor mounted swiftly, explosively, and Andrew lifted her off her feet and carried her up the stairs.

THREE

November 1799

Life was simultaneously pleasant and frustrating. Andrew had lived with Beatriz de Santos for a month, ostensibly sleeping in the second bedroom of her house, and in spite of their intimacy, their physical desires remained strong. He frequently accompanied her on walks and shopping trips, sometimes escorting her to the homes of her friends for an evening, and everywhere he was accepted at face value as a French planter who owned property in the southwest corner of Louisiana.

The Spanish authorities had abandoned their search for the American river devils who had escaped from jail, and Andrew could go where he pleased in New Orleans without fear that he would be recognized and taken into custody. Nevertheless he was unhappy, principally because he was embarrassed by a lack of funds. Beatriz was giving him lodging and food, and he tried to repay her in the only way he could by rebuilding her dilapidated barn, a task that occupied most of his days, and then enlarging the pantry off the dining room.

He felt useless in spite of this work, however, and had no money to buy her a token gift or take her to a tavern for a meal. On a number of occasions Beatriz had suggested that they spend an evening at one of the city's eating and drinking places, but Andrew refused, unable to tolerate the prospect of seeing her pay for their entertainment.

His inability to learn more about her background and life was yet another source of irritation. If she was a courtesan, as he had at first believed, she managed to conceal her vocation from him, and he knew of no attempts on her part to arrange private meetings with others. It was obvious enough when they attended the receptions of her friends that many men found her attractive, but they retreated when they heard he was a guest in her home. Again and again Andrew told himself she could not be a real lady; only a woman of flexible moral standards would remain unconcerned about the damage to her reputation caused by allowing a man to live unchaperoned in her house.

She suffered no lack of money, he noted, and her dressmaker was a frequent visitor, making new gowns for her or altering older clothes whenever merchant ships from Europe arrived with news about the rapidly changing styles in Paris. Even when he asked her direct questions about her income she gave no direct replies, and he knew literally nothing about her finances.

Andrew's existence was not completely without meaning, however, and he knew it. His stay with Beatriz was no more than a passing interlude, and he could not allow himself to wonder whether he felt more than a temporary sense of attachment to her. He was not in a position to think of marriage to anyone.

Whenever he became impatient, a strong desire to return to the United States welled up in him, but he resisted it, aware that he had reached a major turning point in his life. All that awaited him was a river devil's lot, which he detested, and which had no real future for a man who would reach his thirtieth birthday in two more years. Given his choice, he would return to a city on the Atlantic coast of the United States, but he would be cast into a debtors prison if he went to New Haven, and had no vocation that would enable him to earn a living in Boston or Philadelphia, New York or Baltimore. On the Eastern seaboard there were no positions open on the basis of a man's ability to shoot accurately, use his fists and hold his own in a free-for-all fight.

So Andrew lingered in New Orleans, held there by his affair with Beatriz while he pondered his problem. Perhaps he was fooling himself, he thought, but he continued to hope something might happen that would give him at least a clue to his future. He had no one but himself to blame for his predicament, but, if he could help it, had no intention of wandering aimlessly, wasting more years as a Mississippi River barge guard.

The problem was very much on his mind one afternoon as, clad in his old buckskins, he sawed planks for the new pantry wall. Lucille was working in the nearby kitchen, but paid no attention to him; she had become accustomed to his presence, and apparently accepted his alleged status as a French planter. If she had other thoughts, she kept them to herself.

Andrew worked furiously for more than an hour. Then, as he paused for breath, he heard a rustle of skirts behind him and turned, expecting to see Beatriz. Instead, her friend, Jeanne Valdéz, was approaching him. He had met her on several occasions, and although she, like Beatriz, was in her early twenties, exceptionally attractive with long, black hair, violet eyes, and a slender yet seductive figure, he had felt an inexplicable antagonism toward her which she reciprocated. Her good opinion of herself was annoying, and, because her father was prominent in the Governor's administration, she apparently considered most people beneath her.

Andrew bowed as the unsmiling Jeanne approached him. "I'm afraid you've made a call in vain," he said. "Beatriz has gone out, and won't return until later in the afternoon."

"I know." Jeanne's voice was unexpectedly musical; perhaps her Creole lilt and accent were responsible.

Andrew was faintly puzzled.

"I deliberately chose this time. I've come to have a word with you."

"Oh?" He had no right to invite her into the house, and couldn't ask her to soil her yellow silk gown by sitting on a pile of planks.

She astonished him by addressing him in English. "Why don't you leave New Orleans, Mr. MacCullough? Go back to the United States. Now. Today."

He could only pretend he didn't understand the language, and replied in French. "I'm afraid you'll have to speak more slowly if you use a foreign tongue."

Jeanne gestured impatiently, and a diamond and sapphire ring flashed on the little finger of her hand. "There's no need for the deception, Mr. MacCullough. Beatriz confided in me more than a week ago."

Andrew grinned, but remained on guard. "That was none too discreet of her."

"The indiscretions, sir, are yours!"

He blinked, but said nothing.

"Until you moved into this house, Beatriz was respected by everyone. Do you realize what you've done to her good name?" Jeanne was indignant.

"I never judge others by their reputations, and I don't listen to gossip."

"I refer to fact, Mr. MacCullough, not gossip. You and Beatriz are living alone in this house."

"I also make a point of minding my own business, Miss Valdéz," he said coldly.

She flushed, and in spite of his annoyance he couldn't help thinking she looked particularly attractive.

"You assume too much," he continued. "Since you're familiar with this house, you know there are two bed-chambers in it."

"It wouldn't matter if there were ten. What do you think Don Felipe will say—and do—when he arrives from Cádiz?" In her anger Jeanne stamped a foot. Her slipper became coated with sawdust, but she did not deign to notice the mishap.

"You'll have to enlighten me," Andrew said. "Who is Don Felipe?"

She glared at him, her violet eyes icy. "You mock me, sir."

"I haven't yet," Andrew replied, hooking his thumbs in his belt, "although I wouldn't hesitate if I had the opportunity. Since you've chosen to interfere in matters that don't concern you, I must ask you to be more explicit. I've never heard of someone called Don Felipe."

Jeanne lost a trace of her arrogant self-confidence. "I felt sure that Beatriz told you—"

"Insist if you must, but you're wasting your time—and mine." He realized he sounded a trifle pompous, since he had nothing better to occupy him than a little carpentry.

"Don Felipe de Guzmán is being sent to New Spain as the Deputy Governor of Louisiana. He has been a friend of King Carlos for many years."

"I have no interest in the friendships of kings or changes in colonial administrators."

"Beatriz and Don Felipe are betrothed," Jeanne said.

Andrew gaped at her. "I don't believe it."

She could see he was sincere, and her manner softened. "I'm sorry I had to be the one to tell you this, Mr. Mac-

36

Cullough, but everyone who knows Beatriz has been talking, and I'm sure you're a gentleman who doesn't want to ruin her future."

"If what you say is true, I'm certain there's a reasonable explanation. If not, I can assure you there will be no further need for concern." He remained unyielding, and bowed stiffly, looking somewhat ludicrous as he made the courtly gesture in his old buckskins.

Jeanne started to reply, changed her mind and drew herself to her full height as she gazed up at him. "I'll bid you good afternoon, Mr. MacCullough."

Andrew said nothing as he watched her depart.

A long time passed before he returned to his carpentry, however. If Jeanne Valdéz had told him the truth, it was necessary for him to revise his suppositions about Beatriz. A grandee who was close to Charles IV of Spain and was being dispatched to the New World in a high office obviously would not be planning to marry a courtesan.

Why, then, had Beatriz yielded to him so quickly, and why was she permitting him to live under her roof? Andrew made up his mind to force a showdown when she returned from her shopping.

They stood in the parlor, glowering at each other, and Beatriz made no attempt to curb her anger. "My relations with other people," she said, "don't concern you."

"My relationship with you," Andrew retorted, wiping the palms of his hands on his buckskin trousers, "gives me the right to know more about you."

"It does not!"

He had never struck a woman, but was tempted.

"You wouldn't dare," she said, standing up to him.

Andrew raised a hand.

"You're a Yankee bully—"

He let it fall again.

"—and a coward!"

His own temper was soaring. "I demand to know whether you're betrothed to a Spaniard named Don Felipe de Guzmán!"

"If I am, what do you think you can do about it?"

"If I wished, there are many things I could do!" In spite of his rage, Andrew was beginning to feel a little foolish.

"I won't marry you!" Beatriz shouted.

He laughed at her. "I haven't proposed. It's customary for a man to ask a woman whether she'll marry him before she accepts or refuses him."

"I don't care whether you ask."

A tap sounded at the front door, but they were so engrossed in their argument that neither heard it, and Lucille, who was setting the table in the dining room, responded to the summons.

"If I'd known your situation," Andrew shouted, "I wouldn't have compromised you!"

"You know nothing about me!"

A deep voice sounded from the parlor entrance. "That's the man. Take him!"

Andrew turned to see an officer in the black and yellow of Spanish infantry pointing a pistol at him, and before he could move he was suddenly surrounded by armed soldiers. In the heat of the quarrel with Beatriz he had forgotten to put his pistol in his belt, and the knife in his boot-top was inadequate to ward off so many foes. He thought of starting a violent fist fight in the hope that he might escape during the ensuing scramble, but he was afraid the girl might be hurt. The room was too small for a frontier free-for-all.

The soldiers quickly bound Andrew's hands behind his back.

He was fuming, and some moments passed before it dawned on him that Beatriz had screamed and was watching the scene with horror.

"You are an American called Andrew MacCullough?" the officer asked in heavily accented English.

"I have that honor." It was a very slight satisfaction to reply in a pure Castilian.

"Then our search is ended." The officer turned to Beatriz, removed his helmet and bowed deeply. "You are fortunate we arrived when we did, and I trust you will not forget to mention this to His Excellency. The man is a dangerous criminal."

Andrew realized she was being given an opportunity to disavow him, to claim she had never seen him until now.

Beatriz was too incensed to think clearly. "By what authority do you arrest him in my home?"

Andrew broke in, addressing her in English. "I meant
38

you no harm when I broke in, ma'am." He pointed to a candelabrum of heavy silver that stood on a window facing St. Charles Street. "I saw that as I was walking past the place, and wanted it. I could have sold it for plenty. Enough to eat well for a month."

Beatriz was startled, and even though the situation was grave, started to laugh. His play-acting was convincing, and she knew he was trying to protect her.

"He'll steal nothing from this house," the officer declared, bowing again.

"I feel sorry for the poor fellow." She addressed the officer, but looked at Andrew. "Perhaps you'll allow me to give him something to eat before you take him to prison. I'm told the food there isn't very appetizing."

Andrew knew she was trying to make her peace with him, and responded in kind. "You're very generous, ma'am. I won't forget this."

"She's too generous for your kind. He isn't going to prison, Donna Beatriz, so there's no need to give him food. Besides, there isn't time."

Andrew wondered whether he would be taken straight to a place of execution and be hanged or shot. Spanish justice was more elastic than that of the United States and England, and, at present, was far too elastic for his taste.

"What are you doing with him?" Beatriz apparently had the same idea, and was frightened.

"We intend to obey His Excellency's orders," the officer replied pompously. "Remove him. And you, Donna Beatriz, should rejoice that a friend saw him enter this house and reported promptly to His Excellency's Intendant. These Americans are a greedy lot, and he might have gone off with every stick of silver you own."

So a friend had revealed his presence under Beatriz's roof. Andrew felt a surge of cold anger, and promised himself he would repay Jeanne Valdéz—if he managed to survive.

Tears sprang to Beatriz's eyes, and she seemed on the verge of losing control of her emotions.

The parting was difficult for Andrew, too, but he made a great effort in order to help her, and grinned at her, then winked.

As the officer turned away at the door she tried to wink, too.

With a soldier on each side and another behind him, holding a musket only a few inches from his back, Andrew was marched into the street, the officer in the lead.

For the second time in a month people leaned out windows and peered down from their grillwork balconies to watch the troops of King Charles IV escort a prisoner.

It occurred to Andrew, in passing, that his suit of elegant clothes, for which he had repaid Beatriz in full, had been left behind. He hoped she would remember to get rid of them before Don Felipe de Guzmán came to the New World. But he could not concentrate on such matters now. He continued to seethe over the perfidy of Jeanne Valdéz, and knew that if he and his escort should happen to pass her on the street, he would be unable to prevent himself from knocking her to the ground, no matter what the soldiers did to him.

"Where are you taking me?" he demanded.

"No talking is permitted," the officer said curtly, not looking around.

The muzzle of the musket was jabbed into Andrew's back as a reminder that the edict would be enforced.

Necessity forced him to keep silent, and some minutes passed before he realized he was not being taken in the direction of the military headquarters, barracks, and prison, where, he assumed, executions took place. Instead he was being led toward the waterfront wharves, where there were no Army installations.

At last, directly ahead, he saw a river schooner, and flying from her masthead was a flag bearing the sixteen stars of the United States. It was almost too much to hope that he was being reprieved, and would be allowed to leave New Orleans on board the American vessel.

The officer headed toward the ship, however, and when they drew nearer Andrew saw that her main deck was piled high with bags of rice and other overflow cargo. Two civilians were leaning against the rail, watching their approach, and one was easily identified as a trapper. His fur hat, unkempt appearance and shaggy, buffalo-hide shirt were badges of his calling. The other man was exceptionally neat, and at first glance his black suit appeared to be that of a clergyman. He carried a sword, however, and Andrew noted a knife in his boot-top, too. It was impossible to guess his vocation, but he was no frontiersman. Not even the lawyers and physicians of Nashville and Louisville dressed so somberly.

The ship's master came down from his quarterdeck and hurried ashore.

"Here is your American," the Spanish officer said. "Be good enough to sign this receipt for his custody."

The master of the schooner looked uncertainly at the man in black, who nodded almost imperceptibly.

The transfer took only a few seconds, but the Spaniard continued to fuss. "Do not remove the rope at his wrists," he said, "while he is on the soil of New Spain."

The man in black came toward them, and held out his hand to steady Andrew as he jumped onto the deck. "Welcome to the United States, MacCullough," he said.

Andrew was too astonished to reply.

"Will you give me your word you won't go ashore again?" The man drew his knife from his boot-top.

"You have it," Andrew said. "I've seen enough of New Orleans to last me for a long spell."

The rope was slashed, and his wrists were free.

The trapper sauntered toward them. "If you'd like the loan of my rifle, help yourself. You might want to take a shot or two at them Spanish bastards. The name is Gibson," he added casually.

The man in black came between them, moving rapidly. "Don't give MacCullough that rifle," he said sharply. "From what I've heard, he's mad enough to fire it—and send all of us to prison."

"I've got a hankering to put a hole through that officer's helmet, but I won't give in to it, I promise you. It feels too good to be free again." Andrew laughed exuberantly, then looked at the man in black. "How do you know me, sir, and where have you been hearing about me?"

"I'm Abel Hillery of President Adams' State Department," the man said, shaking hands. "And I've been hearing about you for the past two weeks. Is it true that you were responsible for the escape of eleven American river devils from the military prison?"

"Well, now," Andrew replied, grinning, "that depends

on who told you about it."

They moved to the rail as the line holding the ship to the wharf was untied and the anchor was weighed. "Everyone I've met in New Orleans has talked of little else, and I assumed you'd left Louisiana," Hillery said. "But just this afternoon, when I went to pay a courtesy farewell call on the Governor and his Intendant, I learned otherwise. It isn't accidental that you're on board the *Gheen-kho*."

Andrew noted with approval that he pronounced the schooner's Choctaw name correctly.

There was a hint of a smile in Hillery's eyes as he stroked his long jaw. "Don Juan has known since yesterday that you were still in New Orleans, but he didn't quite know what to do about you. From what he told me, you were hiding in the house of a rather prominent lady who is going to become even more prominent when she marries Don Juan's new deputy, who is expected from Spain very shortly."

"It's true enough I found a refuge," Andrew said, "but I know nothing about any marriage."

"Be that as it may." Hillery, the true diplomat, cleared his throat. "The Governor saw a way out, through me, and asked me to give you passage. I gathered he was anxious to avoid a public scandal, which would have been sure to break if you'd been executed, and he didn't want you in a New Orleans jail, either, when his deputy arrives."

Andrew could no longer doubt the accuracy of what Jeanne Valdéz had told him, and was bewildered. Common sense told him there was no valid reason for Beatriz to have placed her own future in jeopardy by taking him under her roof, being seen in public with him and even visiting homes of her friends with him as her escort.

"You owe the United States sixteen dollars for your passage," Hillery said.

"I don't have a penny to my name," Andrew said. "I'll have to work my way."

"The same idea occurred to me, and I spoke to the master of the *Gheen-kho*. But he already has a mate and a crew of six, and isn't authorized to take on any more men."

Andrew measured the distance to the wharf as the ship,

her sails filled, maneuvered toward the center of the broad river. "I reckon I'll have to swim ashore," he said.

Hillery clamped a firm hand on his shoulder. "The relations of the United States with Spain are delicate enough, and we can't afford to give Madrid any excuse to shut the Mississippi to our traffic. We prefer that you owe the money to the Government. I've accepted responsibility for you, MacCullough, and you're going home, on board this schooner, even if I've got to have you clamped in irons!"

FOUR

December 1799

The wilderness was everywhere, and the Mississippi River ruled a vast domain of its own. The men sailing north on board the *Gheen-kho* passed a single convoy of barges from Tennessee traveling in the opposite direction, but otherwise saw no signs of life. For as long as a half-day at a time the journey was made on waters that spread out across mud flatlands for distances ranging from one to three miles, but, now that winter cold was freezing the headwater tributaries far to the north, in some places the mighty river narrowed to a width of no more than three-quarters of a mile.

Beyond it, on both banks, stretching out toward the horizon, lay the virgin forests of willow and pine, cypress and red gum and hickory, and off to the east the monotony of the scenery was varied by a high, flat bluff that rose abruptly from the river delta.

The prevailing winds blew from the west, sometimes the southwest, so the schooner was able to maintain a slow but steady speed. Navigation was the principal problem, however, and either the master or his mate was on the quarterdeck at all times, from the start of each day's voyage soon after daybreak until a halt was called at sunset in the late afternoon. The Mississippi changed her course so frequently, particularly during the spring and autumn flood seasons, that only a sailor familiar with all of her peculiarities could avoid islands that had been submerged and other treacherous underwater obstacles.

Andrew, who knew the great stream almost as well as did the pilots, paid virtually no attention to his surroundings. His adventure with Beatriz de Santos in New Orleans, combined with the treachery of Jeanne Valdéz that had led to his betrayal and expulsion from Louisiana, continued to prey on his mind. And he tried hard to concentrate on his future, knowing he could no longer procrastinate. The hardships and dangers of life as a river devil no longer appealed to him, and he realized that the compensatory excitement he had felt in the past was missing now. Perhaps he was growing soft.

His only alternative, he knew, was that of establishing a homestead somewhere on the frontier. He did not look forward to the prospect of clearing one hundred and sixty acres of forest, building a cabin, and then coaxing corn and wheat, cotton and vegetables to grow in soil that, although rich, never had been cultivated. The life he would lead would be hard, lonely, and somewhat stultifying; he supposed that one who had enjoyed the pleasures of great cities across the Atlantic and the most sophisticated in North America could not be satisfied with the questionable joys of a wilderness existence that might be threatened at any time by savage Indian raids, the encroachments of other, less scrupulous settlers or bad weather that could destroy a season's crops.

He thought, very briefly, of becoming a trapper, like his fellow passenger, Gibson, but quickly dropped the idea. The trade of men who roamed through the wilderness seeking beaver pelts on the banks of rivers and shooting other game for their fur, was not for him. Trappers were a breed apart, restless primitives who had no permanent homes and were content to spend months at a time in the mountains of the West without setting eyes on other human beings.

When the *Gheen-kho* put into Natchez, Andrew went ashore with the rest of the company because he had nothing better to occupy him. But he was surprised, as he had been so often since the place had been taken by Americans, to find it flourishing, growing rapidly. It was no longer the miserable village founded by the French as Fort Rosalie and later a sleepy outpost of Spanish Louisiana. New homes, warehouses and wharves were being built, stores were being established to accommodate the pioneers who were creating farms and plantations for themselves in the adjacent wilderness, and the town's first inn had just been completed.

Abel Hillery treated Andrew to a meal there, and it was surprisingly good. The thick soup, made with vegetables and chicken, tasted and looked like a New Orleans concoction, the broiled flatfish had been taken from the river

45

only an hour or two earlier, and the beef, sold to the proprietor by one of the district's many farmers who raised cattle, was juicy. Natchez had made great progress in the less than two years that it had been under the jurisdiction of the United States, and Andrew tried to comfort himself with the thought that what was being accomplished in the Mississippi Territory could be done in western Tennessee, too.

The schooner's master had intended to resume the voyage immediately after dinner, but instead took on as much additional cargo, principally cotton, as he could carry, so the anchor was not weighed until the following morning. Andrew ate a breakfast of fried flatfish, cornmeal bread and ale, the strongest beverage he allowed himself to drink, and then returned to his tiny cabin amidships to read a book of Latin poetry by Ovid that he had borrowed from Hillery.

The movement of the *Gheen-kho* was imperceptible, the air was soothingly cool, and after a time Andrew stopped resisting the urge to doze off. His appetite had been appeased, there was a roof over his head, and he knew of no reason to stay awake.

A frantic shout from the quarterdeck jarred him into immediate, full consciousness. "River pirates to port!"

In a single movement he bounded out of his bunk and pulled on his boots, all too aware that his knife was his only weapon.

Others were hurrying onto the deck, too, and the mate, accompanied by one crew member, raced below to break out the schooner's cache of firearms, which remained locked in a cupboard except in times of emergency.

Andrew stood at the rail and surveyed the menace with the professional eye of a river devil. Two boats had put out from a wooded island in midriver and were being rowed toward the *Gheen-kho,* one moving toward her prow in order to cut her off, the second edging toward her port side for boarding purposes. In all, the two carried approximately twenty men, about twice the strength of the schooner's personnel, with the larger number in the boarding craft.

Paying no attention to the crew members, who were calling encouragement to one another, Andrew started

46

toward the quarterdeck. Gibson, calmly checking his rifle, already stood at the rail, and a grim Abel Hillery was loading his pistols. "Concentrate your fire on the boat that's trying to cut us off, and crowd on as much sail as you can carry!" Andrew shouted to the ship's master.

"There are too many of them for us. I'd rather elude them, if I can."

"You can't! That's just what they hope you'll do, and then both of them will board you." Andrew's impatience was heightened by the speed of the boats cutting across the water.

The mate and sailor appeared, laden with rifles, bags of powder and several small kegs of bullets.

Not bothering to ask for the right to use a weapon, Andrew filled his pockets with bullets, snatched a rifle and deerskin powder bag, and, jumping down to the main deck, sprinted toward the prow. "Gibson, come with me!" he called, and was reassured by the sound of pounding footsteps behind him as the trapper anticipated his request.

They crouched in the prow, partly shielded by the rising lip of the schooner's hull, in part by boxes of merchandise from New Orleans. Andrew loaded with the speed of long practice, and in the meantime Gibson drew a bead and fired.

"First blood," the trapper announced quietly as the lead oarsman on the starboard side of the boat fell backward.

The river pirates retaliated with a furious barrage, and were excellent marksmen, too. A bullet sang through the air only inches from Andrew's head before cutting through the schooner's rigging, and he crouched still lower, took aim and squeezed the trigger. He was unfamiliar with the rifle, which pulled slightly to the left, and his shot did no damage. Cursing under his breath, he reloaded.

Gibson fired a second time, but his shot merely dug a hole in the side of the boat.

Andrew braced himself, squeezed the trigger again and, having compensated for the tug of the weapon, had the satisfaction of seeing the lead oarsman on the craft's port side slump in his seat. "We're even," he said. "One apiece."

The fusillade from the boat became more intense, and

both men in the prow crouched even lower as they re-loaded.

On the next round each wounded his man, and the boat, with only three of its occupants healthy, began to drift.

"Full sail, Captain," Andrew shouted. "It doesn't matter if you ram the damned boat! Your hull is thicker!"

The master of the *Gheen-kho* finally understood the wisdom of the advice and sent two of his sailors aloft. They added sail, and the schooner began to gather additional speed, but one of the men in the rigging made a perfect target for the pirates, and dropped to the deck with a bullet through his head and several in his body.

The schooner had hesitated too long, and the larger boat was drawing closer, almost within boarding range.

Andrew, bent almost double to avoid the fire of the pirates, ran toward the area on the port side where, he thought, the enemy would be most likely to board. Once again he heard Gibson behind him. Hillery was on one knee at the rail, blood oozing from a slight wound on the side of his face; apparently he had been grazed by a bullet, but was firing his pistols at the foe, reloading and firing again.

"You can't hit them at this range with pistols. Come with me!" Andrew commanded, snatching the rifle of the crew member who had been killed.

He led his companions to several thick bales of cotton, which he used as cover. "These will help absorb their fire," he said. "Mr. Hillery, load one of these rifles for me while I fire the other, and don't waste any time!"

At that moment a frightened seaman joined them, and Andrew directed him to do the same for Gibson.

Now Andrew and the trapper were able to devote their full attention to the pirates in the crowded boat, and they maintained a steady, deadly fire, ignoring the shots that sometimes whistled past them, sometimes buried themselves in the padding of the cotton bales.

With grim joviality they kept score. "I got one o' the buzzards in the arm," Gibson announced, "but it ain't stopped him."

"You'll have to finish him yourself," the disgusted Andrew replied. "All I did was put a bullet into the oar handle of mine."

The trapper took a loaded rifle from the sailor, to whom he handed the smoking weapon he had just discharged. "That there is better," he announced a moment later. "He ain't dead, but I took all the fight out o' him."

"I've gone ahead of you," Andrew said after he had taken aim and fired again. "They'll have to bury mine on the island or throw him into the river."

In spite of their casualties, however, the boat continued to approach, and the survivors in the second craft, taking heart, started back toward the schooner.

"Faster!" Andrew ordered Hillery and the sailor.

Once again the two defenders' rifles spoke, then again. Between them Andrew and Gibson wounded three more of the pirates, and the invaders, finally becoming discouraged, allowed the *Gheen-kho* to pass.

"I've never seen a finer exhibition of marksmanship," Abel Hillery said, stretching and standing.

Andrew unceremoniously knocked him to the deck, and an instant later several shots whined overhead. "Never take chances with river thieves. Always wait until they're out of range."

"Thanks for the lesson—and for saving me." Hillery sat up, rubbing a sore shoulder. "I'll know better, if this should ever happen to me again."

Both of the boats soon were left far behind, and the schooner's defenders counted their casualties. Only the sailor who had fallen from the rigging was dead, and two others were slightly wounded, Hillery refusing to admit that the gash on the side of his face was an injury.

In spite of Andrew's assurances that the cutthroats would make no attempt to pursue the schooner, the *Green-kho* did not pause to bury her dead, and it was not until nightfall, when she anchored for the night, that the company went ashore to dig a shallow grave and listen to a brief service performed by the ship's master. Most of the men were still apprehensive, so no fire was lighted for fear it would reveal their whereabouts, and they ate a cold wilderness meal of jerked beef, pickled mackerel, and parched corn.

A crew member was assigned to keep watch, and, as the others went off to their bunks for the night, Hillery offered Andrew a *segaro*. They wandered down the schooner's deck to the stern, where they made themselves as comfortable as they could on packing cases, and for a time both were silent.

"Your valor and leadership," the State Department official said at last, "were extraordinary."

Andrew was unable to remember how many battles he had fought against the Mississippi brigands. "They're good shots," he said, "and if they gain the upper hand there's no stopping them. But they turn tail and run when they're hurt. The only way to handle them is to get the upper hand right off—and keep it."

Hillery smiled. "War can be less complicated than diplomacy. You either win or lose, and the rewards of victory are tangible."

"It's a way of earning a living."

"Well, you earned your passage today. The master refunded me the Government funds I'd given him for you, and if he hadn't, I'd gladly have paid the price myself. You not only saved this ship and her cargo, but I'd have been killed if you hadn't pulled me down onto the deck."

"That was just being neighborly," Andrew replied in embarrassment. "You can't put a price on helping somebody during a fight."

"All the same, it was my life. Not to mention the others, the price of the schooner and of all the merchandise."

"I don't want to see you cheated, Mr. Hillery. My wages as a river devil are six dollars for a one-way voyage, ten for round-trip. So you—or the master—or both of you are being too generous."

"If we're satisfied, and we are, don't complain." Hillery was intrigued by his honesty, the last quality he had expected to find in a Mississippi barge guard who had been in trouble in New Orleans, and who had astonished him by reading Ovid. Using tact as well as guile, he persuaded the river devil to tell him his background.

Andrew realized what he was doing, but saw no reason to conceal his past, and spoke freely. "So there you have it," he said as he concluded the tale. "In less than four years I spent every last penny it took my father a lifetime to earn and put away for me. And all I have are some gaming debts that still haven't been paid, the taste of gin in my mouth and memories of so many wenches that I can't sort out one from another in my mind. My purse is empty, and I don't even own a pistol I can use to protect myself in the wilderness.'

"I'm making you a gift of the rifle you used today," the State Department official said, adding quickly, "I've already paid for it, and I have no use for it myself."

"It's a good enough rifle, and I'm not so blamed noble that I'll refuse. I'm going to need it."

"You'll keep working on the river?"

"Not if I'm sane, Mr. Hillery. The *Gheen-kho* will be safe enough from pirates when we get a mite farther north, so I'll ask to be dropped at Tennessee Bluffs, where the old French fort once stood. Then I'll find myself a site for a homestead, and go to Nashville to register it. If I'm lucky, maybe I'll be able to persuade my cousin to farm it with me, but I'm afraid he still hasn't lost his appetite for adventure."

"I wouldn't have thought you were the type to set up a homestead."

Andrew's smile was bitter. "As Horace said, *Sic me servavit Apollo.*"

There was no need for him to translate. The literal meaning was, "Thus Apollo preserved me," but Hillery knew he was indicating he had no choice. Since he wanted to give up his life as a river devil, he could either carve a farm for himself out of the western Tennessee forest—or starve.

Secretary of State Timothy Pickering felt ill at ease with the President, but so did most men. John Adams could be verbose enough when he wrote official documents, or even letters, but he was inclined to be enigmatic in conversation with his subordinates. Pickering was not only uncomfortable, but resented him, convinced that others in Adams' official family had more influence in matters of state than did the nominal first officer of the Cabinet. In the Administration of George Washington, whose recent death the whole of the United States was mourning, a man always

51

had known where he stood, but Adams was a master of ambiguity.

As a fellow citizen of Massachusetts, Pickering had thought on many occasions, it should have been possible for him to understand the President, but apparently they had little in common. Like his good friend, John Hancock, the Secretary of State enjoyed a hearty dinner and a good bottle of wine, but the President ate sparingly, and, it was said, used wine instead of red ink when working on his ledgers. Pickering liked the relaxed atmosphere of New York, and would have been satisfied to see it remain the capital of the young nation until the new community, Washington City, was built. But the President preferred the austerity of Philadelphia, where he could walk undisturbed down the streets because people didn't want to embarrass him or destroy his privacy by recognizing him.

Above all, the two men differed on the subject of France, which Pickering loathed. But the President, in spite of a grueling, undeclared naval war with the French that had lasted two years, refused to think of any land as an enemy. And today, just when Pickering was suffering from a headache and indigestion after drinking a few too many rum and sack flips the previous evening, the President seemed determined to talk about France.

"Our reports from four different sources agree," John Adams said, spreading four documents in a neat row on his desk. "The new ruler of France—First Consul, he calls himself—is a rather remarkable man."

"I wouldn't trust him, Mr. President," Pickering said sourly.

"I'm not suggesting it." The President's tone was gently chiding. "I'm merely pointing out to you that he's made his peace with us. I'll grant you it wasn't difficult. All his Foreign Minister, Talleyrand, had to do was notify us that First Consul Bonaparte wanted to renew France's friendship with us."

"General Bonaparte's reason is very simple, Mr. President. He's at war with most of Europe—"

"True enough."

"—and he doesn't have ships to spare for a blockade of our ports."

52

"I find it dangerous to speculate on the motives of a man we know very little about." The President straightened his tailcoat.

Pickering was virtually positive that his superior was staring with cold eyes at his crimson waistcoat, and felt a new wave of annoyance. Just because John Adams chose to dress like a pallbearer at a funeral was no reason the members of his Cabinet had to follow his example. It was astonishing that Abigail Adams, who had been a lively woman with a warm sense of humor, could tolerate her husband, but Pickering supposed he had squeezed the humanity from her.

"It's enough for me," the President continued, "that Bonaparte has promised to stop halting our ships on the high seas."

"A Frenchman's promise isn't worth much," Pickering declared.

John Adams averted his face to hide a flicker of annoyance. Perhaps he had been wrong to keep Washington's Cabinet in office, although the idea had been sound enough in March '97, when he had taken office. But he had suffered Pickering's intolerance and stubborn prejudices for the better part of three years, and was weary of the man. Alexander Hamilton had been right when he'd once said, half in jest, "Pickering is an errand boy who refuses to do errands. You're really your own Secretary of State, Mr. President."

"I think we should continue to send our merchantmen to sea in convoys, protected by warships," Pickering insisted. "Then we won't be relying on a French tyrant's word."

"We don't know he's a tyrant," Adams said with a slight smile.

"All the same, Mr. President—"

"Did you read my memorandum of yesterday?"

"Of course."

The President said nothing more, but sat back in his chair and pressed his fingertips together.

Here was another of his damnable ambiguities, Pickering thought, and in spite of his raging headache tried to recall what the memorandum had said.

Adams called on his last reserves of patience. "The foreign trade on which this agricultural nation depends will wither away unless our brigs can cross the Atlantic singly and at will. We don't have enough warships for convoys, as the past two years of experience have proved, and a brig putting out of Baltimore, for example, will lose too much valuable time if she must join a convoy at Charleston or Boston before sailing for European ports."

Pickering nodded, irritated because the President sounded like a schoolmaster rebuking an inattentive boy.

"Consequently," Adams continued, a note of finality in his voice, "we are obliged to accept the word of General Bonaparte. I, for one, am anxious to do so."

The Secretary hoped his expression didn't indicate his belief that the President of the United States had lost his senses.

"How do you evaluate these rumors about Louisiana?"

Pickering hated it when he jumped from subject to subject, and didn't see the connection.

The President waited.

A light dawned, and the Secretary wondered why he couldn't have been direct. "It wouldn't surprise me in the least if France tried to regain control of Louisiana. The French are the greediest people on earth."

"Don't let the Vice-President hear you say that." For the first time since they had gone into conference, Adams laughed.

"Tom Jefferson's head was turned when he was Minister to France. I don't consider him an accurate observer."

"I do, and in this instance you and he are in perfect agreement. It's his opinion that Bonaparte would like to rebuild the French colonies in the New World, and that the people of France feel the same way. They've never recovered the blow to their pride when England took the Canadian provinces from them."

"France will have to go to war with Spain to get Louisiana."

The President picked up two bulky dispatches and flipped through them. "According to our own Ministers in Paris and Madrid, he's in the process of working out a treaty with Charles of Spain that will give him the territory without a war."

"I studied those reports carefully," the Secretary of

54

State said, "and I can't for the life of me see why the Spaniards would agree to such a cession."

"Because France is strong, Spain is weak and Charles would rather avoid a war. One fair-sized city and an endless wilderness tract are small prices to pay for peace, particularly when they're half the world away from Spain."

Pickering was forced to admit, grudgingly, that the argument was valid, and sighed. "If it happens, we'll have to go to war to prevent France from regaining a foothold in North America."

John Adams' temper finally flared. "That's precisely what we can't do," he said with asperity.

"But the threat to our own security—"

"—may be no worse if the French instead of the Spaniards are in New Orleans! We lack the strength to drive out Spain, so how could we go to war against France?"

"Our population has increased very rapidly, Mr. President, and I'm certain next year's census will show that we have four million people in the country. In all of Louisiana, including New Orleans, there are no more than fifty thousand persons, and that's a very generous estimate!"

"But they'd be supported by the French fleet," the President reminded him, and suddenly laughed again. "I sound inconsistent, don't I, Tim?"

"You do, Mr. President." There was more than a hint of malice in the Secretary's voice.

"Just a moment or two ago I agreed that France must give up her naval war against us because she needs her fleet in European waters. Now I'm saying we can't go to war with France over Louisiana because the French fleet is too strong. Well, I spent half the night gnawing at the contradiction."

With Hamilton, who isn't even in the Cabinet any more, right beside you, giving you advice, Pickering thought.

"And I came to the conclusion that it's not I who is being inconsistent. It's General Bonaparte."

Pickering floundered. "I don't understand, Mr. President."

"France lost her colonies because England sent people to the New World, while the French were content to hold vast tracts of land. The same thing could happen again." Adams paused when he saw that the Secretary was becoming still more confused. "Unless General Bonaparte sends colonists to New Orleans by the thousands, and supports them with his regiments and warships, he won't be able to hold Louisiana. To accomplish that purpose he needs peace in Europe, but he's building so many new ships and creating so many new divisions that I think it likely he'll devote virtually all of his attention to his European enemies and use all of his strength against them."

"Then we can take Louisiana from him."

"There may be ways of obtaining it without resorting to force. We'll have to be alert, keep watch on the situation and learn all we can. Louisiana," President Adams said, "may not mean much to France or Spain, but to us it's a great prize."

FIVE

April-June 1800

The palaces of the kings who had ruled France in the centuries when she had been a monarchy were among the most beautiful and ornamental in a land proud of her architectural heritage. But the new, as yet uncrowned head of the state found that most located in Paris and its environs had serious drawbacks. Versailles was not only expensive to keep open, but reminded too many people of the Bourbons, who had been deposed. The Palais Royal was too small, the Luxembourg reminded First Consul Bonaparte of a barn, the Palais Bourbon, although relatively modern, had inadequate bathing facilities for a man who not only scrubbed himself daily in a metal tub but insisted that everyone around him do the same, and the Palais de l'Elysée was little more than a mansion for a king's mistress, which is what it had been when Madame de Pompadour had occupied it during the reign of Louis XV.

So, more or less by default, the First Consul made the Louvre his official home and set up most of his offices there. The palace was very old, and supposedly had been erected on the site of an old Roman fort. Most of its modern wings had been added by Francis I, and as the great Henry IV had lived and worked there, the First Consul carefully made certain that France knew he slept in Henry's bedchamber and made Henry's private audience room his office. It did no harm for a man to be associated in the public eye with his most renowned predecessor.

The Louvre was far from ideal, however, even though General Bonaparte insisted he was as indifferent to personal discomfort and even hardship as he was when campaigning in the field with his legions. The many relatives who made their home with him and the high-ranking officials who dared to speak candidly in his presence lost no opportunity to remind him that the Louvre was drafty in autumn, almost unbearably cold in winter, damp in spring, and hot beyond endurance in summer. The accumulated dirt of decades covered its high windows, shutting out light and making it necessary to use oil lamps and tapers even in the middle of the day.

It was so large, too, that Foreign Minister Charles Maurice de Talleyrand-Périgord, who had injured a foot in early childhood and still suffered the handicap of a limp, found it exhausting to walk from the auxiliary office he maintained in one wing to the inner sanctum of the First Consul. But the homely, luxury-loving Talleyrand was as discreet as he was resourceful. The son of a distinguished general in the reign of Louis XV, he had been the Bishop of Autun before the French Revolution, had unfrocked himself to become a leader in the Republican cause, and for four years, beginning long before the rise of General Bonaparte to power, he had been in charge of France's foreign affairs. Patient in small matters as well as large, he knew that some day the First Consul would move to more convenient headquarters. Until then he was keeping quiet about such trifling matters as endless corridors and agonizingly steep flights of stairs.

Dropping uninvited onto a divan that stood beneath a magnificent Gobelin tapestry at one side of the office, he smiled bloodlessly at the new master of France. It was his private opinion that the Corsican-born First Consul, who wore military uniforms of his own design every day of his life, was a boor. But Talleyrand also recognized his genius, and had every intention of remaining close to him, although it was difficult to keep on good terms with someone who scorned sycophants and insisted that his principal subordinates show intellectual independence, yet who became angry and hurt when anyone disagreed with him.

"The Spanish Cortes," the Foreign Minister said, holding up a ribbon-embossed parchment document, "has just endorsed the new treaty, and Charles has used all three of his seals beneath his signature to prove to us that he intends to abide by every clause."

General Bonaparte always tried to conceal signs of nervousness, but didn't realize that those who were close to him recognized the significance of an unconscious gesture, that of running a hand forward through his hair. "Have they made any changes we didn't expect, or omitted something of importance? You know the Spaniards."

Talleyrand enjoyed a fleeting moment of pleasure as he ignored the hand outstretched waiting to receive the parchment. Then, leaning on his gold-handled walking stick, he pulled himself to his feet and gave the First Consul the parchment. "My office has checked this with the working copy, and they say it's a faithful reproduction."

"You should have gone over it yourself."

The Foreign Minister turned away to conceal his exasperation. It had been a mistake to admit he had turned the routine task over to subordinates. Bonaparte never trusted details to others, and expected his principal lieutenants to follow his example, forgetting that although he was capable of working twenty hours out of every twenty-four, they needed rest and diversion.

The First Consul scanned the embossed copy of the treaty. "This seems to be in order."

There was little in the world that impressed Talleyrand, but Napoleon Bonaparte's ability to read every word of a complicated state paper at a glance unfailingly astonished him. "We've gained a great deal without firing a shot."

Bonaparte knew he was boasting, trying to claim credit for the treaty, but refrained from remarking that French military victories elsewhere in recent years, combined with a fear of French power, were responsible. Men worked harder for him when they could claim the credit for achievements he had made possible.

"They've even included the clauses on the cession of the Louisiana Territory in North America," the Foreign Minister said. "I was afraid they'd leave it out at the very last, as though by accident, hoping we wouldn't refuse to implement the treaty over something so minor."

The First Consul tugged at his lower lip to prevent himself from laughing. "I don't call a tract of more than eight hundred and twenty-five thousand square miles a minor acquisition."

"I suppose not."

"Your lack of enthusiasm overwhelms me, Charles."

"Your zeal inundates me, First Consul. I'm pleased with the lands we took from Austria and the Pope. The expansion wave of France flows naturally across the Italian states. But all that New World land and the city of

59

New Orleans are worse than useless to us, and impossible to defend!"

"For the present, perhaps. That's why it's so important that no word leak out regarding the cession until next year. By then I hope to be in a better position to send a division of troops and a few ships-of-the-line to New Orleans. They'll discourage the British from attempting an invasion, and the Americans will leave us alone."

"I wouldn't be too sure of that. They're an impulsive people."

When Bonaparte grinned, his charm was magnetic. "I've met very few Americans other than their legation staff—who aren't at all like you professional diplomats."

Talleyrand chose to interpret the deliberate slur as a compliment. "Unfortunately."

The grin broadened, and Napoleon Bonaparte picked up the miniature sword he ordinarily used to break the seals on letters. Absently, scarcely conscious of what he was doing, he carved the letter N on the top of his desk, then drew a laurel wreath around it. "I like what little I know of the United States. She may be impulsive, but she's also hard-headed. Her rulers are realistic men, and they won't plunge into a war if they think they're going to lose it."

"Does any nation?"

"The powers of self-delusion are greater in some lands than in others," the First Consul said softly. "My instincts tell me the United States will accept the cession of Louisiana to France, provided we prepare carefully—and secretly—for the transfer. I want to confront them with the accomplished fact before they learn of it."

It was Talleyrand's duty as well as his desire to find weaknesses in his superior's argument. "Let's suppose we're at peace with England next year, as well as with Austria and Russia. Prussia, too, although she won't attack us unless we move first against her. You could take the risk of sending troops and ships-of-the-line to the New World. That's a decision for your military advisers—"

"I make my own military decisions," Bonaparte interrupted curtly.

"Yes, of course, First Consul." Talleyrand backed down. "But let's suppose, just for the sake of looking at every potential, you understand, and not to be considered seriously, that your divisions are tied down in the German and Italian states, and you need your ships-of-the-line and frigates for a new war with England—"

"I admit the distinct possibility." When Bonaparte laughed he looked unexpectedly idealistic and rather naïve.

Talleyrand knew he was neither. "In that event, what can we gain by owning Louisiana? I can't understand why you insisted on acquiring it. It will be a liability to us!"

"Eight hundred and twenty-five thousand square miles of territory are always an asset. You play cards, Charles?"

"An occasional game of twenty-and-one," the Foreign Minister admitted.

"Then you know the value of holding strong cards, preferably aces. Forgive me," Bonaparte added, always sensitive to nuances and unwilling to hurt a valuable lieutenant's feelings needlessly, "for delivering a little lecture to you on a subject in which you're an expert and I'm still something of a novice. Well, not a novice, really, but lacking in practical experience. I was speaking of cards, was I not, particularly aces?"

"You think Louisiana is an ace."

"Even without New Orleans, which gives us a second ace." The First Consul held up two stubby fingers. "England would love to gain possession of the territory. Spain would like to have it returned. The United States could double her territory by almost one hundred and fifty percent, and would gain the Mississippi River egress she so desperately wants."

Talleyrand always was amazed by Bonaparte's memory for statistics and facts.

"There you have three nations coveting territory that belongs to us, and there are others, less important at the moment. We shall have two fine aces to play, Charles. In a world where territory is the principal medium of exchange, I want my purse filled with it!"

The oak landed with a crash that echoed through the forest and rolled out across the broad expanse of the Mississippi River. Andrew leaned on his ax handle, resting for a few moments, and with his free hand wiped sweat from his forehead and eyes. The June sun was blistering, his naked torso was deeply tanned and it was difficult to breathe in the damp, lifeless air. But there was still work to be done; the task of clearing his property seemed endless, and he wondered whether to stake his claim in the most inaccessible wilderness region of Tennessee.

The idea was not new, and had been plaguing him for months, ever since he had cut his first trees to make his cabin. Perhaps he should have settled farther north, where the weather in the late spring, summer, and early autumn was less warm for a man who disliked violent physical exercise and who had spent his formative years in cold New England. At the very least, he told himself, he should have found himself a property closer to Nashville.

Had he known that his cousin Billy would spend only a short time with him before becoming restless and rejoining the river devils, he wouldn't have gone so far into forests inhabited only by roving bands of Cherokee and occasional trappers. Andrew's nearest neighbor lived more than twelve miles from his homestead, river devils who were traveling on Mississippi barges visited no more frequently than once in a month, and he hadn't seen a woman since his last, brief visit to Nashville.

Inevitably he found himself thinking about Beatriz de Santos again, remembering the warmth of her lovemaking. By now, he reflected, she was married to her damned Spaniard, and he never would learn why she had given herself to him so freely and had risked the destruction of her reputation by presenting him to her friends.

It was unlikely, too, that he would have the opportunity to even his score with Jeanne Valdéz. He still felt deep anger whenever he thought of the Creole girl who had reported him to the authorities of New Spain. Thanks to circumstances over which she had no influence he had been deported from Louisiana; for all she had known, he might have been executed or sentenced to a long term in a miserable Spanish prison. If he had the chance to obtain vengeance against her at some day in the distant future, he would utilize it to the full.

Picking up his ax again, Andrew decided he was too weary to chop another oak before sundown, and instead attacked a stand of hickory and oak that required relatively little effort. His arms and shoulders moved rhythmically, steadily, and he put the heat out of his mind as he cut down one tree, then moved on to another. In two more weeks, if he kept to his schedule, he would be finished cutting the west forty, and, after clearing out the stumps and plowing, would be ready to plant there, as he had on the other portions of his homestead.

Off to the east he heard an unfamiliar sound in the forest, and stopping work, reached for the rifle he always kept near at hand. Unable to identify the faint noise, he dropped to the floor of the forest and held an ear to the ground. The sound was the beat of a single horse's hoofs, and he returned to his cabin, put away his ax and then went out into the forest, where he could see the narrow trail without being seen.

He waited with the patience the wilderness required, ignoring the mosquitoes and other insects to whose bites he had long been immune. The horseman drew closer, and seemed to be heading straight toward the cabin, so Andrew assumed a visitor was coming to see him. He remained concealed, however; in this remote frontier land, a man never took unnecessary chances.

Andrew checked his rifle, and when the rider and his mount came in sight, he drew a bead on the man, whose black broadcloth suit, white stock, and bicorn hat seemed totally out of place in the wilderness. Then, suddenly, he recognized the man, and lowering his rifle, stepped into the open.

"Mr. Hillery," he said, "you're just about the last man in the United States I expected to see."

Abel Hillery drew to a halt, his gelding prancing nervously because of the unexpected appearance of the man from the underbrush. "At last," the State Department official said. "I've spent the past two days trying to locate you, and I was beginning to think you hadn't settled in Tennessee."

"Oh, I'm here," Andrew replied dryly, leading him to the cabin. "It isn't much, but I'm anchored to it. If I'd known company was coming I'd have brought in some supplies from the store about twenty miles down the trail, assuming I had the funds to buy them. I'm afraid all I can give you is some venison I've smoked, or bear bacon. With spring water to drink."

A short time later they sat down to eat beside the stone-lined cooking pit outside Andrew's cabin. "Obviously," Hillery said, "I haven't come in search of you to pay a sociable visit."

"I didn't think you had."

"I wonder if you've heard the rumors about the Louisiana country."

Andrew shook his head. "I don't hear much of anything, and all I really care about is whether the Choctaw or Cherokee are taking scalps again. Is there trouble in New Orleans?"

"Not yet, but there's no predicting what may happen if the stories that reached the Administration are true. The State Department suspects that Spain is ceding the whole Louisiana country to France under the terms of a secret treaty."

Andrew whistled softly under his breath. "That General Bonaparte is a mean one. He's ready to fight anybody, any time."

"We hope he's going to prove sensible," Hillery said, "but we can't be certain."

"Will he try to close the Mississippi to American shipping? If he does, every last man in Tennessee and Kentucky will go to war with him, whether the United States Government authorizes it or not. The same is true in the Indiana Territory and the Illinois country. We can't earn a living unless we use the port of New Orleans."

"President Adams is trying to learn two things. First, whether France actually is acquiring Louisiana. Second, if she is, whether New Orleans will keep open for our shipping."

Andrew deftly cut a slice of hot venison with his knife and slowly ate it. "When the word spreads," he said, "every farmer in the West is going to oil his rifle and make himself some new bullets. The stores that sell bullet molds are going to do one mighty big business!"

"We don't want the word to spread. The President wants no panic, and he's afraid some of our people might resort to violence if they hear the rumor. We aren't strong enough to give France a reason to declare war against us.

And we gather that General Bonaparte is quick to take offense."

"So are we!" Andrew declared, bristling.

"That's what makes this situation so explosive. It's the principal reason that everything I'm telling you is to be kept in confidence," Hillery said.

"I don't talk out of turn. But why come all the way out here to tell me anything at all?"

"We need your help."

"I'm no diplomat, and I'm not acquainted with people who'd tell me the details of secret treaties."

"Our legations in Paris and Madrid have been instructed to find out all they can. But General Hamilton believes there's still more we can do."

"Alexander Hamilton?"

Hillery nodded. "There's none wiser, and the President always listens to his advice. If there is such a treaty, he thinks it likely we can find out more from the Spaniards in New Orleans than we can through our Ministers to France and Spain. Colonial officials aren't inclined to be as close-mouthed as higher-ranking officials in the European capitals."

"Provided they've been told the secrets."

"Of course," Hillery said. "That's something we can only guess. But we want to find out."

"How do I fit into all this?" Andrew wanted to know.

"I thought of you when we had a conference at the State Department. We want to send someone into New Orleans, a man who knows the city, speaks French and Spanish, and is alert and intelligent enough to perform a delicate task of espionage for the United States."

"I don't believe I'm qualified."

"He also must be able to look after himself and prevent the Spanish authorities from learning his real identity or mission."

"Then you don't want me," Andrew said flatly. "You can't have forgotten that I was expelled from Louisiana. It wouldn't surprise me if there was a price on my head, and I'm known to a great many people there."

"You're valuable to us precisely because you are acquainted with them. They think of you as a river devil, nothing more. I've learned that Don Felipe de Guzmán has arrived in New Orleans, so I believe you'd be the last man Governor Almonaster y Rojas would want to place under arrest. He'd prefer to ignore your presence in the city than to revive a scandal he made a considerable effort to stifle."

"Maybe so." Andrew was silent for a moment. "But I refuse to use Beatriz de Santos. If you think I'd strike up an acquaintance with Don Felipe through her—"

"The State Department doesn't care how you carry out the assignment, and neither do I. Handle the matter in any way you see fit."

"Fair enough, I reckon. But I'm trying to put this homestead into shape so I earn a living from it, and I can't afford to leave."

"We'll pay for your services, naturally," Hillery said. "Didn't I mention that?"

"You sure didn't!"

"We'll give you fifty dollars for your expenses, and a guaranteed fee of one hundred dollars. If you find out what we want to know, we'll make it two hundred."

"That's more than I can earn here in the next two years. I could even hire somebody to help me on the farm!"

"If the rumor should be true and France closes New Orleans to us, it wouldn't matter how much you produced on your homestead." Hillery wiped his greasy hands on some dry leaves. "You'd have no market."

"I don't need any more convincing," Andrew said with a tight smile. "You could have saved yourself a heap of talking if you'd told me the fee right off, Mr. Hillery. How much will you pay me now?"

"One hundred dollars plus the expense money."

"In that case I'll be on my way as soon as the next barge convoy comes down the Mississippi."

SIX

June 1800

The leisurely, familiar voyage down the Mississippi had been uneventful, almost dull, and New Orleans seemed unchanged. Two regiments of Spanish infantry and three squadrons of cavalry were still stationed in the city, and the customs officials resplendent in their yellow and black uniforms, continued to treat citizens of the United States with condescending scorn. New homes were being built beyond the gates of the original French settlement, several waterfront taverns and inns had closed, only to be replaced by others, and the plantations of the wealthy continued to expand to the north of the city.

Andrew parted company with his fellow river devils and found himself an inexpensive room at one of the new inns near the wharves. Under no circumstances would he masquerade as a gentleman, he had decided, but would remain in his role of a river devil during his stay in New Orleans. Although he had never before undertaken an espionage assignment, common sense told him he would be complicating his lot if he disguised himself in any role other than that which was most familiar to him.

The food of New Orleans was still the best he had ever eaten. He dined on a thick vegetable and chicken soup, a paella of seafood spiced with garlic and saffron, and larded beef that had been marinated for several days in wine. He slept well, and early the next morning, after eating a light breakfast of broiled fish, smoked ham, bread, and goat's milk cheese, he started out toward St. Charles Street, a brace of pistols in his belt and his rifle in his hand. There had been ample time for him to determine his course of action, but he had a personal errand to perform before he started to work on his assignment.

He had no idea whether Beatriz had married her grandee from Spain, and could only proceed one step at a time. Uncertain whether she still lived in her house, with or without a husband, he stationed himself a short distance from it, near the canal that ran parallel to it. Don Felipe, if he was her husband by now, would depart early for his office in the Hall of the Cabildo, it being the custom of Spanish administrators to start their workday early and take a long rest period for their noon meal.

After a wait of about a half-hour, Andrew saw Lucille leave the house for her usual morning marketing, so it was relatively safe to assume that Beatriz still lived in the house and that, even if married, she would be alone, since the serving woman would not go out if the master were still at home.

He walked quickly to the door and rapped on it.

After a long wait it opened, and Beatriz, wearing a dressing gown of pale green silk, stood in the frame. She stared in astonishment at the blond American giant.

Andrew was the first to speak. "I haven't come to embarrass or harm you," he said. "May I have a word with you?"

Still stunned, she motioned him into the parlor. "I never expected to see you again," she said at last.

"A man must earn a living." He looked at her hands, searching for a wedding ring. "Are you married yet?"

Color rose in her face, and she tugged the dressing gown around her more tightly. "No, I—I've insisted that Don Felipe and I must know each other better before—"

"I see." Unfortunately, neither the knowledge of her betrothal nor the passage of time had dimmed his desire for her.

"I've often wished I could apologize to you, Andrew." It was not easy for her to humble herself. "But I deliberately never told you about him, or—"

"There's no need to explain." He bowed. "I wish you happiness, whenever you marry. I intend to be here for only a short time, but I didn't want you to be concerned if someone you know happened to see me on the streets. I just arrived last night with a barge convoy from the United States, and I'll be leaving soon with another, whenever I can find one that will pay my fee."

"Thank you." Beatriz seemed rooted to the spot.

Andrew bowed again and turned toward the door.

"Wait!" she called.

He paused with a hand on the latch.

"I still have the clothes you wore when you were here. They're packed away in a leather box."

"You should have rid yourself of them," he said. "After you're married, Don Felipe will start asking questions. I would."

"He won't see them." Her long, red hair rippled in waves down her back as she held her head high. "I've been saving them because—well, I'm not sure why. Now that you're here, you can take them."

"I don't want them," he replied honestly. The attire of a gentleman, if found in his room at the waterfront inn, might make the authorities curious about a river devil.

"But they belong to you!"

"Burn them, give them away, do what you will with them—but get rid of them."

Beatriz's green eyes reflected her perplexity. "I don't understand why—"

"Men in my trade," Andrew cut in, "aren't very elegant, and the coat alone would make a perfect target for river brigands if I wore it on board a barge." He saw she accepted his explanation, and decided there was no reason to avoid obtaining information from her in order to save him time and trouble. "Tell me, is Ramón Valdéz still the Governor's director of the port?"

"Oh, yes, he's held the post for many years."

"His daughter still lives with him?"

"Jeanne? Yes."

A man need not have known her well and understand her moods to recognize her jealousy. Andrew wanted to offer her an excuse that would make his question appear impersonal, but decided it was better, for the sake of his ultimate purposes, to say nothing more. Beatriz looked so hurt, however, that he could not resist returning to the living room, sweeping her into his arms and kissing her.

She returned his embrace and kiss, her passion matching his, then broke away from him with a vehemence that startled him. "Don't touch me!" she cried. "Ever again! Remember that I'm going to be married!"

"Life would have been much simpler for both of us if you'd remembered it last year." Andrew started toward the door again.

"Go to Jeanne! Or to one of the river harlots!" Her anger appeared uncontrollable.

He let himself out of the house and closed the door behind him. Had he planned the brief meeting, he knew, nothing would have been more effective than to make advances to her after showing an interest in her closest friend. Eventually she would be sure to say something to the Valdéz girl, and would help set the stage for the drama he intended to play. Nevertheless he felt ashamed, even though Beatriz had been reckless at his expense, as well as her own, when she had allowed him to make love to her without telling him she was betrothed.

Putting her out of his mind as best he could, he started toward the Avenue de Bienville, and steeled himself with the reminder that he had a score to settle with Jeanne Valdéz, who had betrayed him to the authorities. He walked rapidly, paying little attention to traffic, and a horseman swerved to avoid running him down.

The man, who was in uniform, cursed him in Spanish.

Andrew recognized him as an officer he had met when escorting Beatriz to various social events. "Captain de Metínez, my apologies. I was careless."

Captain Cristoforo de Martínez glared at him, saying nothing.

Andrew had no idea whether the officer knew him, and didn't care. Turning away, he increased his pace, walking rapidly until he reached the Rue St. Pierre, a small side street off the Avenue de Bienville. Then, slowing, he admired the handsome three-story brick house and landscaped grounds of Ramón Valdéz's home. The director of the port, like other officials in New Spain, lived exceptionally well. If and when France recovered Louisiana, no one would regret it more than would the present administrators of the colony.

A servingmaid answered Andrew's summons, and the woman's eyes widened when he asked to see Jeanne. Obviously she was not accustomed to visits from American riverboat scum. He was ushered into a small chamber adjoining a large, formal drawing room, and after a brief wait the woman returned, then led him up the stairs to a smaller sitting room with an adjoining balcony overlooking an inner courtyard garden. There Jeanne was sitting, reading, but immediately jumped to her feet when she saw Andrew.

It was difficult, he thought, to hate a girl with such a spectacularly attractive face and figure. "Apparently you remember me," he said, removing his hat but not bothering to bow.

"I hoped New Orleans had seen the last of you!" she declared indignantly.

"Sometimes our fondest hopes in this world are frustrated." He strolled out to the balcony.

Jeanne saw the servingmaid lingering in the sitting room, and dismissed her. "If you've come back here to annoy Beatriz again, I warn you, sir—"

"Save your breath," Andrew interrupted rudely. "I just paid a brief visit to her house, and she knows I have no intention of causing her embarrassment or trouble." He walked to the nearest chair, and although not invited to sit, made himself comfortable.

Jeanne's violet eyes narrowed. "I don't trust you."

"You've given me no reason to have faith in you, either, you know." He tried to prevent himself from sounding bitter. The success of his entire scheme depended on her reaction to him in the next few minutes, so it was essential that he hide his real feelings. "You may not believe I knew nothing of Beatriz's betrothal until you told me about it, but that's the truth."

"Does it matter what I believe?" She was disconcerted because he had sat down, but was reluctant to make a scene by requesting him to leave.

"As it happens, it matters a great deal. I can also give you my solemn word that I won't go to her house again, and won't even speak to her if I should meet her in public."

"Then you're more considerate than I believed possible," Jeanne said.

He curbed his temper. "Perhaps you were wrong," he replied, "to judge someone you don't really know."

The girl hesitated for a moment. "Perhaps," she conceded, then became belligerent again. "Why have you found it necessary to come to me with all this?"

"There are several reasons," Andrew said. "I expect to be in New Orleans for a few days, and I don't want to be

71

placed under arrest again. If I am, the treatment one receives in your Spanish prisons might make me less kind—less discreet."

She murmured something to the effect that she couldn't blame him.

Andrew felt he was making progress. "There are other, more urgent reasons," he said. "The most important of them should be obvious."

Jeanne was unable to avert her eyes as he continued to gaze at her. "I'm afraid it isn't."

"Why does a man usually pay a call on a woman?" he demanded.

She flushed, unconsciously raising a hand to make certain her dark hair was in place.

"I was drawn to you when we first met, but I was loyal to Beatriz, as you were. Had I known then what I later discovered . . ." He allowed his voice to trail off.

Jeanne recovered her aplomb. "Have you nothing better to do than pay court to ladies, sir?"

"Is it a crime for a man to recognize a woman's beauty?" Andrew retorted. "Certainly I'm not alone in thinking you lovely. You can't condemn me for thinking about you. You've been on my mind, constantly, ever since I left New Orleans and returned to the United States," he added truthfully.

As he had hoped, it was impossible for her to remain immune to such flattery, and she became flustered.

"I'm not one of your fine Creole gentlemen, but I hope I'm not entirely lacking in civility."

"Beatriz told me you were educated at the Sorbonne, which surprised me, sir. I mean, I assumed that someone who worked as a guard on a Mississippi riverboat—"

"I pray that misfortune never strikes at you as it did at me." Andrew had been uncertain how to approach her, but felt he was treading solid ground now. "My work may be rough, but I earn my living honorably, and I can't accept all the blame for an arrest that was caused by a misunderstanding." He spoke very rapidly, giving her no opportunity to find weaknesses in his rationalization. "As for my escape from prison, anyone arrested on false charges would be obliged to do the same. Don't forget that I caused no permanent injury to anyone."

Jeanne seemed impressed by his harangue.

"I'm here," Andrew continued, "because I would like, very much, to take you to dinner this noon. I've been working hard, I've saved money and I can afford the prices of any inn or tavern in New Orleans. So I'd feel honored if you allowed me to escort you somewhere."

The girl hesitated.

"Of course, you might be ashamed to be seen with someone in buckskins. But I never felt at home in the clothes I wore when I was last in the city," he lied. "I believe it wrong for a man to pretend he's something that he isn't."

The last of Jeanne's defenses were destroyed. "I—I suppose it would do no harm," she said, and smiled.

Andrew felt positive she was gloating over Beatriz, and would lose no time telling her friend about the dinner engagement. At least the life he had led before necessity had driven him to the frontier had taught him something about women.

He arranged to return for her in two hours, and took care to make the deep bow that had been conspicuous by its absence when he had first arrived.

He was in high spirits as he left the Valdez house. Everything was going according to plan, and he had good reason to hope that he could use Jeanne as an instrument in obtaining the information the State Department wanted. He would obtain vengeance, too, and even the knowledge that he was deliberately intending to become a cad did not spoil his mood.

A mounted man was sitting just outside the fence of the Valdéz property, and Andrew recognized Captain de Martínez, the officer who had almost knocked him down. The Spaniard was glaring at him, and, before Andrew could speak, he spurred his horse and quickly rode off down the cobbled street.

The meal had been excellent, and Jeanne had been such a charming, gay companion that Andrew was forced to remind himself repeatedly that it was she who had betrayed him, that his whole scheme depended on her.

"I had no idea you were an accomplished linguist, sir, or that you knew so much about literature."

*"Nos vertus ne sont le plus souvent que des vices dé-
guisés,"* Andrew said wryly.

"Our virtues are often only vices in disguise. I see you
know La Rochefoucauld, too."

His expression was unchanged. "I had a knack for letters and languages, but I failed in everything else." He had
not intended to tell her so much about himself.

"What a pity you didn't pursue a literary career,"
Jeanne said, "or become a teacher of languages."

She was a complete romantic, he decided. "I have no
talent, and professors subsist on wages so low they almost
starve."

"Surely you'd earn more than you do as a riverboat
guard, and it's more genteel as well!"

He had to admit she was right, but could not tell her
that teaching lacked the excitement that had been so vital
to him at the gaming tables and that he had found again,
in another form, as a river devil. Instead he described his
farm to her, and was surprised when he suddenly realized
that what he disliked about his homestead was the dullness
of day-to-day existence.

They strolled slowly, their conversation roaming from
one topic to another, and when they finally reached the
Valdéz house, saw that a coach bearing the royal Spanish
seal stood in the driveway.

"Papa hasn't gone back to work yet," Jeanne said.

"I should like to meet him." Andrew's progress promised to be more rapid than he had hoped.

The girl hesitated briefly. "Another time."

He guessed what was in her mind, that she wanted to
prepare her father for a meeting with an American in the
rough garb of the frontier. "Perhaps you'd allow me to call
this evening."

Her smile was radiant. "I'd like that very much."

Her happiness made him feel guilty as he turned away
and started back toward the street a few moments later.
Even a fresh reminder that she had been responsible for
the arrest that had led to his deportation from New Spain
did not ease his conscience, and it occurred to him that the
task he had set himself might be more difficult than he had
imagined.

As Andrew reached the street and closed the gate behind him he stopped short. About twenty yards away, beneath a huge cypress, was Captain de Martínez, who immediately wheeled and rode off.

It was evident to Andrew that he was being watched, and he was afraid his time in New Orleans might be even more limited than he had assumed. If the Spaniard had been assigned to keep him under surveillance, he might be imprisoned or deported at any moment. But he was determined to return to the United States with the information regarding the possible French treaty that Abel Hillery had directed him to obtain.

SEVEN

August 1800

American frontier buckskins suddenly became fashionable in New Orleans when the new Deputy Governor began wearing them on recreational hunting trips into the wilderness of the Louisiana interior. Don Felipe de Guzmán was openly contemptuous of the effete leanings of his colleagues, and it was rumored that he had been sent abroad because his enthusiasms were those of an earlier age of grandee and in no way resembled the likes of Charles IV and his court. He was a burly man of about forty with a hearty manner, booming laugh, and energetic devotion to work that contrasted markedly with the lethargy of most Spanish colonial administrators.

Andrew saw him only from a distance, Beatriz sometimes accompanying the Deputy Governor as he rode through the city or made an appearance at one or another of the many festivals held in New Orleans. It was difficult for the American to refrain from using his former relationship with the girl to become acquainted with Don Felipe, who would be certain to know, if any official of New Spain had heard, of the supposed cession of Louisiana to France.

But there were limits a man could not transgress. Andrew found it impossible to forget that Beatriz had helped him escape from prison and had given him a sanctuary as well as herself, so he could not take advantage of her, even though his original scheme was progressing far more slowly than he had hoped. Instead of spending only a few days in New Orleans, he had been in the city for the better part of six weeks, and still had not learned what he had come to find out. His original assumption had been riddled with naïve weaknesses.

He had been right to the extent that it would be possible to court Jeanne Valdéz and arouse her interest in him. He saw her daily, frequently escorted her to festivals, theatrical performances and concerts, and was a regular visitor to her home. Jeanne gave every indication that she was falling in love with him, and he had to remind himself several times each day that she deserved the betrayal he was attempting to perpetrate.

What was taking him longer than he had anticipated was his attempt to strike up a friendship with the girl's father. Ramón Valdéz was an elderly, arrogant Castilian who had come to New Spain three decades earlier with Governor Almonaster y Rojas, and although he had supervised the growth of New Orleans from a sleepy colonial port into one of the largest and most active trade centers in the Americas, he still maintained a stiff reserve with foreigners. In his eyes the young American was such a foreigner.

But Andrew had embarked on one line of endeavor, and, having committed himself, could not try other methods. He continued to press his attentions on Jeanne, scrupulously treating her with the respect that a young lady of strict moral background expected, and meanwhile utilized every opportunity to ingratiate himself with her father.

But his patience was wearing thin, the allowance Abel Hillery had given him for his expenses was virtually exhausted, and soon he would be forced to dip into the one hundred dollar sum he had been paid for his services, money he had intended to improve his Tennessee homestead.

In addition he was irritated by the frequent appearances of Captain de Martínez, who continued to maintain a close watch on him near the Valdéz home. At least once each day Andrew found him loitering in the vicinity of the gate when leaving the house, and the officer's conduct was invariably the same: he looked at the American venomously, then rode off in haste. It was still impossible to learn whether the Captain was acting in an official capacity, but Andrew was growing tired of being observed so closely, and was rapidly losing patience with the situation.

His inability to strike even an approximation of a close rapport with Ramón Valdéz prompted him to take more drastic measures. He knew they would compound the ultimate humiliation of Jeanne, but believed he had no choice. It was true that he had grown fond of her, but his

77

own country's future was more important than the feelings of a Creole girl, even one who, in all probability, had not given him away maliciously, but had succumbed to the impulse of a moment.

After returning to the Valdéz house with her from a fireworks display in the plaza of the Hall of the Cabildo early one evening, he decided the time had come to step up the tempo of his activities. He and Jeanne settled down for a chat on the balcony of the second-floor sitting room, a pitcher of watered wine on a table between them, and Andrew, knowing her father would return home within a very short time from the same festivities, pretended to be plunged in gloom.

Jeanne made several attempts to find out what was troubling him, but he remained uncommunicative as he walked to the grilled ironwork railing of the balcony and stared up at the stars in the soft summer sky.

The girl joined him there. "Please, Andrew, tell me what's wrong. Have I offended you?"

Instead of replying he turned abruptly and took her into his arms.

Jeanne made no attempt to free herself, and eagerly accepted his kiss.

He had expected her to struggle against him, and although the kiss was sweet, even passionate, he had an uneasy feeling that he was achieving a victory too easily, and that complications would ensue.

"I was beginning to think," she said as he released her, "that you'd never kiss me."

Andrew saw that she was radiant.

"After the way you and Beatriz—" She broke off and started again. "I thought you didn't really like me."

There was just one response he could make. "I don't feel toward you as I did toward her," he said truthfully, remembering the explosive quality of his physical relationship with Beatriz. "I think too much of you to kiss you casually."

"I wonder," she said breathlessly, "what Papa will say."

Andrew had hoped to use her more directly in his attempt to gain her father's friendship, but she was suggesting something far more permanent, and his heart sank. However, he could not back down without spoiling every-

78

thing he had worked to achieve. "I intend to speak to him, of course," he said lamely.

Jeanne's haste was almost indecent. "I'll take you to him the moment he comes home," she said, moving into his embrace again, "and then I'll leave you alone with him. I believe it's improper for me to be present when you two speak."

It was simpler to kiss her again than to protest that he had not proposed marriage.

A quarter of an hour later they heard Valdéz calling to a servant from the drawing room on the ground floor, and Jeanne immediately took Andrew's hand. "Don't be afraid of him," she said as she led him down the stairs.

He felt apprehensive, as he would if he seriously intended to marry her.

Ramón Valdéz, stiffly erect in spite of his advanced years, saw at once that his daughter and the American were holding hands, and he frowned.

Jeanne said something to him, and a moment later Andrew found himself alone with the Spaniard.

"Sir," he said, "I would like to request your permission to pay formal court to Jeanne."

Ramón Valdéz tugged at the broad black sash that Spanish aristocrats preferred to waistcoats. "I thought," he said, "that's what you've been doing for these past weeks."

There was no escape from the icy, penetrating eyes. "Perhaps I should have spoken to you sooner."

"You wish to marry Jeanne."

Andrew realized he had to make a definite, binding commitment which would be impossible to break without the loss of honor, but there was no choice. "I do, sir, although my prospects aren't good, by your standards. I own a homestead in Tennessee, and I hope to farm it as soon as I can start operating it."

"I must admit," Valdéz said, making no effort to conceal his contempt, "that the occupation of a farmer is preferable to that of what you Yankees call a river devil."

Andrew tried to stifle his resentment.

"What funds do you possess, MacCullough?"

"I have enough to buy livestock, improve my house and hire a man to help me on the property." Andrew saw no reason to be more specific.

79

But the girl's father was dissatisfied. "You expect Jeanne to bring you a large dowry, then."

"In my country we don't believe in the dowry. I don't want a single copper, thank you." Andrew, too, became contemptuous.

Valdéz raised a patrician eyebrow and fell silent.

Andrew could see that his comment, made in all sincerity, had impressed the man.

"Sit down," Ramón Valdéz said abruptly, and walked to a sideboard.

"I don't drink, sir," Andrew reminded him.

"Is that true?" Again the black eyes became penetrating. "I've had the feeling you have merely tried to make me think more highly of you. I have seen American river devils since your country gained her independence almost twenty years ago, and I have never known one who did not drink huge quantities of whiskey and rum."

"Think what you will," Andrew replied, still annoyed, "but I'm the river devil who never touches hard liquor."

Valdéz poured a glass of wine for himself and moved to a chair opposite his visitor. "Jeanne is my only child, and I seek her happiness. She has told me something about you, and it is a comfort—small comfort, to be sure—to know that you are somewhat better educated than the American rabble who swarm through New Orleans."

Andrew bit his lower lip so a fiery retort would not cause an immediate, irrevocable break.

"I cannot give my consent to a marriage between you and Jeanne now," Valdéz said, "but I am willing to test your feeling for one another, as well as your sense of honor, which is important. If you and Jeanne feel as you do in a year's time, I won't stand in the way of your marriage. I had higher hopes for her, but perhaps this is the best solution of a problem that has been vexing me."

Andrew didn't know what he meant, and waited.

"I must have your word that you will repeat nothing of what I shall say to you. Jeanne must not know."

"I give you my word, sir," Andrew replied automatically.

"In one more year I will be returning to Spain, and if Jeanne is not married, I will take her with me. It will be difficult enough for me to live there after spending three decades in the New World, and I have been concerned about her. Here she is a lady, but it makes me uneasy to think of her reception at court, where the manners of our grandees are so much more polished than they are in New Spain. Jeanne knows no other life than that which she has led here, and she loves it. She was born here, and her mother is buried here. It will be very difficult for her to learn new ways in Madrid. I have presented a number of suitors to her in the past few years, but she has shown interest only in you. So be it, MacCullough. We shall see what happens in the next year." Valdéz paused. "Do you accept my conditions?"

"Of course, sir. You give me no choice."

"Including the sacred vow to make no mention to Jeanne of a life in Spain?"

"Yes, sir." Andrew had nothing to lose by making a delicate probe. "You're retiring next year?"

"Not of my own will."

Suppressing his excitement, Andrew forced himself to speak calmly. "I see. Madrid is sending a replacement to take your position in the government."

"Your eyesight is faulty," Valdéz said testily. "There's nothing wrong with my health or my mind, and I needn't retire for another ten years. What's more, my replacement, whoever he may be, won't be sent from Madrid."

Espionage, Andrew decided, was a simple art. He was hearing all he wanted to know, and all that was still necessary was some confirmation of the basic facts. "Surely Governor Almonaster y Rojas recognizes your worth, sir."

"He has no voice in the matter."

Every word Valdéz said confirmed Andrew's belief that the French would take possession of Louisiana the following year. "The Americans who come to New Orleans know you've been fair to us, sir, and efficient. Aside from the customs service, which isn't under your jurisdiction, as I understand it, we have no complaints. If it would help, I can get most of the Americans in the Mississippi River trade to sign a testimonial letter to the Colonial Ministry in Madrid—"

"No one in Madrid," Valdéz said with finality, "not even the King himself, will have a voice in keeping me at my post here. If you're going to become my son-in-law I should treat you with greater candor, but I cannot. Next year you will understand, and if you and Jeanne still want to marry, it may be I will be so discouraged that I will come to live with you at your farm. Is it true that one can see the Mississippi from your land?"

"A bit of it." Andrew was positive now he had found out what he had come to New Orleans to learn.

"After spending so many years here, I would find it very hard, too, to live again in Europe." Valdéz drifted off into deep thought, roused himself and drained his glass. "Go now," he said. "If I know Jeanne," he added with a faint smile, "she has been trying to listen to us from the corridor, and is waiting for you."

Andrew bowed and left the drawing room. As the girl's father had predicted, Jeanne was waiting in the antechamber, and was so elated as she threw herself at Andrew that he felt ashamed of the deception he was perpetrating.

"I expected Papa to order you out of the house," she whispered. "I had no idea he would be so gentle. I can't imagine what has happened."

Andrew realized that Valdéz's own world was in the process of collapse, but could neither discuss the hints he had been given nor the suspicions entertained by the United States Government. Stunned by the realization that, regardless of his private intentions, he had gone through the motions of becoming betrothed, he could only murmur, "A year isn't a very long time."

"It will pass quickly," Jeanne said, hugging him.

He felt trapped. "I must leave now, or your father will think I'm taking advantage of our agreement."

She was reluctant to see him leave, but thought his suggestion was sensible, and walking to the door with him, accompanied him to the front stoop. "Will I see you tomorrow noon?"

"I—uh—yes. But now that everything is settled, I must return home as soon as possible." He wanted to leave for the United States in order to submit his report to Abel Hillery as soon as possible, but he forced himself to concentrate on what a man truly in love would say under these circumstances. "I want to get my farm in shape for you as quickly as I can."

Even though they could be seen by a few pedestrians on the Rue St. Pierre, Jeanne embraced him.

He would pay her one final, token visit, Andrew thought, before going back to the United States, never to return. Even a girl who had betrayed him to his possible executioners deserved some semblance of consideration now that she thought she would be marrying him.

Promising to return at noon, he bade her goodnight, and waited until she closed the door before starting toward the street. If he could, he would find employment as a river devil to defray the expenses of his journey north, but if no post was open in the immediate future he would obtain a horse at his own expense and would make his way northeast through the Indian-occupied lands to the northeast. Now that he had obtained reasonable confirmation of the American State Department's conclusions about a Franco-Spanish treaty, there was no time to lose.

He discovered he felt sorry for Jeanne, but told himself the disappointment she would suffer when he left could not be helped. She would forget him after a time, and eventually might even realize that he had repaid her for her perfidy. Strangely, his victory gave him no pleasure.

The pedestrians were gone now, and the Rue St. Pierre was deserted as Andrew started toward the Avenue de Bienville. When he had walked about half the distance to the intersection, however, a rider moved out of the shadows of a tree at the side of the road, and this time Captain de Martínez did not canter off.

"Yankee," he said furiously, "you are a coward and a pig."

Before Andrew could react a heavy whip cut him across the shoulders.

The Spanish officer raised the rawhide whip to strike again.

But Andrew was ready, and in spite of the searing pain across his shoulders and back he jumped aside as the whip descended. He caught hold of it close to the handle and jerked with all his strength.

Captain de Martínez was pulled from his saddle and tumbled to the ground.

"Are you mad?" the indignant Andrew demanded. "What harm have I done you?"

83

The Spaniard did not reply, but, as he hauled himself to his feet, drew his sword and a pistol.

The thought paramount in Andrew's mind was that, no matter how great the provocation, he could not kill or seriously wound his antagonist. Abel Hillery was waiting for the news he had obtained, and it would be catastrophic to be cast into a New Orleans prison. The authorities, he knew, took a grave view of the killing or maiming of a Spanish officer.

So, rather than draw one of his own pistols and arouse the entire neighborhood with a firearms duel, Andrew grasped his rifle by its muzzle. Using it as a club, he knocked the pistol from his foe's left hand, but, before he could side-step, sustained a slash in his left arm.

The pain, combined with the mystery of the attack, caused him to lose his temper, and although ordinarily he would have had too much sense to use a rifle butt as a foil in a fight with a man who was armed with a sword, his rage made him reckless. Twice he parried deft thrusts with the barrel of the rifle, but as his anger turned cold and his mind cleared, he knew he could not hold off an accomplished duelist indefinitely with the heavy, clumsy rifle.

Waiting until Captain de Martínez slashed at him again, Andrew reflected the blow. Simultaneously he dropped his rifle to the ground and sprang at the Spaniard, grappling with him before the sword could be brought into play again.

De Martínez was no match for Andrew in the type of free-for-all fighting at which every American frontiersman was expert if he hoped to survive. Andrew wrenched the sword from his opponent, and smashed his free hand into the Spaniard's face. The Captain tried to retaliate, but the furious Andrew, undeterred by his injured arm, gave him no chance.

Fists pounded the Spaniard's face mercilessly, a knee landing in his groin doubled him over, and a sharp blow to the cheekbone sent him sprawling backward onto the cobblestones. Andrew continued to pummel him until he realized the man had gone limp.

Staring at him in the moonless light, it finally dawned on Andrew that his foe had fallen unconscious. Standing, he dragged de Martínez to the side of the street, then carefully replaced the officer's sword in its scabbard and the pistol in his belt. De Martínez had been given a beating he would remember, but he would not be able to claim he had been robbed of his weapons.

Andrew decided to keep the whip, however, and after coiling it, carried it in one hand, the rifle in the other. He made his way back to his waterfront inn, the cut in his arm soaking his buckskin shirt, the whip lash across his shoulders and back throbbing. He made a brief stop at the tavern next door to the inn to buy a small, inexpensive bottle of brandywine, and, when he reached his room, used the liquor to clean his wounds. He washed his shirt, splashed more brandywine onto his injured arm, his shoulders, and his back, and then fell exhausted onto his straw pallet.

In spite of his weariness he remained awake, however, his mind jumping crazily from the Franco-Spanish treaty to Jeanne, from the reward he would be paid when he met Abel Hillery to the unwarranted attack Captain de Martínez had made on him. The first gray streaks of dawn were showing in the sky when he finally dropped off to sleep.

Andrew's first thought was that someone else was in his room, and he reached for his pistol as he opened his eyes. Struggling to a sitting position he felt a stiffness in his left arm, a reminder of the injury he had sustained, but the sight of Beatriz de Santos standing over him drove everything else from his mind.

She was staring at him in disgust, and when he became conscious of the reek of brandywine he realized she thought he had been drinking. Lowering his pistol, he rubbed the stubble on his chin. "This is an unexpected surprise," he said, and hauling himself to his feet, discovered that his shoulders and back felt better.

"I've spent more than an hour searching for you," Beatriz said. "I knew I'd find you in a place like this." She looked at him in disdain, her skirts gathered closely. "I see you were celebrating." Her glance indicated the little brandywine jug, in which he had not replaced the cork.

He was still too drugged by sleep to offer an explanation. "What is there to celebrate?"

Beatriz laughed scornfully, and for the first time he detected her anger. "Apparently you had an even busier night than I thought. First you became betrothed to Jeanne—"

"How did you find out?" Andrew felt stricken.

"She couldn't wait to come to my house with the news this morning!"

Although Beatriz had no right to be jealous, Andrew felt flattered. Grinning, he crossed the room to pick up his shirt, which had been drying in the hot sunlight streaming through the room's one window, which he had forgotten to open before going to bed. He opened it now before donning his shirt, and the breeze swept away the stench of brandywine.

"Then," Beatriz continued, "you attacked Captain Cristoforo de Martínez for no reason—"

"Is that his story? The bastard came at me with a whip after I left the Valdéz house. There it is. He'd been following me for weeks, and for no reason—"

"He claims he knew you only by sight," Beatriz interrupted, "and that he had no idea you were in New Orleans until you dragged him from the saddle of his horse and punched him until he lost consciousness."

Andrew opened his shirt again. "Here's what he did to my arm with his sword, and if you'll look at my shoulders I'm sure you'll see the mark of his whip."

There was a flicker of concern in Beatriz's eyes, but her tone was businesslike as she said, "It will be your word against his, you know. You American river devils have reputations as brawlers, and your name is already on the records. Cristoforo is a member of Don Felipe's personal staff, so you know which of you the magistrate will believe."

"Magistrate?" Andrew became alarmed.

"Cristoforo went to Don Felipe this morning, and if you knew Don Felipe you'd understand how very angry he can become."

Andrew looked at his watch, one of the few belongings of his father's that he had managed to salvage.

"I know Jeanne is expecting you," Beatriz said. "She told me. I regret to say she also told the constables who visited her this morning, so I wouldn't go near the house, if I were you. A squad of soldiers is waiting there to take you off to jail."

"I wonder," Andrew replied, "if I've lost my sanity."

"Cristoforo de Martínez also claims you robbed him of his purse," Beatriz declared.

"Do you believe a damned lie——"

"Does it matter what I believe? I've felt badly for a long time because I couldn't bring myself to tell you about Don Felipe, but I'm repaying the debt now, and this will be the second time I've saved you from a New Orleans prison."

"Thank you." Andrew's mission was prominent in his mind, and he knew he should leave at once, but there were so many other matters to be settled. "How can I see Jeanne before I go?"

"You can't. If she leaves her house again, she'll be followed. Don Felipe is expecting you to try to see her. My future husband," she added too lightly, "is a very thorough man. I'll tell Jeanne that you send your love——"

"I'd rather you didn't." He could imagine Jeanne's reaction if Beatriz brought her the message. "I'll write to her instead."

"From the United States, not New Orleans. You really don't have time to write compositions today."

"I understand." Not bothering to shave, he shoved his pistols into his belt, slipped his knife into his boot-top and checked his rifle. "Before I go, Beatriz, can you tell me why Captain de Martínez followed me for so long, and why he suddenly assaulted me last night?"

"Spanish officers who spend a long time in the colonies occasionally do strange things. But we don't know who started the fight, do we, or which of you to believe?" She moved to the door. "I can't risk being seen here," she murmured, and was gone.

Andrew went to the window and remained there until he saw her quickly walking away from the inn, ignoring the stares of the cargo handlers outside a warehouse.

Then he gathered the rest of his belongings, went to the ground floor to pay the innkeeper for his lodging, and went out into the open. He was forced to take Beatriz's warning seriously, and a suspicion gradually formed in his mind. Was it possible, he wondered, that Beatriz was so embarrassed by his presence in New Orleans that she had either hired or tricked Captain de Martínez to attack him in order to find an excuse that would compel him to flee from the city for a second time?

Perhaps all girls in the place were treacherous.

There were no American barges or riverboats at the wharves, and it was impossible to guess accurately when some might appear. Therefore, Andrew knew, he would be forced to make an overland journey. Before departing, however, he decided to check on the accuracy of what Beatriz had told him, and quickly made his way toward the center of the city.

He passed a number of Spanish soldiers, none of whom paid any attention to him, so he became a trifle more reckless as he turned onto the Avenue de Bienville. When he came to the intersection of the Rue St. Pierre, however, he halted abruptly. From the street corner he could see three soldiers on the Valdéz lawn, and was able to make out several others at the rear of the property, too. Beatriz had not lied when she had told him he would be placed under arrest if apprehended.

Retracing his steps up the Avenue de Bienville, he had no definite plan in mind until he approached a tavern where he and Jeanne had eaten on a number of occasions. If the Spaniards were intending to imprison him for having committed no crime other than that of defending himself against an unwarranted assault, he would give them a real cause to arrest and jail him.

Halting at the hitching post in front of the tavern, he selected the strongest gelding tethered there, mounted the animal and rode off, turning north at the first intersection and heading toward the open delta country beyond New Orleans.

EIGHT

October 1800

Washington City, the new American capital, was "the first scientifically planned metropolis in the world," according to the few men who envisaged broad avenues, handsome buildings, and numerous parks, all laid out in accordance with plans drawn by the architect engaged by Congress, Pierre Charles L'Enfant. But Government officials who moved there in 1800 swore it was an ugly village erected in a sea of insect-ridden swamps, a place where the dampness ate into men's bones and sticky mud clung to their boots.

The only structures as yet completed were the Treasury Department building, which was solid, squat, and utilitarian, the place variously known as the President's House, the Executive Mansion, and the President's Palace, which Mrs. Adams was said to hate, and, at the opposite end of Pennsylvania Avenue, Congress House, where the Legislative Branch of the Government worked in relative comfort. Construction had barely begun on offices for the State, War, and Navy Departments, much less other bureaus, all of which had been forced to seek temporary quarters in buildings that would, in time, become private homes, inns, and lodging houses.

Not even Pennsylvania Avenue had been paved with cobblestones, and the mud was ankle-deep in every road. When it rained, which happened frequently, the roads became even worse, and carriages sank to their axles. Vice-President Thomas Jefferson was working on a device that would be attached to the front of a coach and scoop away the worst of the mud, but he had not perfected the invention as yet, and until he did, most preferred to ride horses or even walk.

One of the oddities of the new capital of the United States was that it was a city virtually without women. Mrs. Adams had taken up residence with her husband in the President's House, and the wives of several Cabinet members had accompanied their husbands to Washington, principally because officers of their rank were entitled to live in the more habitable dwellings that had been constructed to date. Most officials, however, including Senators and Congressmen, left their families back home since, literally, no quarters, suitable or inadequate, were available.

Bonuses were being offered to retail merchants who would open places of business in the town, but only three responded to the lure in the first months of Washington's existence. There was a general store that offered consumers a reasonably wide variety of goods, a meat and fish market, and a greengrocer's shop. The owners of the small inns, taverns and lodging houses that were springing up at a rapid rate found it easier to buy from Maryland or Virginia farmers, and some sent to nearby Baltimore for their supplies. "We dine in Washington City at our peril," Alexander Hamilton declared, "and we escape to New York, Baltimore, and Philadelphia as frequently as we can to seek an edible meal."

Abel Hillery's office, which he shared with two others, was located on the second floor of a shingled building boasting only one coat of whitewash that was known as the "State Department auxiliary," and an official of the Spanish Legation had been heard to remark that "even our peasants are better housed than the highest officers of this benighted, barbaric land."

But the office, like the town's living quarters, seemed luxurious to someone who had spent many long weeks traveling through an Indian-infested forest wilderness, sleeping in the open and shooting game for his meals. Logs burning in a hearth dispelled the damp chill, the visitor's chair beside Hillery's desk was padded, and the cup of sweetened tea brought by a servant was hot and fragrant. Andrew MacCullough had almost forgotten the amenities of civilization.

He told Hillery the full story of his sojourn in New Orleans, and, afraid he might omit something of importance, left out no detail, refusing to spare himself.

Hillery listened carefully, asked a number of questions and then sat back in his chair. "Your evidence is circumstantial, of course," he said at last, "but it satisfies me that

France will occupy Louisiana this coming year. It also fits in with a number of other reports we've had." He took a quill pen from a jar of sand, dipped into a container of ink and handed it to the river devil. "Sign this form," he said, "and between now and tomorrow put the pertinent details of what you've told me into a written report."

"What is this?" Andrew scanned the closely written sheet of paper.

"A requisition for the additional one hundred dollars due you. It will need the signatures of the First Assistant Secretary, the Department's Legal Counselor and the Financial Officer, and then we'll send it to the Treasury. You should be getting your money in two or three weeks."

"Must I stay here that long?" Andrew was afraid he might be tempted to visit some of the prominent seaboard cities if he waited several weeks for his pay.

Hillery smiled cynically. "I'm afraid you don't know the ways of the Government."

"I was hoping I could write a letter to Jeanne Valdéz," Andrew said, "giving her an explanation of some sort to excuse myself for not seeing her before I left New Orleans. And then, after taking it to the Spanish Legation in the hope they'll forward it to New Orleans, I've been intending to leave at once for Tennessee."

There was amusement in Hillery's eyes. "Are you so anxious to go back to your homestead?"

"I'd rather do almost anything else," Andrew admitted. "But I've spent about thirty dollars of the fee you've already paid me, and the total of one hundred and seventy that'll be left won't go very far, I'm afraid. I want to put it into improvements on my property before I fritter it all away somewhere else."

Hillery glanced at the other two men in the office, both of whom were bent over papers on their desks, but might be listening. "Let's go to dinner," he said abruptly. "The treat is on me, and I know a place where the food isn't too bad."

The surprised Andrew accepted the invitation, and they walked up a muddy street, turned onto another and came at last to a one-story tavern of unpainted clapboard called the Liberty. It was crowded and noisy, its tables of unpainted pine were already stained and the floors were bare, but the food, as Hillery had indicated, was better than that served in most Washington City eating establishments. The roasted Chesapeake Bay oysters were delicious, and each man ate a huge platter of them. Their appetites blunted, they didn't mind when the beef turned out to be stringy, the potatoes tasteless and the vegetables old.

Finally, after they had finished, Hillery offered his companion a *segaro* and leaned forward, elbows on the table. "The State Department," he said in a low, confidential tone, "will pay your living expenses if you'll stay here for the four and a half months, or thereabouts. We'll have some work for you to do, not much, really, but enough to keep you busy. I'm afraid we can't authorize wages for you, though, so you'll be taking something of a gamble."

"I swore off gaming a long time ago," Andrew said, "but I'm willing to listen."

"President Adams will take no positive action based on the information you've brought to me, any more than he has after we've given him similar stories about a Franco-Spanish treaty. In all fairness to him, there isn't anything he can do, legally, until he receives official confirmation that such a treaty has been signed and that Louisiana has been ceded to France."

Andrew could understand the President's delicate position in the matter.

"The situation is complicated by the fact that Mr. Adams is spending only a few more months in office. He's indicated he isn't paritcularly interested in serving another term, which is just as well, since he has little support. Anyway, the election will be held in February, and the new President will take office early in March. Unless a formal transfer of Louisiana to the French takes place before then, Mr. Adams will do nothing."

"From what I gathered," Andrew said, "the formal cession will take place in 1801. But if we're caught with our rifles unloaded and no powder in our pouches, General Bonaparte can close the Mississippi to our ships and barges, and we'll have to swallow an insult that will ruin the West!"

"You aren't the only man who is concerned about the

problem," Hillery said. "And the tables here are too close together for conversation. Let's take a stroll, shall we?" He paid for their meal, and they went out into the raw, damp air.

They made their way up a street sticky with mud, and Andrew laughed. "I prefer the wilderness to this."

"So would any sane man. It doesn't much matter where we walk. The whole town is the same." They wandered toward the President's House, where a single sentry in the blue and buff of the tiny Regular Army stood duty.

Andrew looked at the man with interest. "He's a toy soldier, isn't he? Nobody in the Army these days has had any experience in fighting a war, and the veterans of the Revolution are getting too old."

"You've analyzed one of the worst aspects of the problem," Hillery said. "The Congressional delegations from Tennessee and Kentucky held a private meeting with some of us from the State and War Departments a couple of weeks ago, and they felt just as you do. They insist we do something to protect our Mississippi shipping, but they realize they can't call up volunteer militia until an emergency actually develops."

"Bonaparte is a clever rascal."

"Too clever, but we've got to do what we can to be ready in case of trouble. Virginia and North Carolina and Pennsylvania—particularly Pennsylvania—have given their support to Tennessee and Kentucky, so the President has given his reluctant consent to a rather ingenious plan. He's attached one condition to it. He must know nothing about it officially. That means the appropriation we've persuaded the Treasury to give us, and a miserably small sum it is, must be concealed on the ledgers."

Andrew was intrigued by the air of mystery.

"The War Department, with the advice and help of the State Department, is drawing up plans. If Bonaparte occupies Louisiana, and if he refuses to grant us the right to use New Orleans as a terminal inland waterway port for our shipping, we must be ready to move very quickly and occupy the city."

"Ah!" Andrew brightened, forgetting the mud through which they were wading.

"Obviously, militia can't be raised, even if France does take possession. Bonaparte would regard such a move as a hostile step, and we'd be plunged into war with France."

"Are you suggesting we'll have to raise an unofficial corps of irregulars?"

"I'm afraid so." The State Department official was silent for a moment; then he turned to his companion with a grin. "Do you know of any men eligible for such a force?"

"There are the river devils, of course—"

"We think in the same terms, but I know too little about your colleagues. How many are there, in all?"

"Two hundred, maybe," Andrew said. "But I reckon we could find still another hundred who have retired to homesteads, as I've done."

"As you will do, when this business is finally settled. Andrew, I'm going to give you a desk, and I want you to draw up specific plans for a march of river devils on New Orleans. Include the supplies, ammunition, clothing—everything—that would be needed for a campaign. We'll submit the details to the War Department for approval, and after a new President is elected, we'll go to him with the whole scheme. Assuming that France takes Louisiana, which is what we must do, the United States will have to prepare for every measure short of active war.

"We feel certain that Bonaparte is too busy in Europe to declare war against us or issue an embargo closing New Orleans to us—which would force us to declare war. Our fear is that he'll turn back our shipping quietly, without an announcement, and if that should happen, we've got to be ready to reply with our own weapons—using our river devils and others who are willing to risk their lives for the future of the country, without pay or glory or even honor."

"I'll stay," Andrew said, "and I'll do whatever is necessary."

The desks of nine clerks crowded the room that would have been comfortable had it been occupied by no more than four, and the cubicle in the corner, partitioned by rough pine planks, was just large enough for a desk and chair. Dark, airless and gloomy, it had only one advantage, that of affording privacy for the planning of an operation that had to be kept from even the most trusted of

94

State Department employees on the other side of the partition.

Andrew worked and lived alone, almost as isolated as he would have been had he returned to his wilderness homestead in Tennessee. He studied maps and made charts, drew up tables and spent countless hours staring at the pine boards of his wall. Utilizing all he knew of New Orleans and its Mississippi River hinterlands, he tried to think of every move short of open war the French might make, and then planned a counteroperation. Aware of his responsibility and eager to be of service, he wrote dozens of pages in the first days he spent at the task, then sent them, as he had been instructed by Abel Hillery, to the War Department annex located directly across the street.

Having heard that all Washington City activities were hampered by clerks who insisted on making complicated records of every document that passed across their desks, he expected to hear nothing from the War Department for a long time, and was surprised when, only forty-eight hours after submitting his preliminary plans, he was called to the office of Brigadier General Wallace van Meiter, chief of the War Department's planning office.

A handsome man in his early fifties whose white hair made it unnecessary for him to wear a powdered wig of the kind currently in vogue, General van Meiter was a New Yorker, a protégé of Hamilton's, and a former militia officer who had suffered the misfortune of being captured by the British early in the American Revolution and spending the better part of the war as a prisoner at Halifax.

Immaculate in a well-tailored uniform of blue and buff, General van Meiter glanced at his visitor's buckskins and kept him standing.

Andrew took an immediate dislike to him.

"The State Department is erratic," van Meiter said, "and your plans do nothing to increase my confidence in the wisdom of non-military men."

Andrew showed his irritation by sitting before being invited to take a chair.

"You've made no provisions for artillery or the deployment of cavalry squadrons, Mr. MacCullough," the General said, emphasizing his visitor's civilian title.

"I was ordered to think only in terms of operations for irregulars." Andrew remained civil.

"War is an exact science." Van Meiter sounded like a man making a speech. "Infantry, whether on foot, mounted, or carried on river barges, as you indicate in some of your plans, are useless unless they're supported by sappers, artillery, and cavalry."

Andrew wanted to retort that the important battles of the Revolution, including the climactic encounter at Saratoga, had been won by unsupported American infantry regiments. "As I understand it, sir," he said politely, "the War Department is making its own plans for any formal war with the French that might develop."

"There is no other kind of war," General van Meiter replied severely, "and General Bonaparte has already proved he's a genius on the battlefield. Do you suppose he'll use methods here that are different from those that have proved so successful for him in Europe?"

Andrew knew that what he thought was irrelevant; he was dealing with a man who had a closed mind. "Bonaparte doesn't confide in me, General. I was told to draw up plans for irregular operations and submit them to you, which is what I've done."

"The War Department is finding it difficult enough to get a fair share of appropriations now that defense funds are being poured into the New Navy for frigates and sloops-of-war," van Meiter said, sounding angry. "Congress might cut us off completely if we had a hand in any operation that's certain to fail. I shall recommend that we take no part whatever in anything you intend to do, Mr. MacCullough. If the State Department wants to daydream, it can form its own corps of irregulars, without any help, support, or encouragement from us!"

Andrew had no desire to become embroiled in an argument with him, took his leave and reported back to Abel Hillery, who listened in grim silence.

"When I see the men in charge of the War Department these days," Hillery said, "I sometimes wonder how we won the Revolution."

Andrew sighed. "You had a good idea, Abel, but it's wasted."

"I don't care what a fool who spent his war on parole in the taverns of Halifax says! We're going ahead with our plans, and if we must, you and I will raise a force of river devils ourselves."

NINE

March 1801

A new era began when Thomas Jefferson, the third President of the United States, walked up Pennsylvania Avenue to the portico of Congress House to take the oath of office making him the nation's Chief Executive. All Government officials were ordered to follow the example of the new President and lead simple lives, but few went to Jefferson's extremes. A widower whose daughters were married, he lived alone in the President's House, attended by a few servants, and refused an escort when he went out into the streets.

Members of the diplomatic corps were astonished when he received them in dressing gown and carpet slippers, and his dinner guests reported in wonder that, disliking what he called "fuss and bother," his meals were served by means of a device called a dumbwaiter, which he had invented, and which enabled him to eat without servants in the room to wait on him. But the food, the bemused guests said, was excellent. Not only did Jefferson have a good cook, but had brought back a large number of recipes with him from his post as American Minister to France some years earlier.

Only one person defied the President's ban on official extravagance and pomp. But, as everyone agreed, Dolley Madison was so ravishingly beautiful that it was unimportant if she obeyed no rules other than her own. Her dinner parties and receptions made residents of Washington City forget that the town was ugly and provincial, and even hardened bachelors lost their hearts to her.

Her husband, the new Secretary of State, did as much to revitalize the Government as Dolley did to give social Washington a new flavor. James Madison, the principal author of the Constitution that had changed the form of the American Government eleven years earlier, was quiet but dynamic, incisive without raising his voice, active yet contemplative. Slender and only five feet, six inches tall, he looked more like a State Department messenger boy than the first officer of the Cabinet as he made repeated trips each day between his own office and the President's.

"Mr. Madison," Hillery told Andrew, "enjoys the complete confidence of the President. You won't twiddle your thumbs behind a desk much longer."

His prediction came true less than three weeks after Jefferson and his Cabinet took office. "The Secretary wants us," Hillery said, looking into Andrew's cubicle one morning. "Come along!"

Madison, dapper in coat, waistcoat, and breeches of matching green, looked very tiny behind the enormous desk that had been purchased when the tall Timothy Pickering had been Secretary of State. He compensated for his small stature with an ever-present air of dignity, but his manner, to Andrew's surprise, was informal.

"I've studied Hillery's diagnosis of the Louisiana situation, and I've looked through your plans, MacCullough. I can't pass judgment on them because I'm not a military man, but Hillery has faith in you, and that's good enough for me. American interests on the Mississippi must be protected, so I'm recommending the entire plan to the President. He wants to see you first thing tomorrow morning, and he starts his day early, so meet me at the Executive Mansion at seven o'clock sharp."

Promptly at seven the next morning Andrew and Hillery were ushered into the dining room at the rear of the ground floor of the President's House, where Thomas Jefferson and his Secretary of State were already deep in conversation.

The President, who scorned a wig, had red hair turning gray, countless freckles across his face and was the homeliest man Andrew had ever seen. He was also one of the tallest; there were few whose height equalled Andrew's, but Jefferson, when he rose, met him on eye level. And the power of the President's personality was overwhelming when he smiled.

"I've been looking forward to this meeting, Mr. Mac-Cullough," he said. "I've found it difficult to visualize a Mississippi River devil who writes concise recommendations in good English, and who supposedly knows the classics. If I may say so, *Illud maxime rarum genus est eorum, qui aut excellenti ingenii magnitudine, aut prae-clara eruditione atque doctrina, aut utraque re ornati, spa-tium deliberandi habuerunt, quem potissimum vitae cur-sum sequi vellent.* Do you follow me?"

"That's a quote from Cicero, Mr. President," Andrew said. "The number is especially small of those who, either by surpassing genius, or by remarkable erudition and knowledge, or by being endowed with either, have enjoyed the opportunity of deciding what path of life they prefer to follow."

President Jefferson smiled broadly. "I couldn't quibble with more than a word or two of that translation. Sit down and have some coffee."

Grinning, Andrew accepted, although both Secretary Madison and Hillery shook their heads as the President went to a sideboard for a coffee cup.

Jefferson poured the coffee himself from a pewter pot, added hot milk from another and watched his guest closely.

Andrew tasted it, nodded, and took a larger swallow.

"Ah, you like French coffee!"

"Yes, sir. I learned to drink it when I was a student at the University of Paris, and they serve no other kind in New Orleans."

Secretary Madison looked pained, and Abel Hillery shuddered.

The President raised his own cup to his lips and stared out at the trees beginning to bud on the newly seeded lawn. "Do you like the French, Mr. MacCullough?"

"I enjoy their literature, music, and art, sir. I admire their architecture, about which I know little. And," Andrew added brashly, "their women, about whom I may know too much."

The President did not turn.

"What I don't like is First Consul Bonaparte's habit of taking territory that doesn't belong to him."

"Ah, but we're assuming he's acquiring—or has already acquired—Louisiana by legal means," Jefferson said. "We also know he has the legal right to close the port of New Orleans to our shipping once he occupies the city."

"I'm not concerned with legal rights or moral rights, Mr. President." Andrew realized he should speak less

100

vehemently, but had nothing to lose. "Thousands of American farmers will starve if we can't ship our produce through New Orleans."

The President turned, and there was an amused light in his eyes. "I'm a farmer myself, Mr. MacCullough. I was testing you. Now, if I understand correctly what Mr. Hillery has proposed and you've implemented, you intend to march into New Orleans, if necessary, and open the port yourselves."

Hillery, who had taken no part in the conversation, felt it was necessary to intervene. "That isn't quite accurate, Mr. President. If the French should close the port, we believe that the mere appearance of a corps of American river devils will induce them to change their minds."

Jefferson toyed absently with his spoon, his long fingers curling around it, then releasing it into his saucer. "The primary aim of my Administration is to maintain peaceful relations between the United States and all foreign powers. The Secretary of State has already notified the chiefs of all legations that we want the friendship of their rulers and people. Isn't that right, James?"

"You edited my letter on the subject, Mr. President."

"The belligerence of Napoleon Bonaparte makes me somewhat apprehensive, but I intend to give him no cause for war with us," the President said. "The United States is growing more rapidly than anyone anticipated, and we shall become one of the greatest farming nations on earth if we're allowed to develop in peace. The new census indicates we have more than five million people in the country, and immigration is so heavy, particularly from Great Britain, that we'll reach six million in a short time."

"At least two million of them will starve if they can't sell their corn, wheat, and cotton, Mr. President," Andrew said grimly.

Secretary Madison concealed a smile behind his hand.

"No man is more anxious than I that the Mississippi be kept open," Jefferson said forcefully. "But, while I am President, no force will be used to attain that or any other goal of this Government. That is my policy, and it shall be enforced."

Andrew was confused, and in the silence that followed he could say nothing.

101

Secretary Madison came to his rescue. "I believe you have a proverb in the West that there's more than one way to skin a deer, Mr. MacCullough."

"A bear, James," the President said absently. "Or a bobcat, or even a wolf, if you need the fur. But there's only one efficient way to skin a deer."

Andrew studied him covertly. This man who had been the principal author of America's Declaration of Independence a quarter of a century earlier and who had held numerous high offices from the governorship of Virginia to his present post, obviously had the right to think of himself primarily as a farmer. Although the frontier had been pushed hundreds of miles to the west from his home in Monticello, Virginia, it was plain that he was no stranger to wilderness living.

Jefferson turned back to the river devil. "The safety of every American citizen must be made secure," he said, "and so must his right to earn a living for himself and his family. As I told Governor Sevier of Tennessee when he called on me last week, I'll take second place to no American in my determination to keep the Mississippi River open to American traffic at all times and under all circumstances."

His statements seemed contradictory, but Andrew saw that Secretary Madison appeared complacent and Abel Hillery looked undisturbed.

"If I were to organize and dispatch an expedition to New Orleans, either now or after the French occupy it," Jefferson said, "I'd be issuing a direct challenge to Bonaparte. Any ruler, even a man who lacked his pride and his need to prove himself superior to others, would be forced to fight a war. National honor would demand it, and the French have been exceptionally thin-skinned since their Revolution, just as we've been. Any country that makes a major change in its form of government believes itself compelled to establish a new international identity. This has been an unvarying phenomenon since antiquity. The Israelites did it, the Athenians did it, the Romans did it a number of times."

Andrew remembered just enough of the history he had studied to accept the observation.

"Fortunately," the President continued, "General Bonaparte is as aware of this national state of mind as I am. His hold on the French people is based on it as much as on his insistence that there be no curtailment of personal liberties, either in France itself or in the lands he conquers."

The analysis was fascinating, but Andrew failed to see the connection with the problem of keeping the Mississippi open for American agricultural produce.

"There you have it," Jefferson said, and, sitting back in his chair, tugged at the slightly frayed cuffs of his shirt.

Andrew was totally bewildered.

Secretary Madison was accustomed to his superior's brilliance, and knew that others who were less gifted often found it impossible to follow his reasoning to a logical conclusion. What seemed clear to Thomas Jefferson frequently remained muddled in the minds of those to whom he thought he was giving full explanations. "May I spell out our position, Mr. President?"

Jefferson was surprised. "Isn't that what I just did? If you insist, James."

"The War Department," Secretary Madison said, "is being given no part in the protection of Mississippi traffic, and Secretary Dearborn is standing aside. The problem is diplomatic, not military. Therefore only the State Department is actively concerned."

Andrew wanted to protest that diplomacy alone would not assure Westerners of the right to use the port facilities at New Orleans, but the pressure of Hillery's shoe against his boot kept him discreetly silent for the moment.

"I'm limited, of course," Madison continued. "I can call in the head of a foreign legation to express my Government's views, or I can send our legation's minister to see the director of another nation's foreign affairs. In extreme circumstances I can do both. Our citizens, acting in an unofficial capacity and exercising their rights as free men, often can do far more than I."

Andrew began to see the first dim beams of light.

Jefferson, aware that he had been too abstruse, decided to help. "It's true, is it not, Mr. MacCullough, that every man in the West carries his own firearms?"

"Certainly, Mr. President. Anyone who went around unarmed wouldn't live long."

"Isn't it also true that the wilderness man is virtually self-sufficient, shooting game for his meat and finding himself berries and roots?"

Andrew smiled. "Yes, sir. But we buy our flour, and those who don't like the taste of bear bacon buy hog bacon when they can afford it. Wild boars are hard to find out our way, maybe because the Cherokee like them, too."

"When I was a young law student," the President said, "my friends sometimes complained that gunpowder was scarce and that they couldn't find lead to make themselves bullets."

"Fine-grained powder without lumps is still a luxury," Andrew replied, "but we can buy lead in Nashville or New Orleans, if the price isn't too high."

"I think it best if I don't hear the rest of this conversation." The President stood, motioning the others to remain seated. "I'm expected at a meeting in my office. Help yourself to more coffee, Mr. MacCullough. The French blend it with chicory, you know, to give it a distinct flavor. Some day I intend to experiment to find out the proportions they use. I'm curious, although I'm really a tea drinker." His long strides carried him across the room quickly, and he closed the door behind him.

"Mr. Jefferson," Secretary Madison said, "is very strict about remaining ignorant of matters that might prove embarrassing to him. Since he's a very curious man it isn't easy for him, but he's learning that's a price of the presidency." He adjusted his stock, smoothed the lace at his cuffs and then said in a sharp tone, "I could find only one fault with your plans, Mr. MacCullough. The United States cannot and must not sponsor the expedition you outline. I think it will interest you to learn, though, that Henry Dearborn considers them excellent from a military point of view, both strategically and tactically. He—ah—happened to see the copy on my desk a day or two ago."

The new Administration was going to great lengths to keep its official distance from the venture that Hillery had first proposed, and Andrew grinned.

"Since most men in the West are armed and capable of feeding themselves," the Secretary continued, "there would be nothing the Government could do to stop a

104

march on Louisiana—provided we knew nothing about it. That's important to remember."

"I hope mail service from the West improves, Mr. Secretary," Hillery said. "I intend to send you regular reports on my journey of observation, and it would be a pity if some of them were lost."

"Yes, it would be most unfortunate," Madison replied, straightfaced. "But I'm sure you'll keep copies I could show to a minister from a foreign legation if any unpleasantness should develop. I'd want to prove to him that the United States had done everything in its power to keep the peace."

"You can depend on me, sir, to keep a complete record," Hillery said.

The Secretary looked at Andrew again. "It's strange that you mentioned fine-grained gunpowder, lead and flour, Mr. MacCullough. Henry Dearborn was telling me those are the very items any wilderness expedition would need. I regret we can't permit you to help yourself to the ammunition and supplies stored in the new arsenal at Natchez. The commandant there, a captain by the name of Hunter, I believe—you might check on it, Hillery—is rather worried because he's been given such a small garrison to defend it."

Andrew, unlike the Secretary and his subordinate, could not help smiling broadly. He lacked the guile of a diplomat, he supposed, and knew he was incapable of performing their functions.

Again Madison's manner changed; his eyes became hard, and there was a new firmness in his voice as he said, "I want to stress one thing above all, MacCullough. The United States will not tolerate the use of actual force against the French by any expedition, even an unofficial one of which the Administration knows nothing. If the threat of force at the Louisiana border isn't sufficient to insure our use of New Orleans, the expedition should disband. American citizens must not invade the colonial territory owned by a major European nation, and they must not engage in actual fighting."

The order was unequivocal, but Andrew doubted that it could be obeyed. "River devils aren't gentle men, Mr. Secretary," he said. "They lead violent lives, they're accustomed to danger, and they don't give a hang for any authority other than their own. Once they set out to do something, there's no stopping them!"

Madison remained unyielding. "Any American citizen who deliberately impairs the relations of this nation with a foreign power will be prosecuted as a traitor, and if found guilty by the courts, will be punished accordingly. I'm sure you and your friends know the usual sentence for treason, Mr. MacCullough!"

Andrew saw he was in earnest.

"Now gentlemen, you must excuse me, too. Mr. Jefferson is expecting me to attend his meeting." Madison nodded and stalked out of the room.

Andrew and Hillery did not speak until they left the President's House and went to the Liberty Tavern for a belated breakfast. "They've given us an impossible assignment, Abel," Andrew said angrily. "You've seen the boys who guard river barges, and you know what life on the Mississippi is like. How in hell's name could we persuade two to three hundred armed men not to use their weapons if the French—or the Spaniards, or anyone else—tried to close the port of New Orleans to us?"

"It wouldn't be easy," Hillery replied cautiously. "But I've never yet known an assignment from a President or Secretary of State to be simple."

"It can't be done," Andrew said flatly.

"It must."

"The West wouldn't object to a war with France or any other country, and you know it! Diplomacy doesn't mean a damned thing to men whose families will go hungry if the Mississippi is closed! What's more, I doubt if one in a hundred ever heard of General Bonaparte—or cares who he is!"

"I've been wrestling with this problem all week, ever since Mr. Madison first outlined the conditions to me. I said nothing to you because I wanted you to hear the limitations from the President and Secretary of State themselves."

Andrew winced. "We'll have to give up the whole idea."

"We've been given orders by the President of the United States."

106

"You work for him. I don't."

"You're an American citizen, so your obligation is no less than mine."

"How can we manage it, Abel?"

"For one thing, I believe we'll have to postpone the expedition until we know where we stand with the French. We'll do nothing until they take positive action, until they make a move against us."

"In other words," Andrew said bitterly, "we let Bonaparte strike the first blow."

"That's the way President Jefferson wants it done. We carry out policy. We don't make it."

Andrew had been hungry, but lost his appetite, a sure sign he was frustrated.

"I'll come out to your homestead with you, and I'll even make myself useful, heping you pull up tree stumps. Then we'll be close enough to New Orleans to move quickly if and when the situation demands that we do something."

Andrew had no alternative, and swallowed his disappointment. Not only was he being denied the right to make certain that no attempt was made to close New Orleans to Americans, but he was being subjected to an indefinite delay before returning there. That, in turn, meant he would not and could not pay another visit to the girl who, he became increasingly convinced as his separation from her grew longer, meant more to him than he had imagined it possible for any woman to mean.

"Abel," he said, "I'll hold off as long as I can. But I'm still enough of a gambler to risk everything, including my life, when I think the time is ripe. No matter how badly President Jefferson wants to keep the peace with General Bonaparte."

TEN

February 1802

Malmaison, the First Consul's bucolic retreat outside Paris, was a modest estate, so small, in fact, that Napoleon Bonaparte hoped its diminutive size would discourage too many visits by his greedy brothers and sisters, whose demands on his resources were insatiable. Unfortunately, his wife's demands were even greater.

The West Indian-born Josephine Bonaparte was reaping the reward she believed her due for having married her husband after recognizing his genius when he had been an obscure Brigadier. A love of opulence was her principal vice, and she filled so many rooms with clothes, furs and jewels, furniture upholstered in silks, rugs from the Ottoman Empire and bric-a-brac from every nation on earth that she crowded the General out of his bedroom suite, which she used to store her belongings.

He slept in a small chamber suitable only for a junior aide, and whenever he came out to Malmaison from Paris for a few days, he found her friends in every guest room and making themselves at home in the dining salon, drawing room and library. At least his original hope had been fulfilled: no quarters were available for his relatives.

Josephine and her sycophants understood that the study at the rear of the ground floor was exclusively his. He permitted no one to enter it without his explicit permission, and made it painfully clear to the artists, actors, and unemployed minor gentry with whom she consorted that anyone caught looking at the confidential state papers he kept there would be subjected to a military court-martial. His cynicism was so great that, certain that someone would ignore his warning, he kept sentries posted outside the study, regardless of whether he was in residence.

Whenever possible the General's immediate subordinates avoided summonses to Malmaison. In spite of his claims that the change of scenery and country air refreshed him, they knew he argued interminably with his wife over her extravagances there, was kept awake at night by her roistering friends and exacerbated a chronic stomach disorder because of the rich food Josephine served.

Talleyrand had become particularly adept at avoiding calls to Malmaison, making a habit to leave Paris for one or another hidden country retreat of his own as soon as he was certain that the General had departed from the city. But the secret police agents who were in the personal employ of the First Consul and swore fealty to him were the most cunning, clever men in France, and it was impossible for anyone to disappear for more than a few hours.

One cold morning when the General was feeling even more restless than usual he wanted to see his Foreign Minister and confidant. The secret police not only found him at a small château twelve miles away, where he had gone with a young woman he called his niece, but they brought him to Malmaison an hour before noon.

"How good of you to interrupt your little holiday, Charles," the General said with a malicious smile. "You have no idea how glad I am to see you. I was afraid I'd have to eat with the gutter scum Josephine brought here this week, but now I shall dine with you instead."

"I'm delighted," Talleyrand replied in the same tone, "that I can be of service to you." He limped to a table and helped himself to some wine, in a cut-glass carafe, that had come from the cellar of an Austrian archduke whose property in Milan the First Consul had confiscated.

Bonaparte had bickered so long with his wife the previous evening that he wanted no quarrel with anyone. "Look at my drapes," he said. "They're an experiment."

The Foreign Minister glanced at the folds of heavy white silk at the windows. "Very attractive, I suppose," he said. "I've never had much talent for appreciating that sort of thing."

"You were a bishop so long you almost became an ascetic," the General told him. "Note the design."

"Are those bees?"

"Yes. I think I'll adopt them as a symbol."

"Why, First Consul?"

"Oh, I'll think of a reason that sounds logical. I'm very pleased with myself, Charles."

"Not in the least unusual."

"Some of my people found a warehouse filled with draperies and hundreds of bolts of expensive cloth at Nantes. You don't recognize the design, obviously. It's the fleur-de-lis of the Bourbons, so to save money I've turned the cloth upside down. Those who recognize the original may assume what they will, and those who don't will be happy enough to accept whatever I tell them."

"You've been wondering again how to extend your term of office beyond the original ten years."

"Yes," Bonaparte said, "I don't like the feeling of impermanence in the very expression, term of office. I couldn't sleep very well last night, and I decided the time is ripe for me to be elected First Consul for life. By acclamation would be the most impressive way, I think. Are you surprised?"

Talleyrand laughed. "I'm dazed."

"One of these days, Charles, your sense of humor is going to upset me." Jutting out his lower lip, the General scowled and ran a hand forward through his hair.

"I'm not amused, First Consul. I'm pleased. I've made a large wager that you'll crown yourself within the next thirty-six months."

Bonaparte's shrug was noncommittal. "There are some things I must do first. Last night, Charles, when I couldn't sleep, I spent most of the night thinking."

The Foreign Minister groaned. "I'll double my staff at once. Have you told the War Ministry yet?"

The General did not smile. "It seems to me the peace we've obtained with the British is very fragile."

"As delicate as the wings of your bees, First Consul. I'm familiar with some of your ambitions—although I'm sure there are others I know nothing about—and I'm positive the British won't tolerate them."

"That's why I want to put my domestic house in order immediately. While I've been waiting for you this morning, I've been writing orders, letters and the like." Bonaparte reached for a pile of documents. "This is a directive to the Finance Ministry. Property taxes are to be increased by sixteen percent at once. This—"

"Why sixteen?"

"Because I'm told that's the limit our economy can tol-

110

erate at present. This is to the Ministry of Marine, ordering the immediate construction of five new ships-of-the-line and eight frigates. This is to the Colonial Ministry, ordering the occupation of Louisiana. We've allowed the Spaniards to stay too long as our tenants. This—"

"One moment." Talleyrand leaned forward, his weight on his walking stick. "When will the occupation of Louisiana become effective?"

"As rapidly as a governor and his staff can sail there, escorted by three regiments in transports. I'm sending troops already stationed at Brest, and as I privately appointed the administrators some weeks ago, they're ready to leave without advance notice. We'll assume charge in six weeks, at the most." Suddenly Bonaparte grinned. "You'll appreciate this, Charles. Our transports will evacuate the Spanish garrison from New Orleans, taking their troops to Cuba or the Floridas, wherever they want to go. I'm instructing the Navy to submit sailing fees to Madrid, through you. I see no point in carrying hundreds of Spaniards free of charge when their King can easily afford any sum we want to charge him."

"Please don't distract me with trivia, First Consul. This is a serious matter. I shall make an announcement of the secret clause in our treaty with Spain, and I'll go back to Paris to draw up a statement as soon as we've eaten dinner."

"You will not." The General's lips scarcely moved, but the harsh ring in his voice reverberated.

"This move will cause major repercussions in London. And in the United States. Apparently you don't realize the gravity—"

"It is precisely because I do realize it that I forbid you to make any announcement until we have presented the world with an accomplished fact. Why give the British the opportunity to send their fleet—which is still larger and stronger than ours—to intercept our transports? Why allow the Americans to march a corps of their curious marksmen who wear uniforms of leather to New Orleans? No, Charles, we shall say nothing, and when we have occupied Louisiana, it will be too late for anyone to interfere."

"I disagree, First Consul." Talleyrand, ignoring his

111

scowl, was one of the very few who dared to defy the monarch, in all but name, who had made himself the absolute ruler of France. "If we surprise the British, they'll assume we have designs on the Canadian provinces—"

"From Louisiana? Do you realize how far it is from New Orleans to Quebec?"

"The Anglo-Saxons are emotional people, First Consul, and don't think logically. The Americans will be certain we intend to invade their country—"

A roar of laughter interrupted the Foreign Minister. "I have a great respect for the American fighting man, if what I've heard of him is correct. But that huge unoccupied forest, Charles! What use would it be to me?" Bonaparte wiped tears of mirth from his eyes, then sobered. "Very well, I shall be patient. Tell me what you suggest as an alternative to my order."

"We wait a week, ten days at the most. Then we make the announcement. By that time it will be too late for a British fleet to intercept us or an American military corps to march to Louisiana. But there will be time for the American Minister to notify his Government, and President Jefferson won't be surprised when he learns we've taken Louisiana. The British Colonial Office can send word to Canada, and the fur merchants in Montreal will sleep soundly in their beds, even when they hear we have returned to North America."

Bonaparte gazed at the drapes for a moment, then made one of his rapid, incisive decisions. "You have done well, Charles. Your thoughts parallel my own, and I was considering doing exactly as you have outlined. You have my permission to call in the British and American Ministers one week from tomorrow, and tell them our news. Separately, of course. England and America loathe one another, but I prefer not to risk forcing them into an alliance."

The charm of the Palais Royal lay in its garden, Robert R. Livingston told himself, and halted on the gravel path to admire the beeches and oaks. There were so few trees in Paris that the American Minister, after spending a year in the place, was homesick. The oaks were spindly, of course, and weren't in the same class with the giants in his

112

native New York, but he had to admit the beeches were handsome. The French spoiled their appearance by pruning the lower branches, but Livingston was willing to grant them an idiosyncrasy or two.

There were squirrels high in the branches, just as he had anticipated, and after looking around to make certain no one else was in the garden, he reached into the pocket of his greatcoat and brought out several shelled, roasted chestnuts he had brought with him to feed the small beasts. There was so little for French squirrels to eat that, in Paris at least, they couldn't afford the luxury of hibernating in winter.

It would be good to go home, Livingston thought, bending low on the icy gravel to scatter bits of chestnut. He missed his law practice, his friends, simple American food. Tom Jefferson had done him no favor, sending him here.

Straightening and brushing his hands, Livingston told himself he might be returning to the United States sooner than he had anticipated. Sir Frederick Atwood of the British legation, who had been called to the Palais Royal earlier in the day, had already told him the news. Livingston wanted to ask some direct questions, and if the replies weren't satisfactory he would sail on the first available ship.

A lackey in a silk uniform escorted the American Minister up the grand staircase to the second floor, and Livingston thought it was typical of Talleyrand to have obtained this most attractive of French palaces for his Foreign Ministry offices. It had suffered the least damage when other homes of royalty had been sacked during the worst days of the French Revolution, it was compact and, being small, relatively easy to heat in winter. Although he couldn't trust Talleyrand, Livingston felt a grudging admiration for him. He had the hard-headed resilience and farsightedness of Alexander Hamilton, combined with the suave graciousness that had marked General Washington's last years.

The walls of the Foreign Minister's private salon were lined with silk damask, and against one was a priceless Gobelin tapestry that, he claimed, had belonged to Henry IV. Chairs and divans had been salvaged from the property of the decapitated Louis XVI, and reupholstered in

113

silks that matched the walls; the tables came from the reign of Louis XIV, since the Foreign Minister freely admitted he had a weakness for secret locks and drawers. There was no desk in the room, no sign that the chamber was used as an office.

Livingston bowed to the man who rose to greet him. "Your Excellency."

"How good of you to call, Chancellor!"

The American immediately was on guard. He had been Chancellor of New York for a number of years, and only his friends, who knew how much he had enjoyed the post, called him by that title. "You sent for me," he said bluntly.

"I hoped you could find time to see me this afternoon," Talleyrand said, correcting him, "and I'm pleased you're here."

Livingston had no intention of helping him break the news, and merely nodded.

"The First Consul has written a letter to your President. You'll want to read it before I seal it."

The American Minister accepted the folded sheet of heavy parchment and scanned it slowly, learning nothing he hadn't already known. France, under hitherto unpublished terms of her treaty with Spain, was taking possession of the colony of Louisiana, which she had founded more than eighty years earlier.

Talleyrand was watching his visitor closely. "You're not surprised by our news, Mr. Livingston," he said, speaking in English.

Livingston refused to give him satisfaction. "Nothing Napoleon Bonaparte does surprises me, Your Excellency."

Talleyrand appreciated the riposte.

"I can give you no official reaction until I've communicated with my Government and receive a reply giving me instructions."

"Of course."

"Whether I lodge a conditional protest with you now depends on a number of factors. What is the attitude of the French Republic on questions concerning American citizens living in Louisiana and American property there?"

"Anyone who lives on our soil, anywhere in the world,

114

is guaranteed the liberty, equality and fraternity pledged to all men in the Revolution. You'll find a reference to those guarantees in the First Consul's letter to your President."

"The reference was a trifle too vague."

"The usual courtesies extended to foreigners will prevail. They must obey our laws while within our borders, and it goes almost without saying that anyone who conspires against the regime will be prosecuted. But law-abiding Americans will enjoy personal freedoms as great as they know in their own country."

That was an exaggeration, but Livingston did not argue the point. France granted far greater liberty to individuals than did Spain, so Americans in Louisiana would find their status improved.

"American property owners," Talleyrand said, "will be protected, and there will be no discrimination against them. They will be required to pay the same taxes that our own property owners pay, naturally. And whether foreigners of any nationality will be allowed to purchase new holdings hasn't yet been decided by the First Consul. The Maritime Ministry is somewhat concerned because so many New Orleans warehouses are owned by Americans, but let me stress that those who hold such property will be permitted to keep it."

The point was valid, and Livingston nodded. "Only one issue remains to be settled, Your Excellency, that of granting Americans complete freedom of navigation on the Mississippi River."

"For the present there will be no change in any of the policies of Spain."

The American Minister was alarmed. "For the present?"

"The First Consul," Talleyrand said, "has ordered all ministries to review the policies and customs of the Spaniards. At least three of them have instituted studies of the Mississippi River problem."

"It becomes a problem only if we're denied access to New Orleans for the export of our merchandise!"

"I don't necessarily mean to imply that your citizens will be denied the privilege of using the port—"

"Your Excellency," Livingston said, aware that an interruption was considered a grave discourtesy in diplo-

115

matic intercourse, but realizing even more strongly that he could not leave the point unchallenged, "the unrestricted use of the river by our citizens is not a privilege. It is a right."

There was a long, strained silence. "Are you threatening the Republic of France, Mr. Livingston?"

"No, sir! You threaten the economic welfare—the very existence of the United States!"

"I appreciate your concern," the French Foreign Minister declared, "but surely you, as an attorney, recognize the legal right of a sovereign power to make any requirements it deems essential for the use of its territorial waterways by another power."

"In this instance, Your Excellency, I can concede no such right," Livingston said firmly. The Mississippi is neither your river nor our river. It belongs jointly to the United States and France."

"Our legal experts would say that such a claim is preposterous, Mr. Livingston."

The American remained calm. "For the sake of argument, Your Excellency, let's suppose that the United States decided to divert the course of the Mississippi. Let's suppose we were able to send thousands of men to build dams and dig a new channel so the river emptied into the Gulf of Mexico far to the west of Louisiana. New Orleans would wither, and the Louisiana hinterland would become useless and barren."

"I must stretch my imagination to the limit in order to envisage such a possibility, Mr. Livingston." Talleyrand believed he was in control of the situation, and remained cool, almost detached.

"Nevertheless, let us for the sake of argument assume we were capable of performing such an engineering feat, ridiculous though it might be in realistic terms. What would France do?"

"I have no doubt that the First Consul would send an expedition to teach Americans they couldn't destroy a French city without paying a high price," Talleyrand said.

Livingston smiled, but his eyes remained serious. "I believe I've made my point, Your Excellency."

"Are you suggesting that the United States would dare to invade Louisiana?"

"I'm merely making it as plain to you as I can that my

116

Goverment will not permit our states and territories in the West to become atrophied and die."

Talleyrand took a snuff box sparkling with gems from a waistcoat pocket and offered it to his visitor.

Livingston politely declined.

The Foreign Minister helped himself to two liberal pinches, inhaled and then spent several minutes sneezing. Finally he took a lace-edged handkerchief from his sleeve and blew his nose vigorously. "Delightful," he murmured.

Livingston knew he was stalling, trying to find the right remark to make in an exceptionally delicate situation. "I trust you're using American tobacco, Your Excellency."

"Perhaps I am." The comment surprised Talleyrand, but he made a swift recovery. "I dare say it comes from Martinique, though. Madame Bonaparte is very loyal to the land of her birth, and most of our New World imports are grown there."

The assertion was nonsense, and he knew it, Livingston thought. A small tropical island could not produce all the timber and tobacco, furs and corn that an expanding France needed, and the very claim indicated Talleyrand's growing recognition of his country's increasing dependence on American trade. England, although officially at peace with France at the moment, was pursuing a quiet policy of stifling her imports, and Bonaparte had a growing need for American lumber to use in building his warships, American grain to feed his swelling legions. All of the cards were not held by the more powerful nation.

"The First Consul," the Foreign Minister said, "is seeking new sources of revenue. He might decide to charge a fee for the use of New Orleans by American shippers."

"We've used the port free of charge, and our Western farmers would claim the rights of precedent. In other words, they wouldn't pay tribute."

"You make this very difficult, Mr. Livingston. You insist on challenging France."

"On the contrary, Your Excellency, France appears determined to challenge the United States. Please don't. We'll try to hold our West in check, but our people there aren't noted for their patience."

"Neither is the First Consul."

"If he doesn't put a chip of wood on his shoulder," Livingston said, "we won't be obliged to knock it off."

117

ELEVEN

July 1802

Presiding Judge Andrew Jackson of the Tennessee Supreme Court was universally regarded as Nashville's first citizen, and the people of the western part of the state instinctively turned to him in times of trouble. A pre-statehood settler and Indian fighter, lawyer and farmer, former Federal Congressman and United States Senator, he stood far above his bitter political foe, Governor John Sevier, in the opinion of his neighbors.

Sevier, who had won distinction in the American Revolution and had fought campaigns without number against the Indian nations of the West, believed that rifles solved every problem. So, when Tennessee heard that the French had occupied New Orleans and taken jurisdiction over Louisiana, no one was surprised when Sevier made an address to the Legislature advocating the dispatch of an expedition to "rap Bonaparte on the head." He meant every word, of course, but calmer men hesitated, realizing the United States would become involved in a major war it could ill afford.

No one who knew Judge Jackson claimed he was soft or lacking in martial spirit, and his friends privately admitted his hair-trigger temper was uncontrollable in personal disputes. But the West considered him a statesman in matters involving the lives and property of others, and no one, including those who would be thrown into bankruptcy if the Mississippi was closed to American traffic, wanted to act without his approval.

Unfortunately for the impatient, the Judge was "riding the circuit," holding court in the remote wilderness towns which he visited each year during the summer months. A delegation of his fellow citizens went in search of him, but he offered them no immediate comfort when they found him. He urged that Tennessee reflect on the situation and do nothing in haste that might be regretted; he would

118

think, too, and would discuss the matter with his friends when he came home.

Scores of frontiersmen, most of them farmers whose crops had been harvested and who had nothing better to occupy them, traveled to Nashville to wait for him, talk with one another and prepare for the worst. Lodging houses were crowded, as were the homes of families who took boarders, and as many as five and six men were sleeping in each room of the town's two inns. A score or more, unable to obtain accommodations of any kind, slept in the forest, near the banks of the Cumberland River.

Andrew MacCullough and Abel Hillery were fortunate. Among the first to arrive, they had obtained a room of their own at the ramshackle Nashville Inn, whose proprietors were planning to replace it with a new brick structure if the city continued to grow and prosper. Andrew had come to Nashville reluctantly, having wanted to organize a force of river devils and march on New Orleans as soon as word had reached his homestead that the French had landed in Louisiana. Hillery, more cautious, had insisted on coming to Nashville so he could send a letter to Secretary Madison by special courier, asking whether to proceed according to plan.

Andrew, bored by months of hard labor on the homestead, found it difficult to wait idly in Nashville until Judge Jackson returned, and found a number of kindred spirits who shared his desire to storm New Orleans. But no one marched. The Judge had asked that there be no action until his return, and in the West his word was an unbreakable law.

Finally, one afternoon late in July, he rode into Nashville, the lower half of his body in buckskin trousers and home-made boots, the upper portion encased in a black coat, white shirt and mottled waistcoat. One of his saddlebags was filled with law books, court records and other tokens of his profession, but the frontier dwellers who cheered him as he rode down Market Street knew he was one of them. He carried a long rifle across his pommel, pouches of powder and bullets were hanging from his neck and jammed into his belt were two heavy pistols.

He promised to make a speech the following morning, and went directly to the inn, where he plunged into a se-

ries of long conferences with congressmen and state legis-
lators, several merchants who owned fleets of Mississippi
River barges, and Judge John Overton, one of his close
friends and law partner.

That evening Andrew and Hillery saw him, at a table
with Overton, when they came into the inn's dining room
for supper. Andrew, who had expected to see an imposing
figure, was disappointed. At the age of thirty-two Judge
Jackson looked much older. Tall but almost painfully thin,
he looked something like a scarecrow, an illusion that was
enhanced by an exceptionally long jaw and nondescript,
sandy hair with red highlights.

He raised his head to glance at the newcomers, curious
because Hillery had changed from buckskins into attire
better suiting a State Department official. And only when
Andrew's gaze met Jackson's for a moment did the power
of the Judge's personality manifest itself. His eyes were
an unusually pale shade of blue, and so piercing that they
seemed to cut through a man. Andrew had the sensation
that the Judge could read his innermost thoughts, and was
forced to reassure himself that the notion was nonsensical.

Hillery presented himself and his companion, and the
Judge promptly asked them to join him for supper. "I
reckon we'll all be talking about the same thing, seeing
there's only one subject anybody hereabouts has any interest in discussing these days, so we might as well be sociable. Now, what's somebody from the State Department
doing this far from Washington City?"

Hillery explained his mission in the West, hastening to
add that he was acting as an unofficial adviser to Andrew
and other "friends."

The Judge chuckled. "If Tom Jefferson himself sailed
down the Mississippi in a schooner, he'd do it unofficially,
pretending he wasn't President."

Andrew decided he liked the man. "Do you think we're
being too careful, Judge?"

"If we've got to fight," Jackson said, "I believe we need
the full power of the United States behind us. We'll need
Regular Army troops as well as militia from every state
and territory so we can take Louisiana and hold it. But as
I was just saying to John, all this talk of war is a mite premature. Let's send a barge—just one, mind you, and

loaded with corn fit only for hogs, so we don't lose much if the French take it from us—and send it down the river. Then, by the Eternal, we'll know where we stand!"

"I want to be on board that barge," Andrew said quickly. "In fact, I'd like to see somebody keep me off!"

There was so little shipping on the Mississippi River that even the brigands who made their living preying on American commerce turned, at least for the present, to stealing livestock from farm and plantation owners. Men were reluctant to risk the possible loss of their merchandise by sending it downstream to New Orleans, but those who heard that a heavily laden barge was sailing south to test the intentions of the French gathered on the banks to cheer the five men making the trial voyage.

Scores congregated at Natchez, and would have delayed the voyagers by giving an ox-roast and jamboree in their honor, but Andrew, who was in command of the little expedition, refused to tarry for the purpose. There would be ample opportunity to celebrate, he said, if he and his companions returned unscathed after finding no change in conditions at their destination.

The voyage was resumed, and Andrew braced for trouble. No one knew the precise location of the boundary between the Mississippi Territory and Louisiana, and when Spain had owned the delta country, no one had cared. One stretch of wilderness was like another, the forest stretched out toward the horizon and, aside from a few roving bands of Indians in search of game, the whole region was uninhabited.

Andrew's hunch proved correct. After sailing several hours downstream from Natchez he saw a newly constructed log fort on a long spit of land that jutted out into the river, and it was small consolation to realize that its garrison, unfamiliar with the tendency of the Mississippi to change course during the spring and autumn rains, might be inundated in a few months.

A warning shot fired by a small cannon landed about fifty yards ahead of the barge, and a soldier stationed on a small watchtower beckoned.

"We might be able to squeeze past them," Andrew told the others, "but we won't try. And remember, lads, we're

121

trying to find out just how mean they're going to be, so we've got to keep our heads, no matter how much they may provoke us."

They directed the barge toward the fort, from which the tricolor flag of the French Republic was flying, and when they drew closer they saw two boats tied up at a makeshift wharf. The larger of them, a miniature schooner, carried two five-pounder cannon, each of the little guns powerful enough to destroy any river shipping. Behind the low wall of the fort Andrew also caught a glimpse of the barrels of two howitzers, powerful guns that could sink any vessels that might be sent downstream by Americans.

In the event of a major dispute, he thought, it would be exceptionally difficult to attack the fort from the river. But he made a mental note of the fact that no attempt had been made to clear away the forest that crept down to the river's edge behind the little peninsula. Experienced frontiersmen could reach a point only a few yards behind the fort before launching a surprise attack on it.

It appeared that a full company of troops, numbering approximately fifty men, was stationed at the fort, and Andrew suppressed a broad grin as he studied the French soldiers. All were dressed in immaculate white tunics and breeches totally unsuitable for wilderness living, and the officers wore plumed helmets of shining brass that picked up the sun's light and gleamed at a distance. American marksmen whose dirty buckskins blended with the background and made them almost invisible would find such foes easy targets.

Although the French had come to the New World in force and obviously were far better prepared for emergencies than their Spanish predecessors had been, they demonstrated no real understanding of the wilderness. Andrew felt reasonably certain they could be overwhelmed by frontier dwellers in spite of their superior, modern armaments.

"Identify yourselves and tie up to our wharf," an officer called in French. "We intend to inspect your cargo."

Andrew, hoping he might glean more if he pretended not to understand the language, looked blank. "Do you speak English?" he replied, cupping his hands and shouting in return.

122

The officer, looking scornful, repeated the directions in heavily accented but intelligible English.

"By what right do you plan to board us?" Andrew demanded.

"You are in the territorial waters of French Louisiana, and are subject to our laws."

Shrugging, Andrew threw a line to a soldier standing on the rickety wharf and allowed the barge to be made fast.

A younger officer was summoned, and came on board with a squad of soldiers. The troops searched thoroughly, but Andrew made no protest until they began jabbing bayonets into the corn that was stacked high near the stern. "Your bayonets are sharp," he said mildly, "and will ruin our grain."

"I must obey my orders," the young officer replied, and there was a hint of sympathy in his voice.

"Are you looking for something?"

"Weapons."

Andrew laughed. "Even if we had them to spare, do you think we'd be carrying rifles to the people of New Orleans?"

"Perhaps. I don't know. Our orders were issued to the War Ministry before we left France—by the First Consul himself." The officer's attitude indicated that orders from that source were obeyed without question.

The older officer beckoned impatiently. "Come ashore to register your names and nationalities."

It would be wise to set a precedent immediately, Andrew decided, and made no move. "We'll wait," he announced, "until the inspection of our cargo is finished."

The commander seemed irritated, but the reaction was logical, and he did not press the point.

When the squad was done and had marched ashore, Andrew led his companions onto the wharf.

"Come with me into the fort," the officer directed.

"Not so fast. I want to leave two of my boys here to guard our cargo."

"Do you suppose we would steal it?"

"You have your orders," Andrew replied, "and we have ours. The owners of the barge don't want it left untended." Having established the principle, he told two of

123

the men to wait, and, with the others, accompanied the officer.

The interior of the fort was remarkably comfortable by frontier standards. The office of the commandant was furnished with chairs, tables, a desk and several oil lamps that had been brought into the wilderness from New Orleans, perhaps from France. To Andrew's amazement there was a luxurious rug on the floor, too, and he concealed a smile when he thought of what would happen to it when the river rose in the autumn.

He signed a registration book, then inscribed the names of his companions, who could neither read nor write. "May I ask why this registration is necessary?"

The officer looked blank. "We have been instructed to record the names of those who travel on the river."

Andrew decided not to tell him that the fiercely independent American frontiersmen would give false names, more often than not, because they hated being regimented.

"Now," the commandant declared, "we shall inspect your weapons, and take from you those we think unnecessary."

"The hell you will." In spite of Andrew's good intentions, the words slipped out before he could stop himself. "Captain, I realize you're trying to do your duty, but let me give you some advice. Touch an American's rifle or pistols, and you'll have a fight on your hands. We're just the first to come down the river. Behind us there will come hundreds of others, maybe thousands, and every last man believes he has the right to carry whatever firearms he pleases to protect himself. One of these days somebody will get shot, and then the whole border will explode. I don't reckon you want a war any more than we do, but I warn you that this fort won't stand for a week if you lay your hands on any American rifle or pistol."

There was a long, tense silence.

The younger French officer, who was standing in the entrance, said in his own tongue, "The Yankee makes sense."

His superior shrugged. "But we can't disobey our instructions."

"Orders written in Paris look very different in this forlorn place."

Andrew bit back a grin. "Our people," he said in English, "fight only in self-defense. Take a man's rifle from him, and he'll think you want to do him harm. That's when he becomes dangerous."

The commandant weighed the problem, then shrugged. "Keep your weapons," he said, then added to his assistant, in French, "These Yankees are little better than savages, so it may be best not to arouse them. When they reach New Orleans, General de Maniton will draw the sting from their vipers' fangs."

The casual statement had an ominous ring.

New Orleans was changed, and the Americans sensed the difference as they maneuvered their barge toward the wharves. The Spanish customs guards were gone, and in their place squads of self-confident young French troops patrolled the waterfront, the bayonets on their muskets gleaming. Other troops were on duty near the warehouses behind the wharves, a senior officer was in charge of the operation, and it was evident that the new masters of Louisiana were purposeful, alert men who expected their orders to be obeyed.

After the barge had been made secure in her berth a boarding party appeared, and Andrew was forced to tolerate a second inspection of his cargo, more thorough than the first. He protested when the corn was prodded with bayonets, but the troops paid no attention, and an additional platoon moved toward the wharf, ready for action in the event trouble developed.

Andrew made arrangements to have his cargo moved to an American-owned warehouse a city square distant, and the moment the negotiations were completed a young officer wearing the gold and blue sash of a General's aide-de-camp appeared at his elbow. "Your assistants will remain on board your barge," the officer said politely, speaking excellent English, "and you will be good enough to accompany me." He made the statement flatly, not as a request but as a command, and obviously expected it to be obeyed.

A horse was provided, and Andrew rode with the aide through the familiar streets of New Orleans to the Place d'Armes, where smartly uniformed, superbly drilled

French troops stood sentry duty. They entered the military headquarters building, from which the French flag was flying, and Andrew was escorted to a spacious antechamber, where he was asked to wait.

A few moments later he was shown into the office of Major General Jean de Maniton, the commander of all French troops in Louisiana. A veteran of First Consul Bonaparte's campaigns in northern Italy and Egypt, the General was a lean, hard-faced professional soldier; he glanced at the buckskin-clad American, and, wasting no time, spoke in a crisp voice.

"You are the first of your nation to come to New France," he said, "so you will be the first to obey the new rules imposed by the War Ministry on foreigners. A warehouse at the river has been sold to us by one of your fellow Americans, and is being converted into sleeping quarters. You and your men may remain there overnight, and may purchase food—which you can cook outside the building. You will not be permitted to go elsewhere in the city, and you will depart for the United States no later than twenty-four hours from the time of your arrival. All Americans who come here in the future will be obliged to obey these same rules." He nodded in dismissal.

Andrew was as astonished as he was angry. "You forbid us the freedom of the city?"

"We do." General de Maniton began to read a bulky report.

"And you're limiting our stay here?"

De Maniton jerked a thumb toward a huge portrait of a scowling Bonaparte on the wall behind him. "Direct your complaints to the First Consul. He knows you Americans want New Orleans, and he has no intention of allowing you to gain a foothold here."

The French regulations were preposterous, and Andrew found it almost impossible to curb his temper. "I have the honor to be betrothed to a lady here," he said, ignoring the fact that Jeanne had never replied to his one letter. "The daughter of Spanish port director Ramón Valdéz."

The General lost interest in the document he was reading. "We're employing Valdéz in another position."

It appeared that Jeanne and her father were still in New Orleans.

"How convenient that an American river bargeman should be betrothed to a lady of stature. Do you have any other friends in the city?"

Common sense dictated a soft reply to the General's sarcasm, but Andrew was too angry. "Yes, Donna Beatriz de Santos, who was planning to marry the deputy Governor of New Spain when I was last here."

"Well." The French commander-in-chief scrutinized his visitor. A minor, routine matter suddenly had assumed greater significance. "Don Felipe has remained behind to help us transfer authority from Spain to France."

Beatriz, in all probability, had not left Louisiana, either, and might be married by this time.

"I plan to see Don Felipe later today," General de Maniton said. "Tell me your name again, so I may find out how well he knows you."

"I doubt if Don Felipe has ever heard of me."

De Maniton's laugh was unpleasantly grating. "That's what I thought. You're a clever rogue, but not clever enough. Americans aren't welcome here, and we particularly don't want your kind. You'll be taken back to the waterfront, and if you're wise you'll stay there until you leave tomorrow. We're allowing you and your countrymen to use our port, but don't strain our hospitality."

Andrew was too incensed to be articulate.

The General rang a small bell, the aide reappeared, and his superior nodded in Andrew's direction. "Provide the Yankee with an escort, and make certain he doesn't leave the foreigners' bivouac between now and the time he sails for the United States tomorrow."

For the moment there was no choice. Andrew inclined his head in a token gesture of farewell, and fumed as he left the office.

Neither he nor the aide-de-camp spoke on the ride back to the waterfront, but as they neared the wharves he broke the silence. "Americans," he said, "won't tolerate these restrictions."

The young French officer, accustomed to unquestioning obedience, looked surprised. "The First Consul has his reasons for every decree he issues."

"I have no quarrel with Bonaparte," Andrew replied, "but if he wants to keep his new colony, he'll have to start learning that Americans aren't the same breed as Europeans. We don't take to any laws that bind us or restrict our freedom."

"The whole world fears him!"

"We aren't afraid of any man who walks this earth on two feet. And if Bonaparte doesn't yet know it, he'll soon find out!"

The warehouse was dark, damp, and unbearably hot. One small window, set high in a wall, provided the only ventilation, and in the far corners rats could be heard groveling for grains of dried corn. Andrew and his fellow rivermen sprawled on the hard dirt floor, and with no candle or lamp to provide illumination, were forced to become accustomed to the almost complete absence of light.

"I got to admit the meat and fish they sold us tonight weren't too bad," one said, "even if they charged us twice what we'd have paid at the market."

"Ten cents, American, for a gallon of ale was too dear," another muttered. "When there's enough of us who come down together on a barge convoy, we'll tear down the walls of this place. It's like a prison."

"There are similarities," Andrew said, "but take it from somebody who knows, a New Orleans prison is worse. All the same, I'm itching to get some fresh air."

"Tomorrow, when we head north," still another of his companions told him, "you can get your fill of it."

"I need air tonight. Right now." Andrew couldn't quite see the others, but felt them looking at him.

"The French ain't aimin' t' let us go no place t'night, Andy! There must be a whole platoon out there makin' sure we spend the night in this here barn."

"I have a hankering to see the sights of French New Orleans," Andrew said. "If a couple of you lads will hoist me up to the window—and then make a noise at the warehouse door to distract the sentries, I'll see you in the morning before we're obliged to sail north."

"You know New Orleans better'n any of us," one said in alarm. "And you know there's no sights worth seein'."

"Don't forget the target practice them soldiers put on for our benefit tonight," another reminded. "These

Frenchies ain't Spaniards. They can shoot with their muskets blame near as good as we can with our rifles. And they ain't bashful, neither."

"Nobody," Andrew said, "is going to restrict me to a riverfront shed. Here. You two steady me while I shinny up to the window. That's it. Now hand me my rifle." He waited until they obeyed. "All right, boys. Now go to the door of the warehouse and start an argument with one another."

His companions understood his refusal to bow to French authority, but were reluctant to obey him, knowing he would be in serious trouble if apprehended.

"I can't perch up here all night like a damned bat!"

The bargemen went to the door, and if their mock argument lacked conviction, they compensated for it by roaring at the tops of their voices.

Andrew, peering out of the window, saw French troops converging on the entrance. He squeezed through the window, balanced on the narrow ledge for a moment and then dropped to the earth below. He had aimed for a clump of bushes, but landed on the hard ground just beyond, and the breath was knocked from him. He managed to keep a firm grip on his rifle, however, and, jumping to his feet, quickly walked away from the warehouse.

The continuing shouts of his fellow bargemen rang in his ears, and he grinned as he headed toward the center of town. Not one of the twenty-five sentries assigned to guard the first Americans to visit French Louisiana saw or heard him.

Now that he had thumbed his nose at French authority, however, he was uncertain where to go. If he visited an inn or tavern, a French officer dining there might become suspicious and report him. He did not dare go to Beatriz de Santos' house for fear she was already married or, at the very least, that Don Felipe de Guzmán might be visiting there. If so, the Spaniard would be certain to notify General de Maniton at once.

That left the Valdéz house, but he found himself curiously reluctant to face Jeanne. He had more than repaid her betrayal, and his one brief letter explaining his abrupt departure from New Orleans after his last visit had been

129

enough, combined with his silence, to convince her that he had been toying with her affections for ulterior purposes of his own.

Perhaps, he thought, he was ashamed to face Jeanne, even though she had deserved his crude treatment. Or was it possible that he could not allow himself to see her when the prospect, although very remote, of spending a few hours with Beatriz caused his blood to race? He did not know.

The loud, shrill notes of a trumpet call broke the silence of the night, and in a moment other trumpets began to answer. Pedestrians stopped to listen, and Andrew halted, too, until it occurred to him that the first trumpet had sounded from the direction of the wharves. His guess was confirmed when a troop of French cavalry approached from the direction of the military barracks and, as people took refuge in doorways and against the walls of buildings, thundered toward the river.

His absence from the warehouse had been discovered, and the garrison was being called out to hunt for him. He needed little imagination to know the French would make a more thorough, systematic search than the Spaniards had been capable of doing.

He supposed that, having proved himself capable of defying the authority of Bonaparte, he could make his way back to the waterfront, and, with luck, go on board the barge. He might be able to hide in its tiny cabin, and when the troops searched it, as they inevitably would, he could pretend to be asleep there. But General de Maniton appeared to be a man with a limited sense of humor, and would impose as severe a punishment on the transgressor as he would for a more prolonged disappearance.

Andrew found himself continuing to walk toward the center of the city, and cautioned himself to move less rapidly. As he approached the Avenue de Bienville he had to move to the side of the road to let two full companies of infantry pass, and the sight of the muskets and bayonets, the grim expressions on the faces of the mounted officers and the sense of purposefulness displayed by all of the troops convinced him he had been wrong to give in to his initial impulse. On French soil no one thumbed his nose at the First Consul.

Scarcely realizing where he was going, Andrew soon found himself on the Rue St. Pierre, and cursed himself for his stupidity. Jeanne, who had given him away once, would be even more inclined to do the same again, now that he had scorned her. But he no longer had any choice, any freedom of action, and could only throw himself on her mercy, hoping that she resented the transfer of Louisiana's sovereignty from Spain to France, and therefore would give him refuge until he could decide what to do next.

He climbed over the fence into the side yard of the Valdéz property, and, staying in the shadows close to the wall, went to the front door. He had been careless as well as shortsighted, he told himself angrily; not until now had he noticed that the moon was almost full, making outdoor concealment far more difficult.

Steeling himself, he tapped at the door.

The serving woman who answered his summons recognized him and was startled, but quickly led him into the house and up the familiar staircase to the sitting room on the second floor.

Jeanne was there, and so was Beatriz.

Both girls stared at him, too shocked to speak.

Andrew made a gallant attempt to recover, removed his broad-brimmed wilderness hat and bowed low. "Your servant, ladies."

Jeanne stood with a hand at her throat, still speechless.

Beatriz rose, and forced a laugh that sounded metallic. "We should have known," she said, "that he'd be on board the first American barge to arrive here since the French occupied the city." She turned from Jeanne to Andrew, her temper flaring. "Surely you must know that General de Maniton insists on confining all foreigners to the waterfront area!"

"So he told me this afternoon." Unaccountably, Andrew's spirits rose, and he grinned.

At last Jeanne recovered her voice. "Those trumpets," she said, "are sounding because of you."

"I believe so," Andrew replied. "The French are remarkably efficient."

"They are also ruthless," Beatriz told him. "This isn't the New Orleans you knew!"

"General de Maniton is so strict," Jeanne murmured.

"I was wrong to come here," Andrew told her. "I have no right to embarrass you or your father." His smile had frozen on his face and, feeling foolish now, he turned away.

"Wait!" Jeanne said.

"Where will you go?" Beatriz demanded.

Andrew shrugged. "This is a big town, and I should be accustomed to hiding from the authorities by now. I'll find a place, and after the excitement dies down I'll go back to my barge."

The girls exchanged swift glances.

"You're mad," Beatriz said.

"Troops will be stationed at every approach to the Mississippi," Jeanne said, "and cavalry will keep watch on every exit from the city. Last week a merchant was robbed by a very clever thief, but General de Maniton caught him. Bonaparte's Governor and his staff are just as determined. Papa says that cold wine flows in their veins."

"You should hear Felipe," Beatriz said.

"I'll take my chances," Andrew told them.

Jeanne hurried to the door, blocking it, and Beatriz caught his arm.

"I can't permit either of you—"

"Nonsense," Jeanne said firmly.

Beatriz was equally adamant. "If you go out into the streets, you'll be shot!"

"Who saw you come in?" Jeanne wanted to know.

"Only the old serving woman—"

"Carmen? I'll see to it that she says nothing." Jeanne communicated silently with Beatriz.

"Wait," Andrew said. "I don't know what you have in mind, but I can't let you jeopardize—"

"You speak to Carmen," Beatriz said to Jeanne, "and I'll show him to the attic."

"I know the way to the attic," Andrew said angrily, "but I refuse—"

"Papa will be home soon," Jeanne interrupted, "and if he finds you here it will be his duty to notify General de Maniton. The French are being very kind to Papa, allowing him to stay as the civilian adviser to the General, and he—"

132

"All the more reason for me to go," Andrew declared.

Beatriz lost her temper. "You always were a bully, and you're still a madman. We'll bring you some food, and you'd best be prepared to stay in the attic for days, if necessary. We'll find out the situation tomorrow, and if you can't go then, you'll have to stay until they stop searching for you."

"If they stop," Jeanne added, and caught her breath. "Please do as we ask, Andrew. I—we—wouldn't want your murder on our consciences."

"She's right," Beatriz said soberly. "This is a serious matter, so please go. Now."

Desperately sorry he had allowed himself to be put in such an awkward position, Andrew finally agreed. He made his way to the top floor of the house and let himself into the dark, stuffy attic. Stumbling over a box, he managed to make his way to the far side, where other boxes and a broken chair were piled on an old mattress. His eyesight improving in the dark, he moved the various items, then stretched out on the mattress, his rifle and pistols beside him.

The trumpets continued to blare, but their sound was muffled, and they seemed far away. Brushing a spider from his face, Andrew's self-anger increased. He was in a vulnerable position, with his life threatened, and he wondered if a brief glimpse of the girl he loved was worth the risks he had taken and the uncertain future he now faced.

Time was losing its meaning, there was no difference between day and night in the attic, and Andrew, trying in vain to curb his mounting impatience, felt an increasingly strong urge to make a break for freedom, regardless of the consequences. Only the pleas of Jeanne and Beatriz kept him in his hiding place. On three occasions Jeanne brought him cold meat and bread, and twice Beatriz appeared with food; the girls remained in the attic for only a moment or two on each visit, and their news was uniformly discouraging. The French were continuing to push their hunt for him, the city was being scoured, and, finally, a reward was offered for his capture.

His chances of making a successful escape from Louisiana seemed remote, if the information Jeanne and Beatriz

133

were giving him was accurate, but his sense of frustration was overwhelming. He had found out what he had come to New Orleans to learn, that France would permit Americans to use the port facilities of New Orleans while severely limiting the personal freedom of United States citizens in the city, but the data was meaningless unless he transmitted it to his fellow Americans.

Men in Tennessee, Kentucky, and the territories were anxiously awaiting word from him, and his mission was a total failure unless he reported to them. He had no idea whether the other bargemen had been released or were being held as prisoners, and neither Beatriz nor Jeanne could give him any news of them.

The girls continued to insist that he remain in hiding until General de Maniton assumed he had gone and gave up the search, and their advice was sensible, but virtually impossible to accept. Andrew felt like a useless coward, and, aware he had spent at least a day and a night in the attic, perhaps longer, made his own private plans. Saving part of the food brought to him, he sneaked out of the attic long enough to determine that it was midafternoon, which suited his purposes. He would force himself to sleep for a few hours, wait until he received his next meal and then vanish from the Valdéz house after dark.

It was difficult for him to drop off, but he knew it might be a long time before he had the opportunity to sleep again, so he emptied his mind and at last lost consciousness.

Strong hands grasped Andrew, and as he suddenly became wide awake he heard men speaking in both French and Spanish.

"This is the man," one of them said in the latter tongue. "We'll share the reward."

Andrew remained limp, pretending he was still asleep until he gained a better idea of what was happening. Very cautiously he opened one eye slightly, and saw the face of Captain Cristoforo de Martínez only a few inches from his own. The Spaniard was wearing civilian clothes, and was accompanied by at least two other men, similarly attired, one of whom was carrying several short lengths of rope.

Obviously the group hoped to take the American by surprise, bind him and hand him over to the French.

Andrew went into action swiftly and violently. He smashed a fist into the face of de Martínez, toppling him, and simultaneously kicked the man with the ropes in the pit of the stomach, sending him staggering backward into the attic wall.

Reaching for his rifle and pistols, Andrew discovered too late that they had been removed; consequently he would have to depend on his physical prowess alone. Before he could gain his feet, however, two men pounced on him and pinned him to the mattress. There were more of his foes in the party than he had thought.

He fought them viciously, using all of his strength as well as the skills he had acquired in frontier free-for-all contests. It was relatively easy to dispose of one Spaniard, who retired from the fray with a broken nose after absorbing several punches delivered in quick succession. But his companion, a burly Frenchman, was more resilient, and Andrew slowly gained the upper hand as they rolled over and over on the attic floor, grappling and wrestling, arms flailing and legs trying to obtain a pinning hold.

In the meantime, however, de Martínez and the fourth man had recovered sufficiently to attack again. The Captain was careful not to come within range of Andrew's fists, but the ropeholder was less cautious, and his weight, added to that of the Frenchman, started to turn the tide.

At this point de Martínez became more active, and Andrew felt his ankles being bound. He kicked savagely in an attempt to free himself, but one of the men was sitting on his legs, and escape was impossible, even though he delivered punishing blows to both of his assailants.

Eventually de Martínez managed to make the ropes secure, and joined the other two in trying to immobilize Andrew's fists. The American continued to pound all three, landing blow after blow on their faces and heads, but even a man of greater than normal strength could not win when the odds against him were so great. The powerful Frenchman managed to pin Andrew's right arm to the floor, while de Martínez and the other man at last gained control of his left.

135

It was simple to truss him and stuff a gag into his mouth, and he was rendered completely helpless.

Removing their prisoner from the attic took more time. For whatever their reasons the quartet apparently wanted no one to know what they were doing, and while the man with the broken nose went ahead to make sure no one was in sight, the others cautiously carried their victim down the stairs. They took him from the house by way of the rear entrance, near the kitchen outbuilding, and the fuming but impotent Andrew was surprised to see that night had already fallen. He had slept longer than he had thought.

The group's horses were tethered behind the barn at the far end of the Valdéz property; throwing the prisoner over a saddle and, still taking no chances, binding him with longer ropes, the men mounted their own horses. The Spaniard with a broken nose was not accompanying the others, so it seemed that Andrew was being removed on his horse.

As a parting gesture, however, the wounded man took a pistol from his belt and began to whip the helpless prisoner across the face and shoulders with its butt. The pain was excruciating, but Andrew knew it would be useless to cry out for help, and, too proud to admit he was in pain, he made no sound.

Captain de Martínez watched the beating and laughed softly under his breath before giving the order to move off.

The group used side streets, but rode closer to the center of town, and Andrew, his face and shoulders throbbing, had no doubt regarding their destination. Directly ahead were the former Spanish military barracks, now occupied by the French, and the prison from which Beatriz de Santos had helped him escape.

De Martínez called a halt at the barracks, and soon officers and enlisted men came running from the nearest building. The ropes that bound Andrew to his horse were cut, and then his hands and legs were freed. Swaying groggily, he found himself surrounded by French soldiers armed with muskets and pistols, all pointed at him. It was impossible to break out of the ring of iron, and he felt too ill to try. Wiping blood from his face with his sleeve, he tried to stand erect, but suddenly collapsed onto the ground. The beating he had received had been even more severe than he had thought.

As though from a great distance he could hear someone speaking the French of the aristocracy congratulate de Martínez, and then coins clinked. Obviously the Spanish officer was being paid the reward that had been offered for the capture of the fugitive American.

An order was given, muskets were prodded into Andrew's back, and he forced himself to his feet, first climbing onto his knees, then making a great effort to stand. Still surrounded by troops, he was marched off to the prison, and when he fell, twice, his captors callously forced him to stand and walk again.

The prison was far different now than it had been under Spanish rule. A chief warden and several assistants were in charge, heavily armed soldiers surrounded the building, and a high fence of sharpened logs had been placed about two feet from the walls of the jail. The palisade was at least ten to eleven feet high, and made the possibility of escape even more remote.

Andrew collapsed again, and this time his captors had no patience with his disability, treating him with even less concern than had the soldiers. Two assistant wardens dragged him down the rough floor of the corridor and heaved him onto a straw pallet in a small, hot cell.

There they stood, looking down at him, and as he peered up at them it occurred to him for the first time that one of his eyelids was badly swollen, impairing his vision. He raised a hand to his face and felt it gingerly, realizing, to his surprise, that his nose was broken. The Spaniard who had attacked him had evened the score with him.

"I think," one of the assistant wardens said, "that he requires the attention of a physician."

"This is the hour when every physician in New Orleans is dining. And with the great shoot of that flock of wild ducks yesterday, what doctor would give up his roast duck with herb stuffing to treat the ailments of a Yankee?"

Both Frenchmen laughed.

Andrew refused to give them the satisfaction of gloating over him. "I require no assistance from a physician or anyone else," he said through gritted teeth.

The taller of the assistant wardens nudged his colleague. "You have spoken the truth, Yankee," he said. "After all the bother you have caused General de Maniton, you certainly will be here for a very long time to come. Either you will die of your injuries, or they will heal." He left the cell, chuckling.

The other assistant warden left a small pail of water and, beside it, a half-loaf of bread and a small square of hard but fragrant cheese. Apparently the French, unlike the Spaniards, did not believe in putting their prisoners on starvation rations. "You were very stupid to break the orders of General de Maniton himself," the man said. "He won't forgive you."

A moment later the door closed, a bolt was moved into place and the key turned in the lock.

Andrew knew only that he had failed, and thought bitterly that Jeanne had given him away to Cristoforo de Martínez. Or had it been Beatriz? He no longer could be sure of anyone's loyalty or help in the New Orleans he once had loved, the city that now had become a hostile, threatening place.

TWELVE

October 1802

The troops of Napoleon Bonaparte's legions were resilient, superbly disciplined fighting men who took unbounded pride in the recovery of their nation from the chaos of the French Revolution and in their own achievements. Convinced that France would achieve unprecedented glory under a leader whose genius they had been the first to recognize, they were inspired zealots who carried out every order to the letter.

As a consequence, life for their prisoners in the military jail at New Orleans was uncomfortable, regimented and boring. Andrew MacCullough bitterly regretted the impulse that had caused him to disobey the directive of General Jean de Maniton and stray from the area to which he had been confined for what should have been a single night's sojourn in New Orleans. Had he followed the General's orders, he would have reported on the state of the French occupation of Louisiana to his fellow Americans by now, and an expedition of river devils would be organizing to test the resolve of the French.

Instead he was languishing in solitary confinement, his prospects bleak and his hope of carrying out his mission virtually nonexistent. The only bright spot in an otherwise gloomy situation was that he had recovered his health after weeks of suffering. The bruises on his face and body had healed, and he did not care that his nose had assumed a new shape, although he was still surprised when, three times each week, he saw his reflection in a square of burnished steel as he shaved under the watchful gaze of two alert sentries.

The French, he had to admit, took far better care of their prisoners than had the Spaniards. Once each week he was allowed to bathe in several pails of water brought to his cell for the purpose, and the straw of his mattress was changed regularly, too, so he was not plagued by the lice that made imprisonment by the Spaniards so unpleasant.

His food, which consisted principally of bread, cheese, and thick soups, was more than adequate, and he exercised daily, to the best of his ability in a limited space, in order to avoid putting on weight.

Yet his incarceration was a torment far worse than any torture he had ever imagined. His jailers were not permitted to speak to him on any subject other than his daily care, and they obeyed the regulations so carefully that he no longer tried to draw them into conversation. He had no idea what might be happening in the outside world, and could not learn whether the bargemen who had accompanied him on the voyage down the Mississippi had been permitted to leave New Orleans. His one hope was that they had returned to the United States, and even though their knowledge of what had happened in Louisiana might be limited, men like Andrew Jackson and Abel Hillery would waste no time launching a semi-military expedition once they gleaned an approximation of the true state of affairs.

With nothing to read and nothing to occupy his long days, Andrew found himself dwelling on the past. But he had learned it was a frustrating, infuriating pastime to think of Beatriz de Santos or Jeanne Valdéz. Whether one or both of them had revealed his whereabouts to Cristoforo de Martínez was almost irrelevant to his situation. He should have known better than to accept their help, and was paying a staggering price for his incredibly naïve conduct.

Self-recriminations solved none of his problems, and he tried to think of ways to escape from the prison, only to abandon each idea in turn. The principal jailer had served in a similar capacity in France, and on his daily tour of the cells he boasted that no man in his charge had ever made a successful break for freedom.

Heavy bars now covered Andrew's one window, and directly beyond the opening was the palisade of stout logs. Strong sentry details were posted inside and outside the prison, and one of the assistant wardens had hinted on several occasions that dogs trained for the purpose of attacking escaping prisoners were being used, too.

So the unhappy Andrew, with nothing to read, nothing to fill the void from the moment he awakened in the morning until he stretched out on his pallet at nightfall, felt the change of season in the air, saw rain fall more frequently, and dreamed of freedom. Sometimes he thought his sanity was threatened, principally because he had no idea how long he would be kept prisoner. The warden had admitted to him that General de Maniton had passed a formal sentence on him, but he did not know whether he would be kept behind bars for a month longer, another year or the rest of his days.

Finally, in late October, a visitor arrived to break the monotony of his empty routine. Andrew was astonished to see Ramón Valdéz, and was even more surprised when Jeanne's father cordially shook his hand.

Two assistant wardens lingered in the open door of the cell, but Valdéz dismissed them with a curt wave. "You may lock me in here with the prisoner," he said, "and I'll tap at the door when I'm ready to leave."

The Frenchmen obeyed him without question, an indication that he was still a personage of stature in Louisiana, even though a Spaniard.

"When we last saw each other," he said when he and Andrew were alone, "there seemed to be a distinct possibility that by this time you would become my son-in-law. But First Consul Bonaparte has changed both our destinies. I wouldn't have believed that I would be permitted to remain in New Orleans, holding a post of great responsibility. And I'm not the only one. There are others from Spain who have been kept in the administration of New France."

"You'll forgive me," Andrew said, "if I fail to share your enthusiasm for Bonaparte."

Valdéz smiled fleetingly. "I cannot say I approve or disapprove of him. He is both good and bad. Protestants may worship freely in Louisiana now, as may Jews, and no one cares what a man's faith may be, which is a far cry from the system that prevailed under Spanish rule. But let someone utter a single word criticizing the First Consul, and he is sent to prison for years. Cells in this very jail are occupied by men who have dared to speak of him with scorn, in public."

"I've met no one here. The warden isn't very convivial."

"So I'm told." Valdéz opened a basket and spread its

141

contents on the one small table in the cell. "Jeanne has sent you this roasted chicken and two sausages. This small keg of ale is a gift to you from Beatriz de Santos. I'd have brought more, but even this much is usually forbidden, and I've been allowed to break the regulations only because I am the civilian assistant to General de Maniton, helping him keep order among the Creoles and the Spaniards who elected to remain here when the colony came under French rule."

"I'm grateful to you," Andrew said. "And please thank the young ladies for me."

Valdéz heard and understood the bitterness in his voice. "If I could, I would tell you who revealed to Cristoforo that you were hiding in my attic."

Andrew was uncertain whether he meant he did not actually know or preferred not to say. Perhaps it was best not to pursue the subject, particularly when there were more urgent matters to discuss. "I'm here, so it doesn't much matter how I got here. What is important is whether the men who came to Louisiana with me have gone back to the United States."

Valdéz shook his head.

Andrew felt as though he had received a severe physical blow.

"For weeks no one knew what to do with them. The Governor wanted to release them, since they had broken no laws, but General de Maniton insisted they be kept in New Orleans. He was afraid there would be a great outcry if they returned to the United States and told their story."

"He was right," Andrew said grimly. "Where are they being held?"

"Not in this prison, but more than that I can't tell you. Let it be enough that they have greater freedom than you enjoy, and more privileges. But they will not be given their freedom until First Consul Bonaparte is convinced there will be no attack on Louisiana by the United States."

"As long as American citizens in Louisiana are treated like cattle—and like criminals—that day will never come."

Valdéz nodded sympathetically. "I know. I have learned much about your countrymen in the many years

142

I have lived here. But the French are new to New Orleans, and don't understand."

"They'll understand our rifles!"

"Quietly." Valdéz was alarmed. "If you should be overheard, years will be added to your sentence."

"No one has ever bothered to tell me my sentence," Andrew said.

The older man looked surprised. "That is wrong. I shall have the matter investigated."

"Don't bother," Andrew said, "provided you'll tell me."

"You were sentenced to five years in solitary confinement, but you won't be set free until peace between France and the United States is assured. Since you also escaped when New Orleans was Spanish, you are considered a very dangerous American agitator."

"Five years," Andrew said, seething, and thought he would become dangerous, indeed, if he was ever able to win his freedom.

Valdéz looked at his watch and stood. "General de Maniton gave his personal approval for this visit in return for my promise that I would stay no longer than ten minutes. But I'll come again."

"Thank you, sir. It's good to know there's one real human being in New Orleans."

"There are many others," Valdéz said with a tight smile. "Jeanne and Beatriz want to know if there is anything I can bring you when I come again."

"I'd like some books, please, and some newspapers."

Valdéz looked dubious. "I'll do what I can, but the French are very strict, and prisoners who are held in solitary confinement are permitted no reading matter, as a rule."

"They prefer that a man go mad in less than the five years of his sentence."

Valdéz shook his hand. "Be of good cheer. You have friends who are working for you. Is there anything else you would like me to bring you?"

"Yes, sir!" Andrew replied promptly. "For the past month I've had a great craving for a *segaro*. I didn't smoke them often before I was brought here, but a prisoner down the corridor has a supply of them, and whenever I smell one I feel a great desire to smoke."

143

"That is one wish I can fulfill without difficulty." Valdéz took a tooled leather case from the inner pocket of his coat. "A friend in Hispaniola knows my fondness for *segaros,* and sends me a packet every month."

Andrew carefully took one *segaro* from the case. "You have no idea how much this means to me."

"Here. Take the other two as well. I have many more at home." Valdéz, delighted to be of service, pressed the remaining contents of the case on the younger man.

Again Andrew thanked him, and when the assistant warden came to release Valdéz, the official told him to light the prisoner's *segaro* with a tinderbox and flint.

Alone in the cell again, Andrew savored the flavor of the strong Caribbean tobacco, and, sitting on his pallet, stared at the food supplies on the table. Within a quarter of an hour his entire situation had been altered drastically, and his sense of hopelessness vanished. He had no intention of rotting alone in a French prison for five years, and he knew how to win his release, provided he made every move with exceptional care.

"Is straw so scarce in New France that I must feel the ground under my body when I sleep?" There was scorn in Andrew's voice as he pretended indignation.

The assistant warden who was dragging sacks of fresh straw from cell to cell shrugged. "The chicken you ate for your supper last night gave you strength, eh?" He peered into the cell. "But you haven't yet eaten the sausages. Don't tell me you prefer our soup and bread!"

"I'm saving them," Andrew said. "I don't want to use all my treats at once. Now, will you give me enough straw? Remember I'm taller than most in this place."

"Help yourself, and throw your old straw into the corridor." The assistant warden placed one of the sacks in the entrance, as prisoners were not permitted to go beyond their own doors.

Andrew took the better part of the sack's contents, and threw out just enough of his previous week's bedding to lull the man's possible suspicions.

"Now that you're a man of property, I suppose you want me to light your *segaro* for you, too."

"I'll wait until I've eaten supper," Andrew said. "I prefer to smoke after a meal. If what you give us here can be called a meal."

"Do you work for your food? No! You're lucky we give you anything to eat." The door closed and was locked.

Alone again, Andrew arranged the fresh matting on top of the old straw, then tamped it down by rolling on it. So far everything was working according to plan, and he cautioned himself to remain patient.

An hour passed before the assistant warden reopened the door to hand him a bowl of half-cold pea soup and a chunk of bread.

"Eat quickly tonight," the Frenchman told him. "I'm going off duty soon."

"Oh? Is something special happening tonight?"

Conversation about the jailers' lives outside the prison was forbidden, but the assistant warden's pride made him careless. "General de Maniton is holding his first reception since he arrived here. And I'm invited. What do you think of that?"

"Congratulations," Andrew replied, hoping he sounded sincere. "It must be a great honor."

"Well, others will be there, too," the assistant warden admitted. "I hold the rank of sergeant, you know, and everyone of my rank or a higher one will be there."

"You'll enjoy yourself," Andrew said, and told himself his luck had finally turned. With officers and noncommissioned officers attending a social event at the house of the commanding general, there would be fewer men of authority on hand to deal with emergencies.

He ate his soup quickly, forcing himself to down it, even though the taste left him with no appetite. It was important that he maintain his strength.

But he concealed the bread beneath the straw of his mattress, and when the assistant warden returned for his bowl and wooden spoon, Andrew was waiting for him.

"Do you suppose you could light my *segaro* now?"

The assistant warden was faintly irritated, but gave in. "Oh, well, why not?" He hurried off for a tinderbox and flint. "Now be quiet for the night, Yankee. I'm going off duty, and have no more time to wait on you!"

Andrew smoked the *segaro* very slowly, puffing on it

145

just enough to keep it lighted. Night came, and he looked at his watch, the one personal possession he had been permitted to keep. The better part of an hour passed, and when the *segaro* had burned to a stub so small he could scarcely hold it, he lighted the third and last. He smoked it slowly, too, in spite of his growing tension, and when he had consumed about two-thirds of it he knew the time to act was at hand.

He stuffed the bread and sausages into his pockets, then carefully moved the straw bedding to the outside wall. Breaking the table into the smallest pieces he could without tools, he put them to one side and opened the window. Everything was in readiness for his daring escape attempt.

Puffing hard on the *segaro,* he held the burning end to a clump of straw, which started to smoke. For a moment he was afraid he had acted prematurely, and cursed himself for not waiting a few more days until the straw became drier.

Suddenly, however, the clump in his hand came alive, and burned brightly.

Andrew placed the burning mound on the ground, and gently fed the flames with additional straw, adding chunks of wood as he built the fire higher. The flames crackled, but he was afraid the wooden wall would not catch fire unless the fire grew still larger very quickly, so he hauled off his shirt and fanned the straw. Now all he had to do was wait, and he donned the shirt again, choking and coughing as a breeze blew the smoke in through the open window.

The slight wind was all that was needed, and Andrew felt a surge of grim but triumphant joy when he saw that the wall had caught fire. The cell was growing hot, so he backed off to the far side, near the door, and watched the results of his handiwork. Within a short time the entire wall was enveloped in a sheet of flame, and the fire, now raging, spread to adjoining cells.

Just as the outer wall in front of Andrew collapsed, he heard men starting to shout. Uncertain whether they were sentries or fellow prisoners, he knew that in a few moments, at the most, the fire would be discovered by the French. He could wait no longer; even though he could not see through the flames and smoke clearly enough to

146

see whether the palisade beyond the burning wall had been destroyed, too.

He poured his gourd of drinking water over his head and face, took a deep breath and dashed out through a sheet of flames. The heat was searing, but he cleared what remained of the wall and then, scarcely able to breathe, saw the obstacle of the palisade looming directly before him. The logs were burning, and although the fire had penetrated to their core, they were still standing upright. Andrew had no weapon or tool he could use to knock down or punch a hole in the wall of flames, and the heat was far too intense for him to even think of scaling the palisade.

There was only one thing he could do. Holding his breath again, he shielded his face with an arm and plunged forward, smashing a shoulder into the blazing logs.

The palisade gave way, the upper portion collapsing and sending a shower of sparks and burning bits of timber flying in all directions, but Andrew discovered he had broken through into the open. He threw himself on the ground and rolled on it to extinguish any flames that might have set his clothes on fire, simultaneously smothering his smoking hair.

To his astonishment he seemed to be unscathed, and jumped to his feet again. The success of his scheme depended, above all, on speed as well as daring, so he moved off into the shadows away from the glare of the fire before he paused for a moment to assess the situation.

The entire prison was burning now, and the flames appeared to have spread to the nearest of the barracks beyond the jail. Civilians as well as French soldiers were running toward the conflagration across the parade ground, and in the distance a great commotion was stirring. The first concern of New Orleans was the fire, not the recovery of prisoners who might be escaping, and as the alarm spread the bells of churches began to toll furiously. The better part of the city had been destroyed by two major fires within the span of less than ten years, and although there had been no loss of life, due to the prompt evacuation of homes, property damage had been staggering.

Consequently the first aim of everyone in New Orleans was that of controlling the fire. Men of all ages, schoolboys, and even girls were voluntarily joining soldiers in impromptu bucket lines being formed at wells in the neighborhood, and the pandemonium became worse as clouds of dense, black smoke rose toward the sky.

The confusion was intense behind the Place d'Armes, and officers of the garrison forgot their dignity as they raced their sergeants to the scene. General de Maniton's reception had been spoiled, but would be long remembered.

It was a simple matter for Andrew to move against the current, but he slowed his pace to a slow stroll, stayed in the shadows and avoided the main avenues and streets. It would take time to put out the spreading fire, and would be still longer before the warden could make a count to determine whether any of his prisoners were missing. By that time it would be essential for Andrew to be gone from New Orleans. Under no circumstances was he willing to ask help from either Beatriz or Jeanne.

After he had gone a half-mile from the jail he walked more rapidly, still not risking a run or trot, however, and cut through narrow side streets and alleyways as he headed northward. At last he reached the open farm country beyond the city, and only then did he break into a run.

For a quarter of an hour he maintained the fastest pace he could achieve, and only when he thought his lungs would burst did he pause, gasping for breath, near the protecting bulk of a large cypress tree. Behind him, in the city, he could see the glow of the fire reflected against the dark sky, but it was no longer spreading, and he knew that as soon as it was safely curbed, the authorities would begin a search for him.

Only now did he realize that his left shoulder was smarting, and for the first time he saw that a hole had been burned through his buckskin shirt. His skin was raw, and he winced slightly when he touched it. Both hands were blistered, too, but their burns were less severe, and he realized he was fortunate. He might have sustained a serious injury that could have immobilized him.

Starting out again, he deliberately maintained a course parallel to the Mississippi, but about one mile from its

148

bank, knowing that when a hunt began in earnest, patrol boats would cruise the river in a search for him. He walked steadily, not wanting to tire himself by running again, but realizing that his one hope of reaching the United States would be to go as far from New Orleans as he could before morning.

An hour or two after midnight he was hungry, and ate some sausage with his bread while he continued to plod across fields of tobacco, cotton, and corn. He avoided the damp, muddier ground where rice and indigo were grown, knowing the uncertain footing would slow him, and he made wide detours around the dwellings of the plantation owners on whose property he was trespassing.

Before dawn he reached the outlying, smaller farms, however, and decided to risk a close inspection of a sprawling, one-story house that was made in part of clapboard, the rest of logs. At the rear, near a shed beyond the kitchen, cords of wood were piled high, and he saw an ax that had been left in a log. Without an instant's hesitation he stole it, knowing that even a long-handled ax was better protection than no weapon.

The kitchen was deserted, so he made his way inside, moving cautiously in the dark, and was relieved when he saw a tub of butter that, apparently, had been churned the previous day. Using the side of a hand he scraped enough off the top to apply a coating to his burns, and then, resisting the temptation to take any food, he resumed his flight.

Shortly before dawn he halted again for more sausage and the last of his bread. Looking back toward New Orleans he could no longer make out any sign of the fire, and realized that in all probability it had been extinguished. He could no longer make out any plumes of smoke, either, so it was likely that the firefighters had completed their work. And, unless most of the other prisoners had escaped, too, a major manhunt for him was well under way.

He plodded on again, and when he saw a small farmhouse ahead, with clothing hanging on a line to dry in a yard behind it, he decided to take still another chance. Approaching stealthily, he saw a man's shirt of heavy wool on the line, and snatched it.

But members of the household were awake, and his

149

luck changed. A woman screamed, a man shouted, and Andrew, still clutching the shirt, ran off across the fields. There were no trees within a quarter of a mile in any direction, the delta country was completely flat, and it was impossible for him to find cover. A musket shot broke the early morning silence, and Andrew shifted to a zigzag course without changing his speed. If someone came after him, or if the farmer roused his neighbors, the situation would become still more serious.

But the man did not pursue the fugitive, having decided, apparently, that the loss of nothing except an old shirt was fortunate, and that a chase wasn't worth the effort.

Andrew breathed a little more easily, but knew he had made his first serious error. The incident was relatively minor, but if French troops visited him later in the day he would be sure to remember the giant in buckskins.

So, although common sense dictated a protracted rest at the first opportunity, Andrew did not halt for more than a few moments at a time until, at noon, he left civilization behind him and plunged into the friendly shelter of the forest. Here, in the pines, he felt at home, but wanting to go deep enough into the woods to make certain he was not trapped unexpectedly, he continued his grinding march for another two hours.

Finally, his legs so weary that they began to tremble, he pressed through a maze of brambles and threw himself onto the ground behind a fallen, decaying log. A moment later, clutching the ax-handle, he dropped off to sleep.

The rustling sound made by a small animal in the underbrush nearby awakened Andrew soon after nightfall, and his sleep had been so deep that it took him a moment to remember all that had happened. Then, suddenly alert, he sat upright, relaxing when he heard the creature moving away. He was ravenously hungry, so he recklessly ate the rest of the first sausage and half of the second.

His hands were healing, but his shoulder continued to throb and had stiffened. Unable to treat it, however, he ignored the discomfort and again resumed his march. He headed closer to the bank of the Mississippi, the forest giving him courage, and continued his journey through the

150

night. With each step northward, he knew, the chances that the French might find and recapture him diminished.

But he had no illusions about the enormity of the task ahead. He was hundreds of miles from home, his food supplies consisted only of a half-sausage, and his only weapon in territory infested with river brigands and bands of savage Indians was the ax. To make matters worse, his shoulder was causing him constant pain.

Forty-eight hours after his escape from New Orleans, Andrew consumed the last of the sausage, and thereafter had to rely on berries and a few wild roots for his food. There were fish in some of the streams that fed into the Mississippi, he knew, and it would not have been too difficult for him to fashion a pole, a line from a strong creeper vine and a hook from one of the innumerable brambles that ripped at his buckskin trousers and stolen shirt, which he had donned after discarding his own, burned shirt.

But he could not afford the time to sit patiently for an hour or two, perhaps longer, beside the bank of a small river. He was in mortal danger as long as he remained in French Louisiana, and could not tarry anywhere until he reached the soil of the United States.

By the third afternoon of his march his hunger was making him desperate, and he knew that without firearms his chances of bagging game were slight. Unlike the wilderness man who had time to spare, he could not set a simple trap and wait for a small animal to fall into it.

So, when he caught a glimpse of the outpost fort of the French near the Louisiana boundary ahead, he decided to take his greatest risk in order to obtain a weapon more efficient than the heavy ax. Stealthily, making no sound, he crept nearer to the blockhouse on the spit of land, halting when he heard the pounding of feet on the ground. A sentry in a white uniform was making his rounds, pacing up and down within hailing distance of the little fort.

In spite of the gravity of the situation, Andrew was amused. The troops manning the post were no longer the crisp soldiers they had been when they first had come to the New World from France. The sentry's uniform was soiled, his brass was dull and he walked with a heavy, list-less tread. Months of isolation in the wilderness of North America had taken their toll.

Making no move, Andrew watched the sentry until he knew the precise line of the man's march. Now it was only a matter of waiting for the right time to strike, and he spent the rest of the afternoon in hiding, as motionless as the Cherokee warriors from whom he had learned the art of stalking other humans.

At sundown the guard was changed, and Andrew continued to wait, wanting the new sentry to grow a little weary before attacking. A man who was rested and alert, obviously, made a more dangerous foe.

At last the sounds emanating from the fort indicated that the members of the garrison were eating their supper, so Andrew moved to a spot only three or four feet from the sentry's worn path. He grasped the handle of the ax with both hands, and when the soldier passed him, swung it with the right combination of strength and accuracy, striking the man with the blunt end at the base of his head, below his brass helmet.

The sentry fell forward on the ground, and as he sprawled there, dazed, Andrew leaped onto his back and pressed his face into the ground to prevent an outcry.

The stunned Frenchman struggled, trying to fight off his assailant, but was no match for his powerful foe. Andrew, holding him with one hand, used the soldier's bayonet to cut off a piece of the uniform tunic that he improvised as a gag, then slashed the cross-webbing, which he utilized to tie his victim's hands and feet. Another strip of the tunic served as a rough but effective blindfold.

Only when the Frenchman's eyes were covered did Andrew turn him over, secure in the knowledge that the soldier would not be able to identify his attacker as the escaped prisoner for whom General de Maniton undoubtedly was searching. Then, armed with the soldier's musket and bayonet, powder pouch and ammunition bag, and still carrying the ax as well, Andrew set out again, continuing to follow the Mississippi northward.

His hunger was unappeased, but he was heartened by the knowledge that he had either crossed or soon would cross into territory claimed by the United States. Nevertheless he took no unnecessary chances. The trussed sentry would be found by the sergeant of the guard within an hour or two, and Andrew knew that if he left a trail easy to identify, the French would not be reluctant to follow him across the border. He had not hesitated to strike, and they would not be reluctant to cross the wilderness border where they could obtain revenge without causing diplomatic repercussions.

Careful to move as silently as a Cherokee brave on the warpath, Andrew avoided stretches of long grass that might break or bend beneath his feet and thus reveal his whereabouts to anyone who followed him. He did not pause until midnight, when the changing nature of the countryside assured him that he had penetrated far enough into American territory to be safe. He had left the delta lands behind, and, on the east bank of the river, bluffs were rising from the flat plain, a sure sign he had arrived in the Mississippi Territory.

But he was too tired and hungry to feel any elation, and found himself a spot to sleep for a few hours. Again he chose a place deep in a bramble patch, and as he drifted off the musket beside him gave him a greater sense of security than he had known at any time since his arrest and imprisonment.

He started out once more at three o'clock in the morning, and knowing the area through which he was now traveling, cut toward the east, where several salt licks were located. Habit caused him to tread carefully, and his caution paid dividends when, from the crest of a knoll, he caught sight of a salt lick in a hollow off to his right.

Several deer were using it, and although the angle was a difficult one, he realized he could not afford to miss. He raised the musket, steadying it, and squeezed the trigger. The sound of the shot reverberating through the forest caused the deer to flee, but one of the creatures had fallen. Andrew came closer, reloaded and dispatched the animal with a second shot.

Using a bayonet as a knife, he skinned the carcass, removing it a distance from the salt lick, then cut as much meat as he believed he could use for two or three days. The basic rules of forest safety made it necessary for him to leave the area in which he had fired the shots, so he started back toward the Mississippi, trudging northward again. After another hour's wait he reasoned he had gone far enough, so he started a fire by rubbing dry, small tree branches together, and added kindling to the blaze once it had started.

He used green branches to make a spit, and changed them frequently as he prepared his meat. Dawn broke, but he was so intent on his meal that he scarcely noticed, and when his food finally was ready he put more meat on the fire. He ate heartily, relishing every bite and reveling in his freedom. He was no longer a fugitive, and it was almost impossible for him to realize that he no longer had to be afraid of pursuers. While he waited for the second portion of meat to be cooked he removed his shirt and rubbed some cooled fat on his burned shoulder.

By the time he finished his meal and was satiated, he was more relaxed than he had been in months, and debated whether to resume his journey immediately or stretch out for another nap.

"Ain't this friendly, now. He's made us a fire, and there's our breakfast!"

Andrew turned at the sound, one hand reaching for the musket and the other for his ax. At the edge of the little clearing stood three husky men, and from their oddly mixed attire of buckskin shirts and city breeches, stout boots and heavy gold watch chains, he knew them to be river brigands. Only men who had acquired loot over a period of time dressed as they did.

"Good morning," he said, trying to sound pleasant. "And welcome." His grip on both weapons tightened.

The leader of the trio took two steps forward into the clearing. "You won't be needin' any more o' that meat, so we'll just take it. And while you're about it, you c'n give us your nice musket and that there ax."

"Here's the ax!" Andrew threw it as he leaped to his feet. Its balance was not true, so his aim was imperfect, but the side of the ax nevertheless caught the river pirate on the temple, felling him instantly.

Before the other two could act, Andrew raised the musket and squeezed the trigger, but the weapon failed to discharge. Aware that even a moment's respite would prove fatal when he was outnumbered, he charged at the nearer

154

of the pair, and his impetus was so great that he drove the point of his bayonet deep into the man's throat, killing him.

It proved impossible to remove the blade, however, and when Andrew whirled he found the remaining brigand raising a pistol. Himself unarmed, he could think of only one thing to do, and kicked the weapon from the man's hand. Then, simultaneously, they lunged at each other and fell to the ground with a crash.

Few men were as tall as Andrew, but his long, arduous flight from New Orleans had weakened him, and his opponent would have been his match under the best of circumstances. They rolled over and over, pummeling each other as each tried to gain an advantage, and when the brigand discovered the injury on Andrew's shoulder he pounded it mercilessly.

Andrew felt himself weakening, and when the brigand finally managed to pin him to the ground, he realized that only a near-miracle would save him. He had killed one of the man's companions and, at the least, seriously wounded the other, so he knew he would be shown no quarter.

The brigand reached down to his boot-top while continuing to beat at Andrew's wounded shoulder, and, as any frontiersman knew, he was intending to draw a knife that would end the fight.

Andrew called on his last reserves of energy and heaved upward. The man was caught off balance because of the awkwardness of his position as he drew his knife, and before he could recover, Andrew managed to roll a short distance from him.

The brigand turned, on his knees, with the knife poised above his head.

Andrew caught him in the stomach with both feet, aware that this blow he could deliver in his depleted state.

The brigand fell backward, and to Andrew's horror his head landed in the fire that was still blazing. The man shrieked in agony and tried to escape, but before he could haul himself out of the flames it was too late.

Sickened by the carnage, Andrew picked up the knife and painfully hauled himself to his feet. His shoulder throbbed, the odor of burning flesh nauseated him and he could only think that he wanted to get away from the scene. Then a slight movement off to his left caught his eye.

The leader, who had been knocked unconscious by the ax blow, had recovered his senses, and a hand was creeping toward his rifle, which lay on the ground beside him.

Andrew reacted instinctively, and threw the knife. In spite of his exhaustion his aim was true, and the blade cut through the man's wrist and pinned it to the ground. The brigand moaned and lay still again.

Cautioning himself not to move too hastily, Andrew gathered all of the firearms within sight, keeping two of the rifles that appeared to be in the best condition. He helped himself to ammunition and powder, too, took a knife from the boot-top of the man he killed with the bayonet and, as an afterthought, helped himself to a bulging pouch of parched corn.

Then, after throwing the remaining weapons as far as he could into the forest, he hastened from the scene, making his way along the bluffs beside the river that led to civilization. There might be other brigands in the vicinity, he knew, since the outlaws usually traveled in fairly large packs, and he realized he was too tired to fight another battle against heavy odds.

Again he was a fugitive, and he trudged wearily, finding it an agony to place one foot before the other. Pain enveloped his shoulder, and some moments passed before he realized that he had not donned his shirt again. Neither had he taken the rest of the venison he had intended to use, but he could not force himself to return for either. The rifles felt heavy in his hands, but they were his only protection, and he did not dare discard one of them.

The land behind the bluffs became wilder, and Andrew forced himself to climb into an area strewn with large rocks. Here a man could find shelter, he told himself, and eventually he came to a huge boulder adjacent to a stand of tall evergreens. This was what he had been seeking, and he crawled into a small hollow between the boulder and trees.

Then, in spite of the ache in his shoulder, he drifted off to sleep.

Dawn streaked the sky when he awakened, which confused him until he realized he had slept for the better part of a day and night. Oddly, he had no appetite, and soon discovered the reason. His shoulder was swollen, and he could scarcely lift it.

Aware that he would die in the wilderness without food, he ate several handfuls of parched corn, and resisting a feeling of panic that surged up in him, tried to consider his situation calmly. He vaguely recalled a journey in the forests of Tennessee that had a bearing on his present plight, and eventually remembered that one of his companions had suffered from an injury to his thigh, the man's body had become more bloated with each passing day.

Now Andrew knew what had to be done. Scarcely stirring from the hollow, he made a small fire, then held his captured knife in the flames until the handle became so hot he wanted to drop it. Then, steadying himself, he made two long, deep incisions in his shoulder.

The searing pain was unbearable, and he lost consciousness again.

Time lost its meaning in the days that followed. Andrew was hot, then cold, wide awake for a short time, then so drowsy he could not hold up his head. He had dim recollections of sunlight and night, and laughed during a thunderstorm because the cold rain cooled his fevered body.

Then, one morning, he awakened to find his head cleared. The swelling on his shoulder had gone down, and he could move his arm again, although the area around the crisscrossed scars remained tender. He was filthy and had lost weight, but the pouch of corn was untouched, and he ate all of it.

Anxious to resume his journey, he soon found a narrow, swiftly flowing stream that fed into the Mississippi. There he cleaned himself, his teeth chattering in the cold water, and, discovering he was thirstier than he had ever been, he drank greedily.

His strength sapped, he could travel only a few miles at a time before stopping to rest. Game seemed to have vanished from the area, and, although he was ravenous, he found no food except some wild onions and a few edible roots. Eventually, in a small lake behind the bluffs, he caught a fish, and was so hungry he found it difficult to restrain himself from eating it until he had cooked it.

One day blended into another, but he continued to plod toward the north, following the Mississippi, and one afternoon he heard voices somewhere ahead. He halted, made sure his rifles were ready for instant use and then advanced more cautiously.

Eventually he came to a clearing, saw a blockhouse ahead and, for a moment, became so confused he thought it was the French fort at the Louisiana border.

Two men carrying rifles emerged into the open and stared in astonishment at the apparition approaching them. The man was naked to the waist, with an ugly scar on his left shoulder, and was painfully thin; his hair was matted, his boots were worn thin and there was a two weeks' growth of beard on his face.

"Who in thunderation are you?" one of them demanded.

Andrew blinked, and his head cleared again. "Isn't that Natchez up ahead?"

"O' course!"

Andrew found himself laughing, and then, his legs buckling, he sat down on the hard ground. "I've been a long time getting here," he said. "As Horace wrote, *Opere in longo fas est obrepere somnum*. He who labors long may be allowed to sleep."

The men continued to gape at him.

"Gentlemen," he said, "I haven't eaten a real meal in at least three weeks, and I'll trade one of these rifles for the biggest dinner and the biggest supper anyone can load onto a table. You won't believe me, but it's taken me all this time to get up here from New Orleans."

"We heard tell there was an American who burned down the jail there and escaped. But that was near a month ago, and he must be dead!"

"If you'll help me to a dinner table, I can prove I'm very much alive. And," Andrew added grimly, "I aim to prove it to the French in New Orleans, too, before I'm done with them!"

THIRTEEN

December 1802–January 1803

Natchez overwhelmed Andrew with its frontier hospitality. The commanding officer of the local militia company gave up a room in his house, the largest in town, to the river devil, the one physician in the area paid daily calls on the invalid and the housewives of the community engaged in a spirited competition to see which of them could prepare the most appetizing and nourishing dishes to restore his strength. Andrew's breakfast consisted of beefsteak, fish, several eggs, and buttered bread freshly baked. His other meals were larger and more elaborate, and he rapidly regained his lost weight.

The physician, amazed that he had survived his ordeal, said that only a man with an enormously strong constitution could have lived after spending so long in the wilderness with virtually no food while suffering from a seriously infected shoulder. But Andrew had been his own best surgeon, there was no need to drain off any more of what the physician called "malign humors," and the shoulder required no medication other than the daily application of a healing unguent that had been made in Philadelphia and carried at great expense to the remote wilderness town.

The people of Natchez refused to permit Andrew to pay a penny for his food, lodging, or care. He had done more than his share for everyone in the wilderness country, they insisted, and lavished him with attention. The local tanner made him a new shirt and trousers of buckskin, presenting them to him as a gift, and the cobbler, who also owned several orchards, gave him a handsome new pair of sturdy boots. The blacksmith forged a pair of balanced knives, and the men of the militia company shared in the expense of a brace of hair-triggered pistols.

By the time Andrew was recovered he learned that the men of Natchez wanted him to lead them on a march to New Orleans, but, after much difficulty, he persuaded them to wait. More than a month had passed since his arrival in Natchez, and he finally convinced the wilderness dwellers that another delay would be helpful rather than harmful. No one was more anxious than he to storm the capital of New France, he explained, but the men of Natchez could not perform the task alone. The French were strong, so a major expedition was needed to drive them from New Orleans.

He intended to recruit riflemen in Tennessee, Kentucky, and the northern territories of the West, he told them, and promised to return with a brigade in the spring. So the Mississippi Territory settlers curbed their impatience and agreed to take no action until they were supported by reinforcements.

An escort sailed up the Mississippi with Andrew early in December, and within two weeks he arrived in Nashville, where the citizens of western Tennessee were gathering to celebrate Christmas. The river devil was given a riotous reception, and Abel Hillery, who was still living at the inn, confessed to him that everyone in the city had been convinced he and his companions on the trial voyage to New Orleans had been killed.

That night Judge Jackson expressed an emphatic opinion when the three men sat down to dinner together at the inn. "If we'd known that you and the boys had been thrown into jail for refusing to accept the French rule denying you the freedom of the city, two thousand riflemen would have taken possession of New Orleans long ago."

"Too bad you didn't." Andrew still appreciated food as never before, and was enjoying every bite of his beef and mushroom pie. "I don't mind telling you I dreamed about an American expedition while I was locked in my cell. And I reckon the lads who went with me are still feeling that way. They're together somewhere in the city, I was told, and they aren't being held in too close a confinement, but they're still prisoners of the French."

Jackson thumped the table with his mug of ale. "They can't do that to Americans. It's reason enough for us to go to war."

Hillery was alarmed. "I feel reasonably certain the State Department can negotiate successfully for their release.

The Administration is anxious to avoid a war with France—"

"The West doesn't give a hang what the Administration wants," Judge Jackson replied, his pale eyes glacial. "I respect President Jefferson. I've admired him for a long time. But he's dead wrong about tugging our forelocks and bowing to France. If Bonaparte throws Americans into jail, we'll make him pay for it. The West won't tolerate such impertinence!"

Hillery tried to calm him. "Judge, this unfortunate incident gives the State Department a splendid opportunity to get something we've been seeking. We can use a demand for the release of the prisoners as an opening to discuss a new treaty that will guarantee free American access to all the port facilities of New Orleans."

Andrew became impatient. "We don't negotiate with river brigands," he said. "The French should be treated the way we treat Mississippi pirates!"

Judge Jackson clapped him on the back.

"If you think I'm going to sit back and wait for diplomats from Washington City to beg favors from Bonaparte, Abel, you're wrong! Not after what his people done to me!"

Hillery's distress mounted. "Surely you remember that President Jefferson and Secretary Madison told you we must avoid war!"

"That was before the French treated me like a common criminal. And when the river devils learn that some of our friends are still being held in New Orleans, there's no power in the United States strong enough to prevent them from attacking the French! You've become a good friend, Abel, but I'm afraid you plain don't understand the way men in the West feel. It was all I could do to prevent the militia company of Natchez from marching on Louisiana alone!"

"I don't rightly know," Judge Jackson said, "whether my wife will release me from my pledge to her. I promised her I'd serve my full term on the bench, but if she doesn't hold me to it, I'll march with you myself!"

"I wish you'd give me time," the desperate Hillery said, "to send a full report to Secretary Madison and find out what the President thinks."

"We can't organize a brigade overnight," Andrew replied, "so there's ample time, provided the President doesn't procrastinate."

"How strong is the French garrison in New Orleans?" Judge Jackson asked.

Andrew told him all he knew.

"And you say they have artillery?"

"Enough for two divisions."

"Infantry, artillery, cavalry." The Judge stroked his long jaw. "They're primed for a war, no question about it. What's more, they're good fighting men. Bonaparte's troops have given a good account of themselves in every battle they've fought."

"They look like professional soldiers," Andrew said. "But we have some advantages. They don't understand our kind of fighting." He explained how he had rendered the outpost sentry helpless and taken his musket. "And they don't rate us very highly. I suspect they have contempt for us because we're amateurs."

"That's because they've never seen us shoot. I'll stand an ordinary frontier settler against the finest marksman in the French army in a contest any day, and I'll wager the new property I just bought for Mrs. Jackson against any sum the French want to put up that our lad will win!"

Hillery tried to dampen the enthusiasm of the two firebrands.

But the Judge refused to listen. "MacCullough," he said, "start recruiting your force right off. All you need to do is tell people what happened to you and the other boys who made the first trial voyage to Louisiana. I'll do the same, starting with a speech I'm going to make at a jamboree on New Year's Day. And, by the Eternal, we'll have more volunteers than we need by spring."

Governor James Monroe of Virginia seemed the best of all men to serve as President Jefferson's Envoy Extraordinary and Minister Plenipotentiary to France in a situation that was rapidly becoming critical. Long a protégé and friend of Jefferson's, he had served two years as President Washington's Resident Minister to France, and Talleyrand knew how much he admired the goals of the French Revolution. His appointment to the special post, in which he was ordered to assist U. S. Minister Robert R. Livingston in obtaining an equitable treaty, was calculated to dampen the ardor of the West for war, too. As a delegate to the Confederation Congress and, subsequently, as a member of the United States Senate, Monroe had been loudly persistent in his demands that the Mississippi River be kept open to American shipping. Unlike most leaders of the Union's older states, he was regarded by the Westerners as one of their own number. And, now that he was free to fulfill the delicate mission after concluding his second term as Virginia's chief executive, his appointment was considered a master stroke by everyone in the Administration.

Monroe did not share the opinion of his peers. A tall, lugubrious man whose homespun attire seemed oddly out of place in the splendor of the First Consulate's palaces, he arrived in France convinced that the views of the two nations could not be reconciled and that war was inevitable. "Somebody must yield," he told Livingston the day he arrived in Paris, "and I know the men of the West. They won't budge."

He managed to conceal his pessimism, however, when he and Livingston made a joint call on the French Foreign Minister, and he responded with unaccustomed affability to Talleyrand's hospitable gestures. They chatted at length about the growth of the United States, the changes in France being wrought by the new regime, and, in some detail, the quality of the Turkish coffee being offered patrons of the cafes that were springing up in every quarter of Paris.

Then, abruptly, Monroe raised the subject that had brought him across the Atlantic. "Your Excellency," he said in his strongly accented French. "I've been directed by President Jefferson to register a number of complaints with First Consul Bonaparte."

Talleyrand contrived to look surprised and somewhat pained.

"First, sir, American citizens are being held in the prisons of New Orleans without cause!"

Talleyrand was prepared on the matter, and replied vigorously. "One of your citizens deliberately disobeyed an order restricting him to the New Orleans waterfront area."

"Why should our citizens be restricted?"

"Does not your country make its own laws for its protection, Mr. Minister? Surely the Governor and Military Commander of our forces in Louisiana have a similar right. Furthermore, this same man burned down the army prison, and nearly set the whole city on fire, a matter of the gravest consequence."

Monroe grinned. "When you were imprisoned during the early days of your Revolution, Your Excellency, I doubt if you enjoyed the experience. Americans are very sensitive to what they consider unjust imprisonment, and they value their freedom so highly—"

"Mr. Livingston has already presented the case to me. The First Consul rejects your arguments."

"What explanation does he offer for the continuing imprisonment of four other American citizens who have broken no laws, sir?" Monroe became grimly somber.

"Their case is under investigation."

"What needs to be investigated, Your Excellency?"

"I assume there must be complications about which none of us have been told. The First Consul relies completely on the good judgment of his Governor and commander-in-chief in New France."

"We don't," Monroe replied bluntly. "And that brings up my other complaint. Why has the right of deposit that Americans enjoyed in New Orleans under Spanish rule been nullified?"

Talleyrand hated to be placed at a disadvantage due to ignorance, but was too shrewd a diplomat to take refuge behind a façade he didn't understand. "I don't know what you mean," he said resentfully.

Monroe glanced at Livingston, whose quick nod indicated that the Foreign Minister was not bluffing. "Your Excellency," the special envoy said, "our official records indicate that seventeen warehouses in New Orleans are owned by American citizens. The merchandise shipped down the Mississippi is stored in them, and when they're filled, in warehouses owned by your subjects. Most of the goods are sent on, either to our states in the East, to the Caribbean or even to Europe in any brigs that put into

New Orleans for the purpose. Our own shipping is limited, as you well know, so most of the business goes to the owners of French fleets. In other words, France makes a handsome profit from our New Orleans trade."

"Are you insinuating it shouldn't?"

"Certainly not, Your Excellency! But we protest the new tax imposed on our warehouse owners. By the time they pay it, their right of deposit, their right to store merchandise, has been canceled, because they earn no profit!"

"If they're dissatisfied, they could sell their properties to French business interests," Talleyrand said.

Livingston coughed behind his hand when he saw his colleague become angry.

But Monroe felt compelled to accept the challenge. "I share the suspicion of the men in our West that the First Consul hopes to squeeze our warehouse owners out of New Orleans by making business conditions impossible for them. I find it too coincidental that the new taxes they're required to pay equal their profits almost to the penny."

"Every nation has the right—the obligation—to protect its own citizens," Talleyrand said urbanely. "If foreign merchants suffer, one pities them, but I certainly can't help wondering if they wouldn't do better to work in their own country. If I were a merchant—a notion that's inconceivable, I grant you—I'd prefer to earn my living among my own people."

"We don't think of New Orleans as foreign territory, Your Excellency," Monroe replied coldly. "Precedent has given us rights there, and they can be contravened only at the peril of those shortsighted enough to deny us the outlet to the sea we need from the Mississippi, an outlet we won't and can't lose."

"Just yesterday," Talleyrand said, fingering the thick gold lace at his cuffs, "the First Consul became very angry because he thought the Austrian minister was threatening him. As it happens, Count von Metzger meant no harm, but the First Consul was deeply offended, and it won't surprise me to see diplomatic relations with Austria broken in the near future."

Alexander Hamilton had claimed for years that Monroe was too candid to be a good diplomat, while Monroe himself preferred to think he achieved more by making candor a major weapon. "I've been expecting a fresh break between France and Austria, and I expect to see you at war with England again before long, too. Perhaps the First Consul's annoyance with Count von Metzger was fortuitous."

"My reason for mentioning the incident is that General Bonaparte believed he had been threatened. If I told him that the representative of the United States sent here to deal with us in a complex and difficult matter informed me that our policies place us in peril, I'm sure I know how he'd react."

The interview was getting out of hand, and Livingston was concerned.

But James Monroe refused to back down. "The First Consul must know the United States wants peace with all nations, particularly with France. We'll never forget it was your help that enabled us to win our independence. But no nation, not even France, can bully us simply because we're small and weak. I'd hoped it wouldn't be necessary for me to mention an aspect of this situation that's explosive, Your Excellency, but you give me no choice. When I said that French interests—and French rule in New Orleans, if you will—are going to be in peril unless you liberalize your policies when you deal with Americans, I was telling you the literal truth."

Talleyrand rested his weight on a new, ivory-handled walking stick, leaning on it with both hands. "With all due respect to Mr. Livingston, who is my friend, and to you, who seem to be a sensible, competent man, I can think of nothing the United States might do to put New France in jeopardy."

There was a brief silence, and Monroe turned to the American Resident Minister. "I was instructed to keep my mouth shut unless I had to tell him, Chancellor. But I see no way of making him realize the seriousness of this situation unless I speak out."

"I'm afraid you're right," Livingston said.

"Your Excellency," Monroe declared, "men in the American West—hundreds of them, perhaps thousands—are mobilizing for a campaign to conquer Louisiana."

The French Foreign Minister seemed unruffled, but allowed himself the luxury of a faint sigh. "How do you reconcile such aggressive acts with your President's claim that he wants peace?"

"The mobilization is unofficial, and the Jefferson Administration is doing all it can to discourage such activities."

Talleyrand's smile was withering. "Really, Mr. Monroe, you must take me for a simpleton. I find it a convenient excuse. Your highest officials prattle about peace, while your people prepare for war. Have you no control over your citizens?"

Monroe's scorn was equally vehement. "During the worst days of your Revolution, Your Excellency, when Paris and the smaller cities of France were ruled by the Terror and armed mobs roamed the streets, was your government capable of controlling its citizens?"

"That was an extraordinary time, an unfortunate period unique in our thousand year history, Mr. Monroe. Are you suggesting that Mr. Jefferson has lost control of his subjects?"

The slip was deliberate, but Monroe refused to be drawn into a needless discussion of the fact that Americans were not the subjects of their President. The central issue on which he was concentrating remained paramount. "As you well know, Your Excellency, the West cannot survive without the Mississippi. When her sons are cast into French prisons without cause, when her merchants are compelled to pay discriminatory, ruinous taxes that bankrupt them, the West becomes impatient."

"They must learn patience when they deal with the strongest power on earth."

"They've conquered the wilderness, Your Excellency. They've braved hardships beyond your imagination, and no one, neither their own President nor your First Consul Bonaparte, can frighten them or prevent them from taking what's due them."

"This is becoming an unpleasant exploration of a complex problem, Mr. Monroe."

"I hope neither of us will have cause to regret it, Your Excellency," the special envoy replied.

"France will hold the United States responsible for any acts performed by the rabble of your West."

"If they knew you'd called them rabble, there would be

no holding them, Your Excellency. May I ask that you repeat to the First Consul what I've told you this afternoon?"

"Never fear, Mr. Monroe. I will! And I'm sure you'll hear further from me."

"I await your convenience, sir."

Bows were exchanged, but no one offered to shake hands.

Monroe and Livingston were silent as they left the Palais Royal, and each was lost in his own thoughts until they had made their way through the palace gardens and reached the narrow Rue de Beaujolais. Then the Resident Minister shook his head. "I don't like this situation, Governor."

"It's even worse than anyone in Washington City believed possible, Chancellor."

"I've sent as many as two full reports to Secretary Madison every week!"

"I know, but the Administration can't accept the fact that any man can be as stubborn as Napoleon Bonaparte."

"He compromises only when he can gain a clear advantage, Governor."

"And the boys in the West won't compromise under any circumstances."

"It seems to me," Livingston said after another silence, "that there's no peaceful solution. This problem will be solved in the way President Jefferson dreads—we'll be pushed or dragged into a war with France."

Louisville, located on the Mississippi's great tributary, the Ohio River, was the oldest American settlement in the West, but was still a raw frontier town, and Andrew Mac-Cullough shared the opinion of his fellow Tennesseans that it was far rougher and less civilized than Nashville. Even physicians, lawyers, and merchants never walked its dirt roads unarmed, and only in the past few years had the more respectable citizens dared to venture out of their houses after dark. But the jail was empty, principally because the constabulary was made up of the best marksmen in Kentucky, hard-bitten men who had followed the frontier westward from the days when the state had still been a

168

part of Virginia, and had learned to survive by using their firearms without hesitation.

The Falls of the Ohio Tavern was vastly inferior to the Nashville Inn, Andrew was convinced, and was astonished when Abel Hillery said he could see no difference in the quality or quantity of the food or liquor that was served with the same abandon. But Abel was a very unhappy man these days, and was no judge of subtleties.

Andrew couldn't blame him, of course, and actually felt a trifle sorry for him. Abel was fighting a losing battle, and no one in any of the towns the pair had visited even listened to his pleas. The time for discretion and caution was ended, and, since the Administration in Washington City seemed unable to obtain rights for all American citizens in New Orleans, the West was being forced to take matters into its own strong hands.

Standing, Andrew banged the butt of a pistol on the rough pine table at which he had been sitting. "Listen to me, boys," he shouted above the din of the crowded taproom.

Gradually the men fell silent, less out of politeness than because no one wanted to argue with a husky giant whose exploits as a river devil and more recent experiences in escaping from New Orleans were known to everyone on the Kentucky frontier.

"Some of you want to start right off for Louisiana—"

A dozen men cheered.

Again Andrew rapped on the table. "We're going, boys, make no mistake about it. But this is one fight that river devils and hunters can't handle alone."

"Why the hell not?" a bearded man in buckskins demanded.

"Because I've seen the French troops in Louisiana, and there are too many of them for a few hundred of us! That means we need the settlers' help. Everywhere I go—and I haven't stopped traveling for the past six weeks—I hear the same thing. Family men want to get their spring crops planted before they go marching off to war. So that's how it's going to be. We'll have a rendezvous at Tennessee Bluffs on the first day of May, and we'll go down the Mississippi in an armada of as many barges and boats as we can build!"

Everyone present, Hillery excepted, joined in a louder cheer.

"Bring your own weapons and powder, and as much jerked meat and parched corn as you can carry." Andrew was making no mention of the planned "raid" on the Federal Government's depot at Natchez, which would give the expedition a boost in spirits at a time when it would be most needed.

"You, MacCullough!" the bearded man called. "Ain't it stupid t' wait so long? The Frenchies will find out for sure that we're comin' their way."

"It can't be helped, so let them find out," Andrew replied. "They still won't have enough time to send any large number of reinforcements to New Orleans before we invade the colony. And there will be enough of us to beat the troops who are already there!"

The roar of approval was deafening.

"We'll take New Orleans—and keep it!" someone shouted.

"Not just New Orleans! All of Louisiana!" another added.

Andrew saw the pained expression on Abel Hillery's face, and knew what the State Department representative was thinking. Inevitably, a campaign to force the French to grant Americans their rights in the colony was being converted into an overwhelming demand that the United States annex the territory. Once the men of the West occupied New Orleans and the rich farming country of its hinterland, only superior force would compel them to leave.

Even a timid foreign ruler would not accept the consequences of such aggressive action, and Bonaparte was the most fearless, even reckless leader to appear in Europe for generations. Andrew was somewhat dismayed by his own role in plunging his country into a major war with the most powerful nation on the far side of the Atlantic, but neither he nor anyone else could stem the flood.

"Save your lead and powder, boys, and bring along every friend who can handle a rifle! And don't forget— we'll meet on the first day of May!" Andrew sat down to resume eating his meal and, glancing across the table, thought it small wonder that Abel had no appetite.

During periods of intense concentration General Bonaparte sometimes remained in his suite of offices at the Louvre for as long as a week or ten days, eating his meals at his desk, sleeping for short periods and returning to his labors with a renewed vigor that left the members of his staff exhausted. His mind functioned with brilliant clarity at these times, but his temper was so short that his relatives and higher-ranking subordinates avoided him, if possible, and his wife and mistresses learned they would regret visits to him.

He stretched out now on the divan in his inner office, unmindful of the marks his boots were making on the white velvet upholstery. His personal aides-de-camp attended to such trivia, and ordered the divan covered anew every week or two. With his eyes closed he reflected none of the personal magnetism that was one of his greatest assets, and, in his shirtsleeves, he looked small, physically insignificant.

His Foreign Minister knew, however, that he was able to rest and think simultaneously, and, aware he might lose his temper over trifles, weighed every word. "I've been reading the London newspapers that arrived at Cherbourg by packet boat yesterday, and I find one comment particularly interesting. In the *Post*. Shall I translate it for you?"

"Do you think my English so poor that a translation is necessary?" The First Consul held out a hand for the newspaper, and when it was not given to him instantly, snapped his fingers.

Talleyrand hated being treated like a servant, but made no protest. This was not a morning to stand on one's dignity. "The article is marked," he said.

Bonaparte held the newspaper before him, and although he found English a difficult language to master, felt compelled to translate aloud to prove he could do it. "France," he read, "has been taking advantage of the Peace of Amiens to extend her borders everywhere. As trustee for the Spanish Netherlands and Belgium she now holds territory directly opposite us, separated only by the English Channel and a small segment of the North Sea.

"In fact, a glance at a map will shock all Englishmen concerned with our security and trade. Bonaparte possesses the entire coastline of western Europe from Rot-

171

terdam to Genoa. He has diminished the strategic power of our fortress at Gibraltar, and neutralizes the effectiveness of our base at Malta. The Mediterranean soon may become an exclusively French sea."

Bonaparte chuckled. "How slow the English are to awaken to reality." Again he laughed, then resumed reading. "Even in the New World he has acquired, from Spain, a vast tract comprising almost one million square miles of territory, including the thriving city of New Orleans, which controls the Mississippi River.

"How much longer can any nation, Great Britain in particular, allow this creeping expansion to continue? How much longer can we stand aside while Bonaparte makes himself the ruler of a domain so vast that, unless we call a halt to his activities, he can crush us at will? We, together with Austria and others who are menaced, even including the United States, must band together and prevent the greedy French from occupying the whole world."

Bonaparte yawned. "I see nothing new here. One English newspaper or another has been saying the same thing for many weeks."

"Did you notice the signature at the end of the article?" Talleyrand asked.

Bonaparte glanced again at the newspaper and, crumpling it, dropped it onto the floor. "Viscount Buchanan," he said with a shrug.

"One of his brothers holds the rank of Rear Admiral in the Royal Navy and holds a post on the planning staff at the Admiralty. The other is a member of the permanent staff at the British Foreign Office. This, of all articles about us, was officially inspired. Without question it represents the attitude of King George's government, and we must view it accordingly."

His eyes closed again, Bonaparte grinned. "You sound frightened, Charles."

"I think it likely that the English are planning to go to war with us again at the opportune moment. They're virtually inviting Austria to join them, and I know they've been making private overtures to the Dutch and Prussians. I suspect they've been in communication with Czar Alexander of Russia, although I can't prove it, and this article indicates they wouldn't object to at least a temporary alliance with the Americans. The situation is very serious, First Consul."

Bonaparte bounded up from the divan, his eyes dark. "I am intending to resume war against the English before summer. My military espionage reports, which are far more accurate than anything your diplomats pick up for me, prove to my complete satisfaction that they plan to go to war with us again. So I'm not going to wait for them to strike the first blow."

Talleyrand instinctively shrank in his chair. "I wish," he said bitterly, "you'd tell me your plans in time for me to do my work accordingly, First Consul!"

"I instructed you a year ago to work for the neutralization of Russia and Prussia, and there has been no change in your orders. Forget the Austrians. They're still upset because we took so much territory from them, and they'll need another thrashing before they'll consent to a permanent peace—which I'll grant them in return for still more of their holdings. Don't waste time on the Dutch, as I must conquer them in order to make my hold on the Low Countries more secure. And from now on, Charles, let me worry about military and naval operations, if you please."

"I want no part of either, thank you." The Foreign Minister felt nervous when Bonaparte stood over him, breathing down at him, and tried to stand.

But the First Consul refused to move. "Just do what's expected of you."

"Have you any complaints about the work of my department?" Talleyrand sounded waspish.

"Not at the moment," Bonaparte replied, suddenly cheerful, and let him escape.

The Foreign Minister stood and limped to the windows overlooking the gardens, now bare beneath a light coating of snow. "Perhaps I can be of greater service to you than you realize. Even you have your blind spots, First Consul."

"Prove it, Charles!"

"Very well. You plan your campaigns on the Continent and at sea with great care. You have plans, I know, that you'll use if the Prussians join the English, and other plans if they don't."

"All military staffs make contingency plans, and my

173

Generals are far more thorough than those of any other country. That's one of the great secrets of my success." Bonaparte was triumphant. "What are my blind spots?"

"You've made no plans whatever for dealing with the Americans, First Consul!"

Bonaparte was amused. "My staff is too busy to exercise needlessly."

Talleyrand drew himself to his full height and looked condescendingly at his superior. "You're mistaken."

"A young nation of a few million people with a Regular Army of only a few thousand men and a Navy so small that one of our weaker squadrons could destroy it offers no threat to France, Charles. If you want to catch me napping, find a better example of my carelessness!"

"You confirm your negligence with every word you utter." It wasn't often that the Foreign Minister won an argument with the First Consul, and continued to sound patronizing. "Just yesterday I had an extremely unpleasant audience with the special American envoy, Monroe."

"Did he threaten us?" Bonaparte was incredulous.

"In a manner of speaking. He swears the men of the American West—the frontier dwellers—are planning a march in force on New Orleans, and when I told him we'll hold President Jefferson responsible, he insisted that the President has no control over them."

"I can't take such statements seriously."

"Neither could I, yesterday. Since then I've spoken to all the men in my department who have visited the United States or have been stationed there. I've even conferred, until very late last night, with two of your regimental commanders who fought beside the Americans during their Revolution. And all of them say precisely the same thing, that Monroe was telling the truth. The men of the West are very independent, and they're furiously angry because of our policies in Louisiana."

"How many will attack us?"

"Who can say? One thousand. Five thousand. Our people, including your military men, say they're excellent marksmen, willing to endure hardships that no European soldier would tolerate, and exceptionally determined."

Bonaparte began to pace up and down. "I want everyone to whom you've spoken in this matter to give me a full report, in writing."

"I thought you'd want such reports, so I've already asked for them, First Consul. It's obvious that if you're going to war against the British and Austrians again, you'll need the fleet and all your divisions on this side of the Atlantic."

"Don't lecture me on basics, Charles!"

Talleyrand had won, and sat again, his expression complacent. "What are your orders concerning the Americans, First Consul?"

"I don't know," Bonaparte admitted bluntly. "First I want to determine the alternatives. Then I'll consider them. Until I do, I won't be in a position to decide whether to whip the United States or find some accommodation with it."

FOURTEEN

April 1803

Tennessee Bluffs, the wilderness site where the city of Memphis soon would be founded and flourish, was the scene of feverish, ever-increasing activity. With Mississippi River traffic at a virtual standstill, river devils and bargemen who had nothing better to occupy them began to arrive early in April, and cleared the forest for the camp of those who were expected later. New arrivals drifted into the bivouac each day, among them hunters, trappers and frontier farmers, young lawyers and physicians in search of adventure, and a surprisingly large number of settlers who only recently had crossed the mountains from the East.

No one was in charge, and no attempt was made to organize the growing band, but the problem of obtaining food forced the men to work together. The best hunters roamed through the forest each day, spreading out over a wide area, while those who remained behind divided such chores as cooking and standing sentry duty. Barges, sailboats, and several small river schooners were hauled up onto the bank of the Mississippi, and men who had nothing better to occupy their time built additional barges.

When Andrew MacCullough arrived at the rendezvous in mid-April, accompanied by an apprehensive Abel Hillery, a force of almost five hundred men had already gathered. Because of his activities as a recruiting agent Andrew was known to the vast majority, and many expected him to assume command of the expedition, but he quickly disabused them of the idea.

"None of us wants to take orders from anybody else," he said, "although I'm sure we've got to have some kind of organization. The best way to do it is to organize ourselves into companies, let each company elect its own officers and then the officers can elect the brigade commander."

The fiercely independent wilderness men heartily endorsed the idea, and it was generally agreed that, with one hundred to two hundred new recruits arriving each day, companies should be formed as soon as possible. Almost inevitably, trouble in the camp hastened the process. Among the volunteers were many who recognized no authority except that based on their own physical prowess, and with little to do before the brigade started down the Mississippi, they drank too much of the corn whiskey they and their friends had made.

Bitter quarrels jarred the serene atmosphere, and several violent fist fights were halted before any serious damage was done. Then, two days after Andrew's arrival, a fellow river devil called him to the top of the bluff. "If ye want t' see some excitement, Andy, come up here!"

Andrew climbed the bluff, then stopped short. Directly ahead, surrounded by a cheering throng of woodsmen, were two frontier dwellers in buckskins, each armed with a knife, circling each other warily. Both were cursing, moving in a crouch and waiting for an opportunity to strike.

As yet there had been no bloodshed, but Andrew knew that one such fight, if allowed to continue, could lead to scores of others, in which firearms as well as knives would be used. The expedition might founder in a series of brawls before it got under way, and he realized that men who insisted on feuding had to be subjected to outside discipline.

He pushed forward through the crowd, ignoring the advice of those who urged him, for the sake of his own safety, not to interfere. As he joined the two combatants he could smell the liquor on the breath of one, a heavy-set farmer with a wispy beard, and he knew it would be difficult to stop the fight.

"Keep t' hell out o' my way," the man muttered.

The other, clean-shaven, merely cursed.

"Boys," Andrew said, "save your weapons for the French. Break this up!"

They paid no attention to him, and the bearded man feinted at his opponent who, more sure-footed, side-stepped.

Andrew edged closer. "If you've got to fight, boys, try a free-for-all, with no holds barred."

Both men seemed deaf.

"Listen to me!" he said, making one final appeal to their reason.

"You was warned!" the bearded man shouted, and slashed at him.

Andrew ducked inside the reach of his arm, caught his wrist as it descended and twisted it so hard the knife fell to the ground. Simultaneously the river devil shoved him with such force that the man suddenly sprawled on his back.

The other fighter wasn't sure whether to attack his fallen foe or the giant who had interfered.

During the brief moment he hesitated, Andrew struck, driving a fist into his stomach and toppling him with a shattering blow to the cheekbone. The man crumpled, and Andrew stooped down to snatch his knife from his hand.

"Now we're going to be sensible." Andrew addressed himself to the crowd as well as to the battered gladiators. "No fighting with weapons will be allowed on this expedition." He hurled the knife, and it landed, quivering, deep in the trunk of a huge oak. Then he bent down, picked up the other knife at his feet and threw it at the same target.

There was a murmur of awe mixed with apprehension as the second knife grazed the first and ended a hair's breadth from it in the tree trunk.

"Are there any river devils in this crowd?" Andrew wanted to know.

About twenty frontier fighters came forward when he beckoned them.

"Boys," he said, "we're forming a battalion of our own. River devils are going to keep order in camp, and on the journey to New Orleans. Anyone who raises a knife or a pistol or a rifle to any other member of the expedition will be responsible to us. And here's what we'll do to breakers of the peace."

He reached down and hauled the clean-shaven knife fighter to his feet, then caught the bearded man, who was trying to make his way into the throng. They struggled in vain to free themselves from his grasp, and he knocked their heads together, the sound audible to all of the spectators.

"Now you know, boys!" Andrew declared. "So keep the peace—or suffer the consequences. Billy," he added as he caught sight of his cousin, "round up all the river devils at the water's edge, and we'll arrange our own patrols. We aim to take New Orleans on this march—not kill off each other, and may the Almighty help any man who forgets it!"

Thomas Jefferson practiced what he preached, and his devotion to the principle of informality was so great that he walked from the President's House to the temporary headquarters of the State Department for an urgent conference with Secretary Madison. Washington City's spring rains had been torrential, so his boots and breeches were spattered with mud. In addition he had suffered one of the mishaps common to pedestrians in the rapidly growing town: a breeze had picked up sawdust and wood shavings from a nearby building under construction, and so many tiny particles clung to his coat that he looked like the supervisor of the crew erecting the structure.

The meticulous James Madison was horrified. "If you had sent for me, Mr. President, I'd have come to you immediately!"

Jefferson preferred to treat the matter lightly. "Your files and reports are here. We'll save time, and time seems to be important. Have you had any additional letters from Hillery?"

"Only one you haven't seen, and it says nothing he hasn't already told us." Madison took a letter from a folder on his desk, and handed it to the President.

Jefferson's ability to read very rapidly always had astonished his friends and colleagues, and he absorbed the communication in little more than a glance. "I find myself wishing I hadn't agreed to the formation of an informal expedition of Westerners, and I very much regret the plan to let them take food and munitions from the Natchez arsenal."

"They'd be marching regardless of whether we approve, and they'd storm the Natchez arsenal if we hadn't agreed to open its doors. At least Americans won't be killing Americans."

The President handed him Hillery's letter. "The War Department believes it might be possible, barely possible, for a force of two thousand irregulars to take New Orleans by storm, provided they aren't required to put the city under siege. For that they'd need artillery, and the discipline of a real army."

"Yes, sir, from what I've read, a siege always requires great patience."

"But the capture of New Orleans won't be the end of this tragedy, James. Not only will the French feel compelled to retake it, naturally, but they're certain to launch a full-scale war against us. That means Boston and New York and Charleston will be subjected to bombardment by their new fleet, and they may try to capture all of our major cities."

"I expect the worst, Mr. President."

"We can't win a short war against a major power, and a long campaign will exhaust us, just when we're beginning to grow prosperous." Jefferson sighed. "I have no real choice, however. The West must be supported. An order to the states for the mobilization of militia is on my desk, ready except for my signature, and so is another incorporating merchant sloops and schooners into the Navy. I'll ask you to help me prepare a message to Congress declaring a state of national emergency."

"How soon do you plan to move, Mr. President?"

"I'm of two minds," Jefferson said. "We must be ready for the enemy, of course, so I'm tempted to act immediately. On the other hand, I don't believe the French will take any belligerent steps until the irregulars in the West actually attack New Orleans. Then, since it will take the better part of a month for the news to reach Paris, and another for an expedition to be sent across the Atlantic, not to mention the time it will take to prepare Bonaparte's forces for a campaign against us, I'm inclined to think we can defer mobilization until New Orleans is assaulted."

"It's a gamble, of course," Madison said.

"True, but we must take it. If we mobilize our full strength now—such as it is—we merely notify France that we're planning to fight her. The longer we can delay, the more time we have to keep trying to reach a reasonable accommodation with General Bonaparte."

"May I be candid, Mr. President?"

"I've never known you to be anything else, James."

180

"You won't be pleased to hear me say this, but I believe your optimism is totally unwarranted. Monroe and Livingston have been inundating me with reports from Paris. Letters they've written jointly, letters they've written separately. And neither of them can find even a hint of any change in the position taken by General Bonaparte. Not only has he refused to accept any of our very modest requests, but he hasn't permitted his Foreign Ministry to discuss them with us!"

"I can't understand this new mood of the French," President Jefferson said, frowning.

"You mean the mood of General Bonaparte, sir. He dreams of great glory—"

"A national leader, to be successful, must reflect the feelings and wishes of his people, James, and don't ever forget it. If Bonaparte wants to expand the borders of his country and make her the greatest power on earth, then the people of France share his aspirations. What puzzles me is their refusal to work out our mutual problems amicably. What's more, she's been our best friend. The—ah —unpleasantness John Adams encountered took place during a transition period in her government, and didn't reflect her true attitudes toward us—"

"Bonaparte's hostility to us seems to indicate he's become far more our enemy than our friend, Mr. President."

Jefferson paid no attention to the interruption. "What's more, she's the most logical and reasonable of all nations."

Like so many others, Madison was exasperated by his superior's love of France and all things French. It was difficult, however, for a Cabinet member to show open irritation with the President. "The French Revolution wasn't reasonable, Mr. President," he said mildly.

Jefferson shook his head. "It was based on logical principles, James. I'll grant you that the excesses of misguided individuals got out of hand, and were shocking. Most of them were men who weren't leaders in the ultimate sense of the word, however, which is why they were deposed, one after another. But General Bonaparte isn't that sort. His devotion to personal liberties, to such democratic essentials as freedom of worship, for instance, is admirable. He's proved himself an exceptionally able administrator as well as a military commander of unusual talent, and I'm convinced he has the almost unqualified support of the French people."

"If so, our task is that much harder," Madison replied wearily. "He won't yield any prerogatives to us in Louisiana, not even the fundamental rights necessary for the survival of the West, which he could do without harm to himself or to French interests. He's been arbitrary and rude, and I can't blame our Westerners for feeling they must take action themselves."

"Neither can I, although I grieve when I think how badly our development will be crippled by another war." The President stood, caked mud falling from his shoes to the floor. Fortunately, there was no rug in the office, so a broom of straws could be used to sweep away the dirt, and the men who tried to clean the offices of Washington City were accustomed to dried mud.

"I anticipate no change for the better, Mr. President," Madison said, escorting his superior to the door.

"Send another letter of instructions to Monroe and Livingston," Jefferson replied. "If Bonaparte can be stubborn, so can I. Tell our representatives to let nothing discourage them in their search for a peaceful, honorable solution. Tell them to persist, to keep trying, to keep seeking, no matter how often their overtures are rejected."

The antechambers of the First Consul's offices were crowded with high-ranking military and naval officers, officials of the merchant marine charged with building new warships for the enlarged French fleet, and several of the Finance Ministry's experts. There were administrators of the conquered Italian states and Low Countries, several prominent manufacturers, and representatives of the two largest gunpowder-making plants in the country.

All sat patiently, conversing in low tones, and everyone seemed reconciled to the inevitability of a long wait. Apologetic aides ushered one visitor into General Bonaparte's inner office as another came out, and occasionally a staff member went from one visitor to the next, explaining that, before the day ended, the General would see every man he had summoned.

A few glanced up when the Foreign Minister limped

into the antechamber, and several rose to greet him. But Talleyrand, showing none of his usual urbanity, did not deign to nod to anyone, and walked straight to the desk of the senior aide, whose desk guarded the entrance to the inner sanctum.

"Inform the First Consul that I must see him at once!"

The Colonel behind the desk was embarrassed. "I'm sorry, Your Excellency, but he's holding a meeting right now, and as you can see, there are a number of gentlemen ahead of you."

"Tell him to cut his meeting short," Talleyrand said, "and never mind how many are waiting."

He spoke more loudly than he realized, and before the Colonel could reply, the door opened. General Bonaparte, dressed in his favorite uniform of Colonel-in-Chief of the Guards regiment, stood in the frame, his expression quizzical.

"You've often told me the first virtue of a diplomat is endless patience, Charles," he said, but stopped short when he saw the expression on the Foreign Minister's face.

Talleyrand brushed past the desk of the aide and went straight into the inner office.

General Bonaparte followed. "I'm afraid I must interrupt our talk," he said to two civilians from the War Ministry. "If you'll be kind enough to wait outside again, I'll call you back very shortly."

They departed hastily.

Bonaparte closed the door, his smile faded and he spoke in a cold rage. "The English have sent Lord Nelson to sea with a large fleet, and another is mobilizing at Plymouth. The Royal Army is calling men to duty, and the Austrians have already sent fifteen divisions to their borders. There can be no doubt whatever that they're going to war with us again, and you know how important it is for us to strike first. Every day is precious, every hour is precious, yet you have the temerity to upset my entire schedule. You've gone too far, Charles, and I demand—"

"Sit down, First Consul," the Foreign Minister said curtly.

It had been so long since anyone had given an order to Bonaparte that he was dumfounded, and sank down onto a divan before his temper blazed still higher. "You forget your place, Charles. You're impertinent—"

"Abuse me after you've heard what have to say. Not being deaf or blind, I'm well aware of the preparations you're making for war, and so is everyone else in Paris. The British and Austrians are ready to evacuate their legations on three days' notice—at any time. But you've made a mistake that can ruin you, First Consul." Talleyrand shook his walking stick in the General's face. "You wouldn't listen to me, and you're not only going to suffer a bad defeat, but you're going to be humiliated. All Europe will laugh at you!"

Bonaparte jumped to his feet, his spurs clanging. "By God, no one laughs at me!"

"I've just received word," the angry Foreign Minister said, "that a corps of American leather-shirts is going to march on New Orleans. No one has any idea how many of them will take part, whether there will be one thousand or ten!"

The sudden change in Bonaparte was remarkable. His fury vanished, and was replaced by a monumental calm that someone unfamiliar with him might have mistaken for indifference. He directed his visitor to a chair with a pointed forefinger, then sat back in apparent relaxation.

"This is your fault, First Consul. You wouldn't listen to my warnings—"

"Compose yourself, Charles." The general spoke quietly. "Most crises are less acute than they're made out to be."

"This one is worse, unless you can spare several divisions of troops, fifty to seventy-five transports and a great many cannon to the New World. I really don't know how many you'd need, but—"

"For a city the size of New Orleans, I'd want fifty, plus as many howitzers. But, as you well know, I can spare no troops, no transports, and no cannon for the protection of New Orleans."

"Then prepare to lose it, while all Europe laughs at the spectacle of invincible France being driven out of her largest and most profitable colony by a mob of half-civilized Americans who can neither read nor write."

"You forget that they can shoot, Charles," Bonaparte

said pleasantly. "In battle I always prefer ten marksmen to one scholar."

Under the happiest of circumstances Talleyrand thought the First Consul's humor crude; at the moment it was groundless and inexcusable. "It's too late for me to teach you the fundamentals of statecraft."

Again Bonaparte's mood changed, and his face seemed to freeze. "There is nothing you can teach me, Charles, but there is a great deal you can learn from me. No one will laugh at France or at me, now or ever, and any man who fails to believe in our future will be sent into exile. Are your passports in order, Charles?"

Talleyrand became pale, but remained firm. "You admit you'll need every man and every ship for the new war against the English and Austrians."

"And their allies. The Dutch are sure to join them, which will give me the reason I've been seeking to occupy Amsterdam, Antwerp, and the Hague. Czar Alexander is jealous of my reputation, and may become a member of the coalition, too, which will cause us some additional problems. But they aren't insurmountable. Nevertheless, as you say, I shall have neither regiments nor warships to spare for an adventure in the New World, much though I'd enjoy it if I weren't distracted elsewhere."

"Surely you don't intend to surrender Louisiana without a struggle?"

"You mentioned the fundamentals of statecraft, Charles. You must know that a ruler, regardless of whether he's a hereditary monarch, an elected chieftain, or someone who holds his post for life, as I do, can't afford to be backed into a corner from which there is no honorable escape. When that happens, a hereditary monarch loses his crown, and often his life. An elected chieftain is repudiated by the voters who put him in office. And if he's in my position, he courts disgrace, followed by oblivion. I'm astonished to find you so naïve, Charles."

Talleyrand ignored the sarcasm. "You've thought of some way to deal with the crisis in Louisiana, then?"

"I've had a number of plans in mind ever since I first heard that bands of American marksmen might descend on the city. The worst of them would be to order the regiments now stationed there to make a stand to the death.

The heroism of martyrs always inspires the general public, which is willing to forgive failure in its awe of those who have given their lives for a hopeless cause. However, I hate losing men needlessly, or giving the Americans a free gift of Louisiana. Furthermore, I'm far too busy today to discuss matters that should be thoroughly familiar to you. Tell me all you've learned about this march of the leather-shirts."

"I know nothing more than I've told you."

"You're quite sure the expedition isn't being officially sponsored by President Jefferson?"

"I'm positive. I expect Minister Livingston to call on me at any moment to assure me that Jefferson disclaims all responsibility."

"Good." Bonaparte felt a familiar, gnawing pain in his side, and, hating to let anyone know he was suffering from a physical disability, turned away as he slipped a hand inside his tunic. Perhaps his physicians were right, and he should eat more regular meals at set hours, although it was impossible when he was in the last stages of preparation for a new war and was distracted, as well, by such problems as a pending conflict in Louisiana. "Can't you find out something more about the size of the corps the Americans are sending to New Orleans? Reconnaissance is useless when it isn't accurate."

"My informants are vague because the Americans themselves don't know how many men they're putting in the field. Small bands spent the winter traveling through the frontier, visiting small towns, and no one will know how many will volunteer until they actually appear for the march."

"The potency of an army of irregulars depends on its leadership. What do you know about the leaders of this mob?"

"Jefferson's adherents in the West have persuaded respectable men to stay at home. This includes veterans of their Revolution, so the leadership is made up of young, untried men who have had little military experience."

"If we weren't dealing with Americans, I'd be inclined to think the few troops stationed in New Orleans could turn the rabble away. But Burgoyne made the mistake of following orthodox European combat principles at Saratoga, and lost the war for the British there. I don't discount American mobs, even when their leadership is somewhat questionable."

The Foreign Minister yawned behind his hand.

"I realize you have no interest in military matters, Charles, but you needn't be so obvious." Bonaparte was very tired, and virtually any display of disinterest was enough to infuriate him anew.

Talleyrand had done his duty, and his one thought now was to escape as soon as possible. "I regret I can give you no additional information, First Consul."

Bonaparte began to pace the room, forgetting he had not removed his hand from the inside of his tunic. "Obviously, if this expedition is being planned for the near future, it would do no good to demand more specific intelligence from your sources over there."

"I've already written for more, naturally."

"By the time letters are exchanged, the campaign could be ended." Bonaparte halted and half-sat, half-threw himself onto the divan. "You've given me something to think about, Charles. Come back in three days, and I'll have decided what to do."

Talleyrand was dismayed. "Three days? Monroe and Livingston are coming to my office this afternoon!"

"Put them off!" the General rasped. "Europe must come first, and I can't give any consideration to America until I've made more important decisions!"

The elected officers of the frontier battalions and companies sat in a half-circle around a campfire on the bluff, and Andrew, standing at the rear of the group, was satisfied that a great deal had been accomplished in a short time. The expedition was scheduled to sail for New Orleans in another week, there were now almost two thousand men in the bivouac, with more still arriving each day, yet the near-anarchy of camp life had been ended.

River devils, working in groups of three and four, patrolled the entire area day and night, and as a result only two fist fights, both of short duration, had marred the serenity of existence at the rendezvous. The fleet of barges and small boats continued to swell, and there was every reason to believe that transportation facilities would be

187

ample, even if as many as another one thousand men arrived before the date of departure.

The food shortage, which had been serious, had terminated abruptly when a wagon train of seventy carts had arrived from Nashville, all of them laden with smoked beef, bacon, rice, flour, and other staples contributed by the city's merchants. Advance scouts had brought word that still another wagon train was due in the next day or two from Louisville, the Kentucky merchants refusing to be outdone by their Tennessee neighbors.

With so many problems solved, it was difficult to believe that very soon the actual voyage would begin, and that, within a month at the most, the frontiersmen would arrive at New Orleans. It was equally hard for Andrew to let himself think of the city, and he swore that never again could he trust a female on whom his life had depended. Either Jeanne or Beatriz, perhaps both of them, had revealed his hiding place in the Valdéz attic to Cristoforo de Martínez, who had become his nemesis. He had a score to settle with de Martínez, and with the girl who had come to mean so much to him—even if he gained no satisfaction other than telling her what he thought of her treachery.

Andrew was jarred back to the immediate present when he heard his name being mentioned by Captain Robert Crompton, commander of a company of Kentucky rifles, and, as the others began to cheer, he turned inquiringly to Captain Felix Black, head of a company of Tennessee Rifles, who was sitting cross-legged only a few feet from him.

"You've just been nominated for brigade commander," Black said with a grin, "and it looks like you're going to be elected by general consent—without a vote."

Andrew became alarmed. "Hold on!" he shouted, and walked quickly toward the fire.

The officers continued to applaud.

Facing them, he raised a hand for silence. "Gentlemen," he said, "I'm grateful to you for the honor of this nomination, and for your confidence. But I withdraw my name."

There was a groan, and someone shouted, "You can't do it, MacCullough!"

"Hear me out! I've been made commander of the devils'

188

battalion, which is enough of a chore for any man. Until we break camp next week, we'll continue to act as the constabulary—"

"And you're doing it damned well!" someone shouted.

There was a roar of approving laughter.

Andrew waited for it to subside. "Once we start down the Mississippi," he said, "we've agreed that every company will look after its own disciplining. That's as it should be. We've also agreed that the river devils will act as the vanguard, since we know the Mississippi—and New Orleans—better than blamed near anybody else. Let me be honest with you, gentlemen. I'm going to be busy enough commanding three companies of fire-breathing, ornery, contrary-minded river devils.

"I'm going to have to stop them from burning down every plantation and farmhouse in Louisiana. I've got to turn them into soldiers before we reach New Orleans, or not one household—and not one woman—in the city is going to be safe! If I can handle my own men, I'll be satisfied."

"If you won't command the brigade, who should?" a Kentuckian called.

"Well, that's a good question," Andrew said. "I've been hoping that Judge Jackson of Nashville would come out to join us, but a contingent from Nashville that just arrived at camp today said he won't be coming. Mrs. Jackson is holding him to a promise not to take up arms until the United States officially declares war."

Captain Crompton, almost as tall as Andrew, joined him at the fire. "The truth of it is, gentlemen," he said, "is that none of us has ever commanded more than a few neighbors in a skirmish with savages. There isn't a blamed man in this camp who has the experience to take charge of at least two thousand men."

There was an uncomfortable silence, and then Major Charles Robertson, a nephew of one of Nashville's founders, the commander of the Nashville companies, cupped his hands. "May I say a word?"

"Come up here, Charley," Robert said. "Nobody can see you in the shadows."

Robertson moved to the fire. "It seems to me that each of us has enough worries right now," he said. "We're trying to make troops out of men who've never taken orders from anyone in their lives. Why can't we wait until we get down to Louisiana before electing our brigade commander and his staff? By that time we'll know each other better, and it'll be easier for all of us."

"I agree," Andrew said. "First let's create our army, and then we'll worry about making Generals and Colonels. We're going to have our hands full training men to take New Orleans from professional French troops, and that ought to keep everybody out of mischief."

FIFTEEN

April-May 1803

Cherry and chestnut trees were in blossom, shrubs were budding and the grass, a deep, velvet-like green, was almost long enough for its first cutting of the season. The garden of the Palais Royal looked its loveliest, but Ministers Monroe and Livingston were in no mood to enjoy the beauties of their surroundings. They walked rapidly, each engrossed in his own thoughts, and when they entered the palace they showed none of their usual courtesy, but asked abruptly to see the Foreign Minister, who, they said, was not expecting them.

The two Americans were prepared to wait for a long time, if necessary, and were surprised when they were shown with almost no delay to the private salon on the second floor. There Talleyrand, although gaunt and bleary-eyed, greeted them cheerfully.

"This is a pleasant coincidence," he said. "I was planning to send a note to your legation, inviting you to pay me a visit today."

"I don't think it will be as pleasant as you might imagine, Your Excellency," Monroe said.

The French Foreign Minister remained unruffled. "Let me send for a bottle of excellent wine from the Bordeaux region that I received as a gift only yesterday."

It was too early in the day for the Americans to drink, and Livingston shook his head. "We'll defer the wine, if you don't mind, and attend to business first."

Talleyrand inclined his head in a gesture of agreement.

"An American sloop out of Baltimore put into Cherbourg last night, Your Excellency, and a special courier brought us a message from President Jefferson. There has been a change, a major change in the policy of the United States." He took the document from his pocket.

Monroe, watching Talleyrand closely, thought he detected a faint flicker of surprise in his eyes.

"In part," Livingston said, "the letter covers ground as

191

familiar to you as to us. It is my duty, however, to remind you of the essentials. Three-eighths of all American trade is channeled through the port of New Orleans. Therefore any nation that is not friendly to the United States in her own occupation policies in Louisiana must, inevitably, become the enemy of the United States."

"Our President and State Department," Monroe added, "are as well aware of the situation in Europe as are informed people here. They know that war will break out at any time between France and a number of powers. Therefore Mr. Jefferson authorizes us to inform you, Your Excellency—"

"Without threats, direct or indirect," Livingston quickly interjected.

"—without threats," Monroe continued, "that in the event we have not reached an agreement regarding New Orleans by the time hostilities begin, it is certain that the United States will be compelled by her own interests to join in the war on the side of Great Britain."

"I've given a great deal of thought to this problem over a long period of time," Talleyrand said with a faint smile, "but I must admit it never occurred to me that England and her former colonies might form an alliance. Extraordinary!"

Monroe saw that the prospect did not disturb him. "You, of all men, Your Excellency, should know that necessity creates strange and unusual marriages."

"I dare say." Talleyrand remained affable. "Does your President offer any solution to our problem in order to prevent this marriage?"

"He does make an offer," Livingston declared, "but it has no connection with the possibility of a future alliance with the British. Our principal aim is that of insuring a permanent outlet for our river commerce. Therefore, sir, the United States is prepared to purchase the city of New Orleans from France, provided you're willing—and the price isn't exorbitant."

Talleyrand was silent for a long moment. "I find it rather frightening that the minds of men so often move in parallel channels." He paused, then asked quietly, "What would the United States be willing to pay for all of Louisiana?"

The question was so unexpected that the Americans were incapable of replying.

"Last night," Talleyrand said, "very late last night, as a matter of fact, First Consul Bonaparte indicated his willingness to sell the entire colony to your Government."

"We don't consider this a laughing matter, Your Excellency," the stunned Livingston said.

"Nor do we, I assure you," the French Foreign Minister replied. "The First Consul has weighed the matter, and believes a sale of all Louisiana to the United States might provide the only amicable settlement of the problem that threatens our friendship."

James Monroe realized the offer was a master stroke. In the coming war Bonaparte would need all his strength and energy for the fighting in Europe, and could ill-afford to divert men, ships and munitions to the New World. So, rather than become embroiled on distant fronts as well as those closer to home, he was willing to make a grand gesture that would preserve American friendship for France without causing him to lose any shred of the reputation for invincibility he had attained. His primary interests were in the Old World rather than the New, and he would have more than enough to occupy him for a long time to come, particularly if he defeated one or more members of the new coalition being formed against him, and absorbed some of their Continental territories.

"Does the First Consul have a sale price in mind, Your Excellency?" Monroe asked.

"He left that to me. I suggested eighty million francs, which he found reasonable and fair."

Livingston caught his breath, and Monroe blinked. Eighty million francs was the equivalent of fifteen million American dollars, a ridiculously small sum to pay for New Orleans, a permanent guarantee that the Mississippi River would remain open to American traffic and the acquisition of a vast tract consisting of more than eight hundred and twenty-five thousand square miles, a portion of it west of the Mississippi. By making such a purchase the United States would become almost one and one-half times her present size.

"Are there any conditions pertaining to the sale, Your Excellency?" Livingston asked.

"France hopes, of course, that the United States will see fit to maintain close trade relations with her."

Both Americans grinned. Bonaparte's legions would need a constant source of raw materials, particularly food, and American grains would be essential to the success of the French war machine.

"You won't find our people lacking in gratitude, Your Excellency," Livingston said. "Americans have always preferred France to England, and this deal will settle our friendship for a long, long time. You can rely on our corn and wheat, as well as our lumber and anything else you want."

"I thought we might work out a separate commercial treaty," Talleyrand said.

"Of course, Your Excellency."

"There is one further condition, and I mention it rather hesitantly. The First Consul has been somewhat concerned about the expedition of irregulars from your West that may invade Louisiana this spring."

"We're equally concerned," Monroe said quickly.

"If they should attack New Orleans, the blow would be damaging to the First Consul's reputation. And he wouldn't be in a position to reward such perfidy by selling Louisiana to the United States. In other words, the sale is directly contingent upon the abandonment of plans for such an attack."

"We'll do everything in our power to see that the peace isn't broken, Your Excellency!" Livingston declared fervently.

"France will do her part, too. We shall send one of our fastest sloops to New Orleans as soon as the agreement is concluded. How long will it take you to obtain approval from your Government?"

Monroe thought rapidly. The exchange of communications with Washington City would take at least seven or eight weeks, and by that time the frontiersmen would have stormed New Orleans, thereby destroying the unique opportunity for the United States to expand her borders enormously and become a power of consequence in the world.

No treaty was valid and binding until ratified by the Senate, and, as a former Senator, Monroe knew that the upper chamber of Congress guarded its prerogatives jealously. Nevertheless he could not imagine any member of the Senate voting against such a treaty. His own authority, as outlined in his appointment by the President, was vague, which had irritated him somewhat before he had left Washington City, but now he saw the chance to utilize the lack of precision in his instructions.

"I'm prepared to sign a preliminary draft of the treaty right now, Your Excellency."

Livingston smiled in approval of his colleague's deft handling of the situation.

"I've already drawn up a preliminary draft," Talleyrand told them, and, pulling a bell-rope, sent a junior aide for the document.

It proved to be a remarkably simple agreement, which wisely left the precise boundaries of the territory changing hands to be determined later, in the final version of the treaty. Monroe and Livingston both declared themselves satisfied, Talleyrand sent for a quill pen, a jar of ink and a small box of sand, and all three men signed the document.

The Americans were still stunned by the change in their country's fortunes, and as Chancellor Livingston sanded the wet ink, he murmured, "This is the noblest work of our lives."

"Our sloop made the crossing from Cherbourg in record time, Mr. President," Secretary Madison said, "and the news is so good I find it difficult to believe."

Thomas Jefferson bent over the joint report from James Monroe and Robert Livingston, reading it a second time. "I didn't dare hope the French would go this far. Overnight we've become a different nation, a huge country with a potential growth that's virtually unlimited. But our future depends on our ability to halt the march on New Orleans down the Mississippi."

"The War Department has sent a team of couriers to intercept the Westerners, Mr. President, and the Navy has dispatched three ships to New Orleans in the hope that they'll arrive before the volunteers can attack."

"I like to think of myself as objective and unemotional, which is sheer nonsense," Jefferson said. "All I know is that I'll either go down in history as the President who bought Louisiana for a token, or as the President who couldn't prevent his country from being plunged into a needless war. The next few weeks will prove whether we have genuine patience, James."

"How soon do you plan to announce the new treaty with France, Mr. President?"

"I'm afraid we'll have to wait. If our people attack New Orleans, France may cancel the entire agreement, and the disappointment would be greater than the country could bear. Tell no one about the treaty for the present, and we'll soon learn whether one of the most ironic pages in our history, or that of any country, is being written."

The delay at Natchez was maddening, but unavoidable. A force of more than two thousand, three hundred frontiersmen poured into the little town, their number more than double its total population. Its facilities were overtaxed, so a bivouac was established on the outskirts of the community, and local volunteers who had been waiting for months to join in the assault on New Orleans attached themselves to the brigade.

Late that night, in accordance with the plans that had been made in Washington City when the venture first had been conceived, the Federal arsenal located on the Mississippi just above Natchez was "raided." Two hundred carefully selected river devils and members of Major Robertson's battalion marched from their camp to the arsenal, thoughtfully bringing with them the expedition's empty wagons, while barges were made fast on the shoreline a short distance away.

The commander of the arsenal and his small platoon of Regular Army troops carefully absented themselves from the premises for a half-hour, and at the end of that time approximately half of the food and three-quarters of the gunpowder stored there had been carted away and packed on board the barges. Everything was in readiness for the final stage of the voyage to New Orleans.

Then, at dawn the following morning, nearly one thousand members of the brigade were too ill to resume the journey. The initial, frantic investigation revealed nothing of consequence, and alarmed officers wondered whether the "river sickness" that had killed so many explorers and trappers more than one hundred years earlier was claiming new victims.

Natchez's one physician and the five who were traveling with the brigade had their own ideas, and by noon made their diagnosis. The volunteers had exhausted their supplies of alcoholic beverages earlier on their journey, the town's small, cramped inn sold out its reserves of whiskey, rum and ale in less than an hour after the vanguard had arrived, and there were too few wells in the vicinity to quench the thirst of the volunteers.

Therefore, acting in defiance of strict orders, the men had been drinking river water. When Andrew MacCullough heard the news, he knew, as did everyone else familiar with the Mississippi, that the column would be forced to remain at Natchez for at least five days. The victims would be ill for three days, then would require another forty-eight hours to regain their strength. Nothing positive would be accomplished, either, by telling them they had themselves to blame. Anyone who drank the muddy waters of the Mississippi, in which rotting vegetation floated the better part of the year, paid for his folly.

The impatient river devils, all of them healthy, were anxious to push ahead, but Andrew insisted they wait for the rest of the brigade. "Seeing there are two hundred and fifty of us," he said, "I reckon we can beat five hundred Frenchmen in any kind of battle, but we can't whip the whole garrison. The brigade has come this far together, and we'll go the rest of the way as one unit."

Through daily association for more than six weeks the officers had come to know each other well, and Major Charles Robertson was unanimously elected brigade commander. He accepted on two conditions, first that no one call him General, as he was too ignorant of military affairs, and second that Andrew MacCullough of the river devils act as his deputy, in addition to his other duties.

Andrew, too, believed he had been backed into a corner, and knew of no way he could avoid the new responsibilities, so he bowed to the will of Robertson and the enthusiastic approval of his fellow officers.

Most of the sick took longer to recuperate than the physicians had hoped, and after the brigade had spent a full week at Natchez, Major Robertson called a war council of his battalion and company commanders. The day was warm and sunny, so they gathered on the lawn of the Anglican church, and sentries were stationed around the perimeter to keep both civilians and uninhibited members of the brigade from eavesdropping.

"Gentlemen," Robertson said, "Captain MacCullough and I have spent the better part of the past two days analyzing our situation."

"Because we've had nothing better to do," Andrew added dryly.

Robertson waited for the laughter to subside. "We're agreed that the French know we're coming. We find it inconceivable that a flotilla of armed men as large as ours could cruise down the Mississippi without attracting so much attention that even French administrators and soldiers unfamiliar with the frontier wouldn't hear of us. So we can expect a rather violent welcome. We have a more immediate problem, however.

"Directly across the Louisiana border stands a French fort, which Captain MacCullough knows well, as some of you have heard. At last report a garrison of approximately fifty men was stationed there, but the commandant at New Orleans—if he has any common sense—has reinforced it by now.

"We've sent several scouts to find out the strength of the fort, and are expecting them to report back to us tonight or tomorrow morning. Captain MacCullough, will you describe our dilemma?"

"Yes, sir. Obviously, gentlemen," Andrew said, "we've got to take that fort, regardless of how many men are stationed there. My river devils are aching to do the job, and they'll call me a traitor for saying this, but I believe there are others who can do the work more efficiently. I'll pit my boys against any troops, anywhere, when it comes to river fighting. But the fort is vulnerable from the rear, and should be approached from the forest."

Several commanders of rifle companies began to speak simultaneously.

Robertson called for order.

"You're jumping ahead of me, gentlemen," Andrew

said with a grin. "Rob Crompton's boys could creep right over the palisades before the French knew they were there, and so could Felix Black's Cherokee fighters. I'm just naming two companies that come to mind, although I'm sure there are others," he added quickly. "If we decide that's how we want to attack, Major Robertson will make the assignment. I won't, so stop jumping up to attract my attention, gentlemen.

"What we want from you, first of all, is an expression of opinion. Do you think we ought to take the fort from the rear, from the wilderness side?"

"Is that what you recommend, Andy?" the commander of a Mississippi Territory called.

"I sure do!"

Robertson called for a vote, and the officers unanimously favored following Andrew's suggestion.

"We'll reach New Orleans within seventy-two hours of the fort's fall," Andrew said, "so we've got to make certain —without fail—that no Frenchmen escape to carry word to New Orleans that we're so close. What are your suggestions?"

A brisk discussion ensued, and it was finally agreed that some of the faster and more maneuverable boats in the brigade's flotilla, particularly two graceful, flat-bottomed schooners, would lie in wait just out of sight during the attack on the fort from the forest. If possible, the members of the assaulting force would silence the French cannon in order to prevent them from damaging the American vessels. Then, while the riflemen threw a cordon around the fort in the forest, the ships would reveal themselves, and, with river devils on board in case a battle developed on the Mississippi, would cut off any possible attempt of the French to send one of their own craft downstream.

The plan was sound, and only Abel Hillery of the State Department, who attended as a silent observer, was glum. Since no one listened to him, he no longer protested that the expedition, conceived as a means of persuading the French to grant concessions to Americans, had become a corps determined to invade New Orleans and drive out Bonaparte's troops. Civilians as well as fighting men on both sides would die, Hillery believed, and property would be damaged, causing the Creoles of the city, ordinarily friendly to Americans, to resent them.

The brigade well might cause more problems than it cured, but it was too late for Hillery to remonstrate. Reason had been abandoned for armed might, and the United States would be forced to pay the price for the expedition's rashness.

SIXTEEN

June 1803

Philadelphia and New York, Baltimore and Charleston demonstrated restrained enthusiasm when they learned the Government had purchased the vast Louisiana Territory from France. Only a few men realized that the United States, which had suddenly expanded to the far reaches of the unexplored Rocky Mountains, had become a very large nation and, if she lived up to her new potential, could become as strong and influential as the great powers of Europe. The majority thought of the West as a vaguely situated area beyond the mountains, a land where financial failures and immigrants established free homesteads, and although they appreciated the unexpected growth of the country, they did not consider the purchase significant.

New England, where President Jefferson never had enjoyed great popularity, was openly skeptical, its attitude somewhat colored by the fear that it might lose its pre-eminence. Many echoed the Hartford *Courant*, which said: *The augmentation of our territory is not altogether welcome. We are ill-prepared to administer and protect this new wilderness, which may impose a burden on all of our citizens.*

The Boston *Advertiser*, which had been founded by Sam Adams, the radical, moving spirit of the American Revolution, had become increasingly conservative in recent years, and took an even gloomier view: *The great strength of America is that the preponderant majority of our people share a common heritage of English customs and law, not to mention the most obvious of benefits, the English language. New Orleans, the only city of our new domain, is populated by Frenchmen, Spaniards and a mixture of the two known as Creoles. We wonder whether it will be possible for them to amalgamate with our already-established citizenry.*

The West went wild when the news spread, however, and nowhere were misgivings felt. Ohio, which had become the Union's seventeenth state on March 1, declared a twenty-four-hour holiday, and farmers, merchants, and factory owners joined in predicting that their own population and wealth would double within a decade as a direct result of the acquisition and the consequent freedom of river traffic from the upper reaches of the Ohio to the mouth of the Mississippi. Schools and law courts were closed for a day in Knoxville and the other towns of eastern Tennessee, and in Nashville, as in Louisville and the frontier settlements of Kentucky, impromptu celebrations were held.

In the Indiana Territory and adjoining Illinois country, men were equally delighted but expressed their joy more quietly. It was possible, the wilderness settlers told one another, that within a relatively few years they would no longer be forced to sleep with their rifles close at hand or build palisades around their towns. They had become so accustomed to danger that no one could imagine a life without it, but the prospect was heartening.

Two of the courier teams sent from Washington City made no attempt to spread the word about the purchase, but devoted their energies to the attempt to reach the invaders of Louisiana before it was too late. Both groups had reached the Mississippi, and while one traveled downstream by water on a flatboat onto which extra sail had been crowded, the other rode along the east bank, changing horses whenever possible and paying exorbitant prices for fresh mounts when necessary.

Only men accustomed to the forests could have tolerated the pace. The messengers who traveled by land suffered the more grueling experiences, resting only a few hours each night, and, not taking time to cook meals, subsisting on jerked venison, cold fatback and parched corn they bought from settlers along the way. They became gaunt and weary, but pressed on, always aware that more than two thousand armed frontiersmen were moving toward New Orleans somewhere ahead of them, and realizing that blood would flow unnecessarily unless they accomplished the near-miracle of halting the expedition in time.

What frustrated them was their inability to close the gap. Each day they heard that the flotilla had been sighted, or had halted for a night's encampment, but the leaders of the expedition appeared to be men determined to let nothing prevent them from reaching their goal. By the time the couriers had reached the Mississippi Territory they were cursing the names of Major Charles Robertson and Captain Andrew MacCullough.

Andrew had not asked to take charge of the detachment assigned to occupy the French border fort, but he had been unable to refuse Robertson's request that he take command. "You're better suited for the task than anyone," the Major had said. "You know the fort, you understand river fighting and no one is more familiar with the wilderness."

So, in the early hours of the morning, Andrew stood on the east bank of the Mississippi, about a mile above the fort, directing the final preparations for the assault. Crompton's Kentucky Rifles, augmented by a score of additional wilderness men from Illinois and Mississippi, were making a long sweep around the bastion, and would approach it from the south. Black's Tennessee Rifles were beginning their advance from the north, and if all went as planned, the two forces would join somehere beyond the defenders' sentry outposts, due east of the fort. Every member of the land party was an experienced woodsman, the equal of the Cherokee in making his way silently through the pine forest, so there was only a slight chance that the French would become aware of the two companies closing in on them.

The river devils, however, were taking a far greater risk. Fifty of them were crowded on board three small schooners which had been camouflaged with the branches of trees, and even the sails had been smeared with dried mud so they could not be seen too readily at night.

Andrew had estimated it would take the boats about an hour to reach the fort, provided they were not delayed by underwater obstructions. The Mississippi was one of the most hazardous of rivers to navigate, particularly when it was necessary to sail in the shallow waters close to the east bank in order to avoid detection, and Andrew knew that much depended on the skill of the pilots he had selected for the craft, river men of long experience who, nevertheless, were handicapped because of the need to find their way at the darkest hour of night.

Standing at the prow of the little schooner leading the procession, Andrew realized that the river devils were suffering from a number of disadvantages. Although the element of surprise was in their favor, his men carried no cannon on the flatboats and would have to rely on their own rifles, which were no match for the artillery of the French. And, even though the defenders were not familiar with the subtleties of wilderness warfare, they were expert gunners who would not find it difficult to strike clumsy, flat-bottomed river boats incapable of being maneuvered rapidly.

The over-all odds were against the French, of course, and Andrew felt certain that his stronger force would be able to capture the fort. But, as he had emphasized repeatedly to his river devils and the men of the rifle companies, the primary purpose of the operation was to prevent the escape of even one Frenchman who might be able to carry word of the expedition's approach to New Orleans. The wilderness men marching on the fort through the forest would have a fairly simple task fulfilling their mission, as they could make the sentries their prisoners and seal off the palisades.

But the river devils would find it infinitely more difficult to prevent the escape of one or more small boats enjoying the protective cover of artillery fire. So the success of the venture depended almost completely on his own boldness and the willingness of his men to take great risks.

The little squadron sailed silently downstream, moving past small islands and submerged, dead trees. The forest on the near bank was quiet, and appeared impenetrable in the half-light; the west bank was almost completely obscured by a thin layer of fog just above the surface of the river.

Soon after four o'clock the schooners reached their initial destination, a small hook of land only a quarter of a mile from the fort. Here the river devils had to exercise a discipline unique to them, as the slightest sound could be heard by the French sentries. Under the best of circumstances their presence might become known, since a guard stationed near the waterfront might happen to glance in the direction of the river, for no particular reason, and discover the approach of the little armada.

The river devils manned oars which were tightly bound in cloth to prevent splashing, and then the schooners, moving now in a single, horizontal line, swept around the hook of land and headed toward the promontory on which the fort stood. This was the critical moment, and the fate of the detachment depended on what transpired in the next few minutes. Andrew had instructed the commanders of the rifle companies to move against the flanks and rear of the French at precisely 4:30, and a quick glance at his watch told him that the boats would reach the bastion from the Mississippi at the same time.

He had no way of knowing, of course, whether either of his companies approaching the place through the forest had encountered difficulties that had delayed them. If so, the French would be able to concentrate the greater part of their strength against the schooners, and his river devils would be subjected to a fierce bombardment.

The palisades loomed up ahead now, as did a new, thirty-foot tower that had been erected since Andrew had last seen the place, but he could detect no signs of life. If any sentries were stationed in the tower, they were either asleep or otherwise lax in their duties. The palisades did not appear to be manned, either, and the French continued to slumber as the schooners closed in.

Andrew was the first to leap ashore onto the little wharf, which did not appear to have been repaired since he had last set foot on it, and it creaked under his weight. His river devils were close behind him, two-thirds of the company coming ashore while the remainder continued to man the schooners. The frontiersmen were at their best in situations that required them to display initiative as well as daring, and it was unnecessary to give orders.

Each of the river devils knew what to do. Several headed toward the four small boats tied to the wharf, cut their lines and hauled them to one of the schooners, which promptly moved off a short distance, the small flotilla in tow. The French had been deprived of their means of transportation to New Orleans by water, and in the event

205

a serious fight developed, those on board the schooner were prepared to sink all four boats at once rather than see them fall into the hands of the French again.

So the primary objective of the group was accomplished within moments of the landing. The French had been denied the vessels that could carry a warning to the military authorities at New Orleans that an American expedition was sailing toward the town.

Meanwhile Andrew and the majority of the river devils headed toward the palisade. Several men were boosted over the tops of the pointed logs, and they, in turn, quietly opened the gate for the rest. Andrew, leading his men into the compound, caught sight of his first French sentry, a luckless young soldier who had already been captured by two of the men who had climbed the palisade. A gag had been stuffed into his mouth, and his hands and ankles were being roughly but efficiently bound, rendering him harmless.

For the first time since coming ashore Andrew felt compelled to take active charge of the operation. Dividing the river devils into two units, he sent one to take possession of the cannon, which stood behind a second, lower palisade; the others started off, simultaneously, making their way toward the log buildings within the compound. The French, demonstrating their usual ability to create the amenities of civilization anywhere, had put up several clapboard structures and had laid out roads within the fort, so the river devils were forced to proceed cautiously, uncertain which buildings were used for military purposes and which were barracks and, perhaps, dining halls.

Andrew watched the latter unit as the men, spreading out, cautiously inched forward in the dark. Then, hastily, he followed the others to the cannon platforms. As he climbed the small palisade he told himself that the men who had built it had not known their business; it was too low to protect gunners from infantry attack, and the pine saplings were too young to form an effective shield against artillery. With all of their military prowess, the French had not yet learned the essentials of New World warfare.

There were faint but distinct sounds of a scuffle somewhere ahead, the first noises made by the river devils, and when Andrew reached the platforms he found that three more white-clad sentries had been taken into custody. Two had put up a struggle, and both were nursing bruises as, gags in their mouths, they were trussed. Other river devils, grinning, were turning the cannon to face the main buildings of the fort.

Andrew made certain they had gunpowder and ammunition at hand in the event they needed to use the guns, but cautioned them not to fire unless they received a direct order to that effect from him. With their comrades spreading out through the compound, indiscriminate firing might kill other Americans.

Marveling at the speed and ease with which the cannon stations had been captured, Andrew raced off after his other men. He could see little in the dark, but the soft padding of footsteps somewhere ahead guided him, and he joined the river devils just as a line of armed men approached from the opposite direction. Both units stopped abruptly, the click of rifle hammers broke the silence, and, as tension mounted swiftly, the first serious clash of the engagement seemed inevitable.

But something out of the ordinary struck Andrew; the men opposite him stood in a half-crouch assumed by wilderness fighters, so he muttered to the river devils nearest him, "Hold your fire. Pass the word."

Then, boldly, he took several paces forward, standing alone in the compound street. "Identify yourselves!" he called softly.

There was a brief silence, then someone chuckled. "I'll be damned," a man said in English.

"Is that you, Captain MacCullough?" another asked.

"Captain Crompton," Andrew said with a quiet laugh, "your boys just came closer to suffering the worst beating Kentuckians have taken since the massacre on the North Fork by the warriors of the Miami."

River devils and riflemen grinned at each other in the dark, their tension evaporating.

"Is Captain Black's company here?" Andrew wanted to know.

"He's sealing off the palisade around the fort," Crompton of the Kentucky Rifles replied. "Me and my boys here, we had nothing better to do, so we thought we'd see the sights of the place."

"Then let's see them." Andrew gave a series of new orders, directing squads to occupy each of the buildings in the compound.

They moved off at a trot, and Andrew, accompanied by Crompton, several river devils and a few Kentuckians, headed toward the commandant's quarters.

An orderly who was sound asleep on a pallet outside a closed door was immobilized with almost absurd ease, and a moment later the man who had been snoring gently in the feather bed that occupied the inner chamber struggled to a sitting position and blinked at the muzzles of a half-circle of rifles.

One of the Kentuckians found a tinderbox and flint, and began to light a number of the exquisite, smokeless French tapers that only the wealthiest of Americans could afford.

The astonishment of the French officer mounted as he saw the rough, attire of the brigands who had invaded his bedchamber, and he began to sputter. "I demand—"

"Permit me to interrupt," Andrew cut in, addressing him in French, "but you're in no position to make any demands, sir. Your garrison has just fallen. And," he added proudly, "to the best of my belief, not one shot has been fired and not one man on either side has suffered serious injuries."

The Frenchman was wide awake now. "Who are you, sir?"

"I happen to be the deputy commander of an expedition of American volunteers. My name is MacCullough, and my men call me a Captain."

The French officer swung his bare feet to the floor, and started toward the far wall.

One of the river devils stepped forward to halt him, but Andrew, realizing what the Frenchman had in mind, stopped his subordinate with a gesture.

The French officer clamped his plumed helmet onto his head, donned his tunic over his nightshirt and reached for his sheathed sword. "Colonel le Brun of the 4th Guards Regiment, Captain MacCullough. It appears that I am your prisoner, sir, so be good enough to accept my sword."

"Keep your sword," Andrew replied in embarrassment, "and you're not my prisoner, either. The United States and France aren't at war. Not yet, anyway, and I have no authority to take prisoners or even occupy this fort longer than will be necessary to insure the safety of our expedition."

Colonel le Brun was bewildered. "Only in this wilderness, where the silence drives one mad, do men make war and insist it is not a war!"

Andrew translated, and the Americans laughed. But the morning's work wasn't yet done, and Andrew gave some additional orders. "Captain Crompton, post sentries wherever we need them. Tell Captain Black to put all firearms belonging to the garrison under guard. And send off word to Major Robertson that the main body can proceed down the river without interference. I want the river devils stationed on the schooners notified they can come ashore, too. And I'll inspect your outposts whenever you're ready."

"Yes, sir!" Crompton hurried away, the other Americans accompanying him.

Andrew was alone with the French commandant. "Colonel le Brun," he said, "I'm afraid I can't offer you much in the way of breakfast, but it will be a pleasure to share what I have." Now that the fort was his, he realized he was ravenously hungry.

Le Brun looked at the bag of parched corn that Andrew opened for his inspection, and shuddered. "Your men have not yet looted my stores?"

"They haven't—and they won't! They may be irregulars, but any man under my command who steals property will be shot!"

The French officer's face cleared. "In that case, Captain MacCullough, I insist you permit me to act as host at breakfast. I keep some chickens whose eggs are always delicious, the wild onions that grow in the marshes are palatable after they have been marinated in a light Chablis that I have sent to me from New Orleans for the purpose, and I've discovered a type of mushroom in the woods behind the fort that has character. I'm afraid I can't give you more than an omelet on such short notice, but my chef baked bread only last night, so it shouldn't be overly stale."

Andrew accepted at once. The fare sounded superb

after months of nothing but wilderness meals, and he felt almost sorry it had become necessary to drive the French out of Louisiana. There were few civilizing influences on the frontier, and a man who savored the pleasures of cosmopolitan living was bound to regret their loss.

SEVENTEEN

June 1803

Abel Hillery made an impassioned address to the officers of the brigade who gathered at a council of war in the fort on the Louisiana border. They had one final chance to keep the peace, he told them, and if they missed it, the full responsibility for a major war between the United States and France would fall on their shoulders. Both nations were proud and quick-tempered, he pointed out, and it would be impossible to maintain peaceful relations if they persisted in their plan to attack New Orleans.

He reminded them, too, of President Jefferson's earnest desire to avoid a war with a powerful European nation, and he stressed the benefits that a period of continuing peace would enable the United States to enjoy. It was true, he declared, that American rights had been abridged and ignored, and American citizens had been abused. But he felt confident that a march to the farms and plantations on the outskirts of New Orleans would cause the French rulers of the city to adopt a more conciliatory attitude. So, he argued, the United States could attain the equivalent of a victory without shedding blood or delaying the nation's progress.

The frontiersmen listened politely, showing no enthusiasm, and then Major Robertson made a brief, sharp reply. The West had been stifled, he said, outlining grievances familiar to every man present, and had shown unusual patience in the hope that France would become more friendly. But First Consul Bonaparte's civilian and military deputies in Louisiana had proved they did not intend to soften their stand against the United States, and the entire future of the West was in danger.

Therefore, he said, the men who depended on Mississippi River freedom of traffic and the right to use the port facilities of New Orleans without restriction could afford to wait no longer. Their survival demanded that they take matters into their own hands and act vigorously, and if a major war broke out, only the French would be to blame.

He put the question of capturing New Orleans to a vote, and without exception the brigade's officers declared themselves in favor of prompt military action. There was no discussion, no argument, and Hillery's advice was ignored.

The only subject for debate was whether the entire journey should be made by boat or whether the expedition should leave the Mississippi and march overland after reaching the farm country outside New Orleans. Andrew pointed out that, either way, the approach of armed Americans would be seen, and that word undoubtedly would be carried to the French authorities. In his opinion the brigade could advance more rapidly toward its ultimate objective by sailing as close to the city as possible before disembarking, moving into battle formation and meeting Bonaparte's legions.

Some of the officers dissented, but everyone familiar with the river believed the plan was sound, and it was adopted by a majority vote. So the expedition started out at sundown after a stay of less than a full day at the border fort. A small detachment remained behind to hold the bastion, maintain a guard over the French garrison and prevent its members from racing ahead to New Orleans.

The brigade sailed downstream all night and rested the next day in the forest, repeating the process the following night. But the Americans were drawing close to the plantations and farms beyond the city now, and a chance meeting with local residents was possible at any time. So, after a few hours of rest shortly before dawn, the volunteers ate a cold breakfast of their usual, dull fare and embarked on the last leg of their momentous voyage.

The sailing order was changed, and the river devils comprised the entire vanguard, with the battalions of riflemen behind them. Andrew placed himself on board the schooner that led the procession, the rest of his battalion on board barges strung out behind. His most immediate concern was that the French might have learned of the invasion. If so, General Jean de Maniton could have prepared an ambush, and his troops possibly were lying in wait for the invaders behind a bend in the river.

In order to prevent the decimation of his ranks in the

event of a surprise attack he spread his barges out, making them less of a target, and he was surprised when the assault failed to materialize. Had he been in the French commander's position, he would have used every means to reduce the strength of the invaders and drive them off before they reached the city itself, where civilians might be caught in a crossfire.

Andrew and Charles Robertson had agreed that the brigade would go ashore when any French troop concentration was seen, but the armada of river boats continued to draw closer to the city, and there was no sign of Bonaparte's legions by the time, in mid-morning, that the spire of the cathedral in the Place d'Armes was sighted in the distance. Although Andrew's luck seemed too good to last, he decided to attempt a daring tactic: he would sail, if possible, to the commercial docks that American river shipping had used in the past, and would make his landing there. There were a number of open spaces in the area that would permit freedom of maneuver, and the large warehouses of the district would provide adequate cover if his river devils were forced to scatter and become involved in a duel of marksmen.

Farmers working their land near the bank of the Mississippi saw the fleet, stopped their labors and stared in curiosity at the Americans. Other Frenchmen smiled and waved, as did Creole settlers, and it appeared that men who had been living in Louisiana for some time bore no grudge against Yankees. Perhaps, Andrew thought, General de Maniton might find it difficult to arouse the civilian population and obtain assistance from volunteer fighting men.

When the flotilla reached New Orleans itself, knots of people gathered on the banks of the Mississippi to watch the procession, and again Andrew was amazed that none of the men carried rifles or muskets. The defenders, he concluded, were remarkably lax.

At last the familiar wharves loomed ahead, and the schooner headed toward them, followed by the barges carrying the river devils, with the rest of the armada closing in behind. It was unlikely that French artillery had been massed behind warehouses in the sector, since General de Maniton had not known where the Americans

213

would land, and Andrew estimated that, at the worst, he would be opposed by rifle and small-arms fire.

He leaped onto a wharf, the other occupants of the schooner at his heels, and the rest of the river devils, responding to the challenge, ingeniously lashed their barges together to make a bridge, thereby enabling them to come ashore more rapidly.

Andrew and the men from the schooner had already taken undisputed possession of the wharf, and the rest of the river devils promptly spread out in the streets beyond it, gaining a foothold. Twenty-five of them under the direction of Billy MacCullough occupied an empty warehouse, which gave the invaders a base of operations, and by the time the riflemen began to come ashore, the river devils held the equivalent of three city squares.

Major Robertson and several other officers joined Andrew outside the warehouse, and the American commander was perplexed. "People yonder are watching us from their balconies and windows," he said, "but I've never seen men less anxious to fight!"

"They're not armed," Andrew added. "And look at their families watching us, as though we were on parade. My boys are ready for battle, but we sure can't fire at women and children!"

One of the junior officers suddenly pointed up a broad street, lined with warehouses, and the atmosphere changed at once. A group of French officers in splendid array were riding at the head of what appeared to be the entire New Orleans garrison. Behind the mounted flag-bearers rode the cavalry, and a river devil who had climbed to the roof of the American-occupied warehouse shouted that the French infantry regiments were massed behind the horsemen.

Somewhere in the distance a military band began to play, and Andrew and Robertson exchanged bewildered glances. "It seems to me, Charley," Andrew said, "that they don't care how many civilians get killed. These are city streets, not an open battlefield."

Abel Hillery, who had come up to join the expedition's leaders, heard the remark, and although he, too, was confused, he sounded excited as he exclaimed, "Listen!"

The French fife and drum corps was playing in the distance, and as it drew a little closer the Americans could hear the strains of "Yankee Doodle."

"I reckon they don't know why we've come here," Andrew said.

"There's just a chance they do," Hillery replied. "Will you ask your men to hold their fire, Major Robertson?"

"Until I find out they're trying to trick us," Robertson said, and gave the necessary orders.

The group watched in silence as the French continued to march toward them, plumes waving and the horses prancing. Then an adjutant shouted a command, the ranks halted and for a moment no one moved.

Robertson, taking no chances, passed the word to his battalions to be alert.

General de Maniton, wearing a glittering uniform of gold-encrusted white, rode forward alone, followed by several members of his staff.

"I reckon he wants to talk," Robertson said, and went forward with Andrew to meet him. "If he's sensible, he'll agree to a truce, so no civilians are hurt."

Hillery, although not invited to accompany them, kept pace with the pair.

General de Maniton dismounted, and returned the salute of Robertson and Andrew. "I did not expect you so soon, gentlemen," he said.

Their confusion became greater, and Robertson stalled for time by introducing himself and his companions. If the General recognized Andrew, he did not admit or show it.

"Your American sloops must be very fast ships," he said. "Official word from Paris reached us only three days ago. The First Consul writes that the transfer of authority is yet to be arranged, but for all practical purposes, gentlemen, New Orleans—and all Louisiana—now belong to you."

The stunned Americans were too flabbergasted to reply.

Hillery's training as a diplomat came to his rescue. "We —ah—know none of the details, General."

De Maniton told them what he knew of the sale of Louisiana to the United States, then added, "I can't turn over the garrison to you until I receive instructions from the First Consul, but we can pitch tents on the parade ground for your regiments, Major Robertson."

Robertson started to reply that his troops were irregulars who had marched to Louisiana on their own initiative, but Hillery silenced him with a quick dig of an elbow.

"We will be grateful for any hospitality you care to show us, General," the State Department official said.

"I have an idea," Andrew added, "that most of our boys will start for home in a few days." He silently promised himself that he would see to it that the frontiersmen did not linger in the city, where idleness and the availability of strong liquor might complicate the most miraculous event ever enjoyed by the United States.

"The people of New Orleans are looking forward to a parade, Major," de Maniton said. "Will you march with us?"

"You lead us, General, and we'll be right behind," Robertson declared, refraining from saying that the volunteers had expected to fight their way through the streets.

The American battalions were formed into a semblance of military ranks, the men cheering when they heard the almost unbelievable news.

Within a short time Andrew found himself marching at the head of his river devils to the beat of the French fife and drum corps. Still dazed by the bloodless acquisition of Louisiana, he was sobered by the realization that hundreds of men might have died unnecessarily. But the march on New Orleans had not been in vain. When the full story behind the maneuvers of the diplomats became known, he felt certain, the pressure applied by the American frontiersmen would be recognized as a major factor in the French decision to sell the colony.

There could be no doubt that the people of New Orleans welcomed the change that was ahead for them. The river devils and riflemen looked like shabby amateurs as they tried in vain to keep their ranks straight, but the men, women and children of the city cheered themselves hoarse as the Americans swept through the streets. The Creoles, Spaniards, and French who had lived in New Orleans for any length of time had been subjected to the influences of the wilderness, too. And, like the citizens of the United States they soon would be joining, they were Americans.

The throngs on the Avenue de Bienville were so dense

that their steady roar of approval drowned the music of the fife and drum corps. But Andrew forgot the crowd, the cheers and the martial airs as he searched for one face in the close-packed throng. He could not find her, however, and wondered if, in spite of his country's triumph, he had come to New Orleans too late.

The civilian French Governor of Louisiana was waiting for the Americans on the steps of the Hall of the Cabildo, and General de Maniton escorted Major Robertson to him, two other French officers walking beside Andrew and Hillery. Here the crowds were at their thickest, and it was impossible for Andrew to hear what the French Colonel beside him was saying. All of New Orleans appeared to have converged on the Place d'Armes, and Andrew thought it was ironic that he, twice a prisoner in the city and twice a fugitive, should be honored by the representatives of First Consul Bonaparte and hailed by the people who soon would become his fellow citizens.

Suddenly he felt a savage blow on his left shoulder, followed by an excruciating wave of pain. He looked down, saw a hole in his shirt and watched a smear of blood spread around it.

The French Colonel was horrified. It was obvious that someone had fired at the American, and that the roar of the onlookers had made the sound of the shot inaudible.

Andrew raised his head, and, recovering from his initial shock, recognized the face of a man directly ahead in the crowd. The shot had not been fired at random, but had been deliberately aimed at him.

"I have a score that needs settling," he said to his escort, and, unmindful of his wound, started off after Cristoforo de Martínez.

The Spaniard slipped off through the throng, but Andrew pressed after him, the crowd parting to let him through. He had no clear idea of what he intended to do, and realized it would be far better to let the authorities, be they French or American, find his assailant, try him in a court of law and punish him. De Martínez had been his nemesis too long, however, for reasons beyond his comprehension, and had caused him too much suffering to let others obtain vengeance for him. A man who had lived for years in the wilderness came to believe in the direct, ruthless frontier code of justice, and acted accordingly.

Soon Andrew found himself in a narrow, twisting lane behind the Place d'Armes. At first glance it seemed deserted, the residents having gone to join in the welcome to the arriving Americans, but a slight movement ahead, in the shadows, told him he was on the trail of de Martínez. Pursuer and pursued made their way into another narrow lane, then into an alleyway where the balconies of the houses almost touched, cutting off most of the daylight.

It occurred to Andrew that de Martínez was not fleeing from him, but was purposely leading him into a trap. It was difficult to see in the half-light, and with the entrance to the alleyway directly behind him, Andrew realized he made a perfect target for someone lying in wait for him.

He threw himself to the ground just as a shot rang out, and a bullet sang through the air no more than a foot over his head. Conscious of the pain in the shoulder, Andrew raised his rifle, and, continuing to remain prone on the cobblestones, waited.

After some moments his patience was rewarded, and he saw a flickering movement ahead, at a bend in the alleyway. He squeezed the trigger, heard a shriek of pain and, dragging himself to his feet, reloaded as he moved forward, taking care to stay close to the walls of the buildings where the shadows were deepest.

Suddenly, as Andrew turned the corner, he came face to face with Cristoforo de Martínez. The Spaniard had been frantically binding a wound in his side, but jerked upright as he caught sight of his foe, and the two men stood for an instant, no more than ten feet apart.

Andrew fired his rifle, but it jammed, and he was forced to reach down to his boot-top for a knife.

At almost the same moment de Martínez fired a second pistol he had snatched from his belt.

Andrew felt blinded, but made a great effort to concentrate. He realized his enemy was moving away, and waited as long as he dared so his vision would clear. When it improved no more than a trifle, he realized he could hesitate no longer, and hurled the knife at his target with all of his skill and what little remained of his strength.

Then, as he collapsed onto the cobblestones, he heard a

babble of voices around him. But, unable to make out what was being said, he thought he must be dreaming. Sharp pains shot through him, but all at once they stopped, too, and he felt strangely at peace as he lost consciousness.

The featherbed was luxuriously soft, the silk pillowcase was cool, and the fragrance in the room was so unmistakably familiar that Andrew grinned weakly as he opened his eyes.

"You're awake," Jeanne Valdéz said, "and you're yourself again."

"I knew you'd be here," Andrew told her. "I've been dreaming about you."

Jeanne smiled as she looked down at him. "It wasn't a dream. I've been here all along. Every day and most nights."

He tried to sort the meager facts he knew. "I'm in your house?"

"Yes, this is Papa's bedchamber. He insisted they put you here so you wouldn't have to be carried up any stairs."

Andrew digested the information, then asked, "How long have I been here?"

"More than three weeks. Almost a month. At first the physicians weren't certain you'd survive, but I told them from the start that you would."

Andrew explored carefully, and found the shoulder that had caused him so much trouble previously was bandaged again, but was only a little tender to the touch. There was a bandage around his head, too, just above his temple, and he looked at Jeanne inquiringly.

"Cristoforo's last shot grazed your head," she said. "If there had been a difference of a half-inch or less, you'd have been killed at once. As it was, the force of the blow drove you out of your mind, and General de Maniton's own surgeon swore that you'd never recover your senses, but he doesn't know you as I do, and I was positive that with enough rest and care you'd become sane again."

He had an uneasy feeling as he wondered what he had said and done during the past month, but there were other, more important matters to be discussed first. "I haven't dreamed that all of Louisiana is becoming American?"

"Indeed you haven't! President Jefferson has sent a score of men to work out the details of the transfer, and until it takes place, until a governor is appointed for the territory, Mr. Hillery is in charge, working with the French. Until then, everyone is working together, and the French are doing everything they can to help us."

"Us?"

"Of course," Jeanne replied proudly. "President Jefferson has offered full American citizenship to everyone who lives in Louisiana, and Papa and I are accepting. So is everyone else we know. We aren't going to be colonials any more, but citizens of our own country. It's time that Louisiana, especially New Orleans, became part of the United States!"

Andrew grinned, impressed by her earnest gravity.

"Everything that's happening," she said, "is almost too good to be true."

He realized she wasn't speaking only of the French sale of Louisiana to the United States, and wondered how much he had said when he had been out of his mind. Unable to face his personal situation yet, he temporized.

"What happened to Cristoforo de Martínez?"

"You killed him when you threw your knife at him. But it wouldn't have mattered if you hadn't. Two of your river devils followed you when you chased after him, and so did the French Colonel who had been assigned as your escort. All three of them shot him—no more than a second or two after you threw your knife. No one knows how you managed to hit him, you know. There was so much blood in your eyes and on your face that it was almost impossible for you to see clearly."

Andrew shrugged, and felt a slight, uncomfortable tugging sensation in his shoulder. "What I don't understand is why he hated me and was so determined to murder me."

"That was my fault, I'm afraid."

He stared at Jeanne, unwilling to believe her.

"Cristoforo had been a suitor, and was violently jealous, even though I'd rejected his proposal of marriage and would have nothing more to do with him."

220

Andrew began to understand.

Jeanne colored slightly. "He's frightened away several others, but you were different, somehow, and he knew it. That's why he gave you away to the Spaniards the first time you tried to hide from them, and then captured you himself the second time, when the French gave him the reward they had offered. I know you thought that I betrayed you both times—"

"Please," he said, and it was his turn to become embarrassed, "that isn't quite true. I suspected that you were responsible but I was never certain in my own mind—"

"You said many things when your mind was wandering, so there's no need to deny it. You hated me, and I know it!"

"I've never hated you!" He raised his voice.

Jeanne reached out and stroked his hand. "If you become excited, I'm under orders to leave the room. The physicians insist you remain quiet."

"I give you my word," Andrew said, "that I won't shout again. Unless you leave the room. If you do, I'll tear down the house." He smiled when he saw her settle back into her chair. "That's better. Now, as you were saying?"

"You did me an injustice, but I really can't blame you for jumping to conclusions, so I bear you no grudge."

"That evens the score."

"Not quite." Jeanne looked at him, the expression in her violet eyes severe. "You preferred Beatriz to me for a long time."

"Well," Andrew replied lamely, "to be candid—"

"You've been exceptionally candid for more than three weeks! You were infatuated with her, or at the very least you were flattered because she gave herself to you so quickly and easily. I'm one of Beatriz's few real friends, even though I've never approved of her morals. She can't stay away from handsome men, and I'm afraid Don Felipe de Guzmán won't have an easy life with her in Madrid."

"They're going to Spain?"

"They were married about a month before you and your volunteer army arrived here, and they sailed on the first ship that left New Orleans after the purchase of Louisiana by the United States had been announced. You hurried her marriage, you know. She'd been postponing it again and again. And I'm sure you were responsible for her quick departure."

"How could I—"

"You talked incessantly when you were out of your mind, and I know she was afraid you'd be indiscreet and say something that would cause Don Felipe to cancel their betrothal." Jeanne's sigh was complacent. "For a long time I really despised her—until it became obvious that you really preferred me."

"When was that?"

"Long before you knew it, I'm sure," she replied demurely. "But a lady is under no obligation to reveal everything she knows."

Andrew was silent again, and finally stirred slightly. "How much longer must I stay in bed?"

"I'm sure the physicians will let you get up soon, now that you've recovered your senses. Of course, the river devils have already left New Orleans—"

"I'm finished with that life."

"Oh?"

"I'll have to farm my homestead in Tennessee. It isn't what I'd have chosen for myself, but I have very little money, so little that I have no choice."

"One day when Papa came in to see how you were progressing," Jeanne said, "you were talking at great length about your future. How you ranted and carried on, saying how much you hate wilderness living. You manage so successfully in the forests that I was surprised."

"It's a fact," Andrew said, "that I prefer cities, particularly this one. It combines everything I like best about America—and the capitals of Europe I know best."

"Papa," Jeanne said, "has been buying warehouses with the money he once thought he'd need to support us in Spain. Now that Louisiana is American, he says, Mississippi River trade will double and treble, and the warehouses will be filled every day of the year."

"He's right."

"He's going to offer you a post as his superintendent, I know."

Andrew's smile was painful. "I have no funds to invest with him."

"He doesn't need money. What he does need is someone who can handle men, someone who understands Mississippi River cargo—and more than anything else, someone he can trust."

"It's good to know he thinks so highly of me," Andrew said. "But how can he be so sure of me?"

Jeanne averted her face. "If he can't trust his son-in-law, I doubt if there's anyone in the world on whom he can rely, and the new business he's building is too big for him to handle alone." She stood abruptly and started toward the door.

"Wait!"

She paused with a hand on the latch.

"If you don't come back," Andrew threatened, "I'll shout, and when the doctors come, I'll tell them you're to blame."

She slowly returned to his bedside.

"When was it decided that I'm to be his son-in-law?"

Jeanne became scarlet. "I've lost count of the number of times you've proposed marriage to me in all these weeks."

"Maybe," he said with a grin, "I wasn't as much out of my mind as everyone seemed to think."

"Of course, now that you've recovered, I wouldn't dream of holding you to anything you said."

Andrew caught her wrist. "When a man and woman become betrothed," he said, "they usually seal the agreement with a kiss. Must I sit up?"

Jeanne bent close to him, and as he put his arms around her he felt no pain in his shoulder or head. His wanderings were at an end, and he had come home.

Author's Note

The Louisiana Purchase, which transformed the United States from a weak, struggling nation into one inevitably destined to become great and powerful, was unique in American history and unusual by any standard of international relations.

Napoleon's new war against England and the Continental powers forming their latest coalition against him is generally recognized as a principal motive for his unexpected "generosity" to the young nation across the Atlantic. He literally needed all of his men, ships, supplies, and energies for the newest round of his unremitting attempt to gain the domination of Europe.

Too frequently, however, the efforts of Americans in creating the conditions that caused him to sell them New Orleans and the vast Louisiana territory have remained unsung or unknown. The West, aware that its survival was at stake, was literally up in arms, and an informal, unofficial expedition was dispatched to New Orleans, arriving there after the preliminary treaty between the United States and France had been signed.

Therefore the base on which this adventure-romance has been created is a true one, and the river devils, who were among the most courageous of frontiersmen, played an active part in the march that, fortunately, ended peacefully. Charles Robertson and Abel Hillery were real men who earned places for themselves in history, and if Andrew MacCullough did not actually exist, it was necessary to invent him. After all, there were so many Americans of his day who were like him.